Like an Untimely Frost

Charles Tabb

© 2023 Charles Tabb

 Gifted Time Books, Beaverdam, Virginia

All rights reserved

ISBN: 9798850936358

Books by Charles Tabb:

The Twigs series

Floating Twigs
Finding Twigs
Gathering Twigs
Saving Twigs
Coming in 2024: *Burning Twigs*

The Detective Tony Pantera Series

Hell is Empty
The Purger
The Whirligig of Time
Like an Untimely Frost

Stand-alone Books

Canaries' Song
Stories I Told Myself: From Humor to Horror

DEDICATION

For my two best friends, the "other" Chuck and Harry. I treasure your friendship.

ACKNOWLEDGEMENTS

This book would not exist without the following, who have gone above and beyond.

To Sue, Chuck, and Trisha, my process beta readers, and Roger, my final beta reader for my Pantera books, thank you for once again keeping me on the right path.

To Kristine Elder, my editor, I am once again reminded how much better you make me look. Your input is always spot-on.

Finally, to my wonderful wife, Dee, your support and encouragement are priceless. Thank you for keeping me from making huge errors of judgment both in my writing and my life.

Death lies on her like an untimely frost
Upon the sweetest flower of all the field.

--William Shakespeare,
Romeo and Juliet, IV, v, 28-29

One may smile, and smile, and be a villain

--William Shakespeare,
Hamlet, I, v, 116

1

Miranda lay in bed, staring at the wall, her back to the sleeping man she'd had sex with. They hadn't made love. That would be much too pleasant a word for what they'd done. She'd collected the money he brought for her—money nobody else would know about—and then had sex for old time's sake.

At least she was not a street hooker like the girls who stood on corners trying to hustle some money from men driving by. That was too dangerous and a poverty chain. Ninety percent of whatever they made there would go to their pimp, if the girls were lucky. The pimp would use some of the cash on drugs for the girls to keep them hooked and dependent on him. That was always the plan.

In this line of work, Miranda was a top-dollar call girl and only nineteen. The cream of the crop, so to speak, if that were possible in this ugly business. Her bosses made sure she spent her time with men who had plenty of money to spend. She was nineteen but looked several years younger, appearing far too young to be in this business. That was exactly the opposite of the girls who worked the streets, who might be her age but looked ten years older at least. Her pimp even paid for her to go to the gym and work out to keep herself in good shape. It was her appearing younger that helped her earn what she did, and she was allowed to keep half of her earnings, all of it tax-free.

That was not the only difference between her job and the ones worked by the street walkers. Her pimp did not allow drugs. He was still a pimp, but the relationship was more like that between an employer and employee. Of course, her employer had certain fringe benefits, just as with any pimp-prostitute relationship. No, he didn't allow drugs, but he did have other ways of controlling the girls that was even easier, like threatening their lives and making sure they understood it wasn't an empty threat.

She had witnessed one girl be "put down," as he'd called it. The girl had become an addict and was, as he'd said, of no use to him, not to mention a security liability. He had gathered his "girls" to witness what happened to those who did not follow the rules.

Of course, he didn't dirty his hands with the killing. He had another man take care of it. At least it hadn't been a slow torture. He'd strangled her with a scarf while she lay naked and nearly unconscious from drugs.

Her pimp worked for a large firm, Circe Enterprises, a worldwide conglomerate that served as a parent company for various businesses. Because of his high-level position, his anonymity was, as he put it, "of the highest degree of secrecy." The message was clear: remain useful, you live; become a problem, you die.

She lay there in the bed of an apartment used for servicing the people who paid for sex. The girls all had their own key to the place, and she'd known none of the girls would be working today. Their work came in spurts when important clients were in town. They had been told to take a few days off. It was one of their lulls, so she'd used the place for this hook-up.

As she lay there doing her best to ignore the man's light snoring, she wondered what had happened to a girl she worked with sometimes. Her name, or at least the name Miranda knew, was Ericka. She doubted it was her real name. Most of the girls took on different names, but Miranda had stuck with hers. She'd always considered it pretty, almost mysterious. Ericka had disappeared a

2

week ago without a trace. Miranda pictured the man with the scarf and pushed the image away.

She rose from the bed and walked naked into the small kitchen area to make some coffee, inserting the k-cup into the brewer and pushing the brew button. When it was ready, she took it into the sitting room between the kitchen and bedroom and sat there, sipping the hot brew and allowing the caffeine to take effect as she thumbed through the pages of a magazine.

A few minutes later, the man appeared in the doorway to the bedroom, naked as well and apparently ready for more fun. She looked at him and he waved her back into the bedroom. Ten minutes later, they shared a shower and dressed.

"I want to show you something," the man said.

"Oh? What?"

"It's not here. I'll take you there."

After getting dressed, they left, and Miranda glanced at the half-finished cup of coffee and frowned. Nothing in her life was truly hers, not even her time.

As she rode in the car, Miranda wondered where they were going as he drove toward a seedier part of town.

Pulling into a secluded area out of sight of the road, he sat looking at her. She wondered what he planned to do now. They'd fucked twice earlier. This was not exactly high-class accommodations. It was downright filthy, in fact, with litter scattered around the place where he'd parked. She was expecting a demand for more sex, maybe oral, and this surprised Miranda. He'd never gone more than once with her, and the second time today had been a surprise. Now there would be a third?

"What?"

"Get undressed."

"You're going for three?" she said, forcing a smile that at least suggested she liked the idea.

"In a manner of speaking."

She suddenly thought she knew what he planned. "You want me to get myself off?" It was a common request, and the one she enjoyed the most when working since nobody touched her but herself. She didn't care who watched, and the best thing was she never had to fake it. She was her own best lover. She'd even made a little money on the side doing that on the internet, though she feared her boss/pimp would find out and demand some of the profits.

"No. Just get naked. You'll see."

She shrugged, hoping his idea of fun wasn't making her walk home naked from here. If that's what he wanted, she would refuse. It wasn't as if he had been vetted by her pimp. This was her own thing on the side, and the money wasn't even for the sex, really, but something else.

As she undressed, he watched her. Beads of sweat began to roll down his face. It was still cool inside the car with its air conditioning going to keep the outside heat at bay, and she wondered why he would be sweating. Was he that anxious about what he intended her to do?

When she was naked, he said, "Now, get out of the car and just stand there."

Oh, shit, she thought. He was planning to make her walk home naked. He would warn her about telling the cops anything about him, especially that he'd made her do this. She liked him but was also afraid of him.

"No."

"What?"

"I won't walk home like this. That's beyond weird."

He smirked. "Get out of the fucking car, or I'll get a tire iron and beat you to death."

Tears welled as she opened the door and stepped out onto the cracked concrete of the hidden parking area.

4

She stood there, waiting for him to drive away, but instead, he got out of the car.

As he walked around the rear to approach her, he was unbuckling his belt. She felt relief wash over her. He just wanted to do it in a fairly public place.

"Turn around and put your hands on the side of the car," he said.

She did as instructed, feeling happy she wasn't going to be forced into public like this beyond leaning naked against the car and getting screwed in this mostly hidden area.

When the belt wrapped around her throat, she grabbed for it, grunting her protests as he squeezed the belt tighter. She could feel herself losing consciousness. The blackness enveloped her and she was gone.

2

Yvette Chapelle, known in the business world she inhabited as Circe, was furious she had been called to Richmond. She'd been notified by Claude, the man who oversaw one of her combination legal/illegal businesses there, that a problem demanded her attention. Why it was a problem Claude couldn't handle was beyond her, and he'd insisted that Ron Widner, his regional boss, could not deal with this either. He would not discuss the situation over the phone, of course, so she had no way of knowing if he was correct that she needed to be in on the evaluation and handling of the problem. If this turned out to be a wasted trip, Claude would wish he'd died of a heart attack.

She'd been forced to fly to Richmond from her home in Paris. To make matters worse, her private jet was being serviced, so she had to fly commercial, which always put her in a bad mood. Claude knew this and was likely dreading the meeting as much as she had dreaded this flight, with all the insane delays from going through security, the layover at JFK, and the bad food.

As her flight touched down in Richmond, she pulled her phone from her purse and pressed the button to call Claude.

"Yes, my lady?" he answered.

"I am on the ground," she said. "Are you here?"

"Of course."

"I will be there as soon as I'm allowed off of this flying bus."

"I have the finest limo for you, my lady."

"Of course you do."

She disconnected the call without waiting for a reply. The limo comment was designed to ease her tensions, but it was ridiculous. He would never pick her up in anything other than a luxury limousine, especially when she would already be angry just because she had to be there.

Gathering her carry-on from the overhead bin, she pushed her way past the other first-class passengers and strode down the boarding ramp into the gate area. Turning right, she walked the nearly quarter mile to the place where friends and family of arrivals stood, craning their necks to see whoever they were here to meet. She spotted Claude, who was doing his best to look relaxed and failing. Perhaps he knew his job now balanced on a thin edge. She considered that if things went the way she suspected they might, his remains, if they were ever found, might require dental records for identification.

As she handed him her carry-on, he said, "I hope your flight was good."

"Don't be stupid, Claude," she retorted and strode ahead of him toward the exit.

"You have no other luggage?"

"I'm staying only one day," she said. "I want to get back to Paris, and I'm not looking forward to another layover at JFK, but it will have to do." She didn't mention that she might stay in New York a few days, where she would purchase more clothes. It was none of his business.

"I swear this is not something that could be handled without your input."

"You'd better be right."

After they were in the limo and headed into town, she said, "So, what is this problem that required me to fly from Paris?"

Claude raised the soundproof glass partition between the driver and the rear of the limo. "I have discovered that Ron is stealing from you."

She sat in silence a moment, measuring the full import of that statement. Ron Widner had worked for her for over ten years. He was an essential cog in the machinery of her empire, much of it illegal. At least it explained why Ron couldn't handle the problem. It also explained why Claude had insisted she come to the states.

Ron handled everything from Washington to Miami on the east coast. The amount of money he oversaw was staggering. She'd always known that those at the top of her organization could skim money for years without detection, but she figured the punishment for disloyalty was enough to deter them from partaking of that ill-advised path.

"Do you have proof or just suspicions?"

"Proof."

Circe herself was a billionaire, but she would not be listed on any Fortune 500 lists. She worked hard for her anonymity. People knew who she was, but not how she made the vast fortune she had, nor did they know its extent.

She owned a number of legitimate businesses, but the majority of her wealth came from her business of obtaining things for others who were willing to pay for them. These things were illegal in every country in the world, so obtaining them required a high price be paid.

She reflected on the last time she was in Richmond. A man named Greg Quinton had needed another identity. His wife had been murdered by the serial killer known as The Purger, and he'd decided he needed to disappear for a variety of reasons he'd not explained to her. She had met with him personally because she'd met him before, enjoyed his very personal company, and he had her phone number. She had made the arrangements, but he'd been killed shortly after they met. She'd worried that someone may have seen them together and would report that to the police, but if that had happened, she was never approached about it.

Now, she was here to take care of another matter. Claude was off the hook, but now she would take out all her anger at having to fly here on Ron and anyone else who'd helped him.

"Where is the proof you say you have?"

"In my safe."

"Are we going there now?"

"Yes."

She spent the rest of the limo ride in silence, so Claude did the same. When they arrived at his office downtown, she took a seat while he opened his safe. He brought her documents and a thumb-drive.

"What's on this?" she asked, holding up the small plastic case.

"Video."

"Of what?"

"A sting operation I set up to get him to admit he was stealing from you."

He plugged the drive into his desktop and opened it. She watched the short video and felt her anger rise even higher. In it, Ron bragged about stealing from, as he put it in the video, "the great bitch, Circe."

"She's clueless as to where her money goes as long as she gets enough to fund her extravagant lifestyle," he said to the young woman, who acted impressed with his deeds.

"Is that a hooker?" Circe said. "Is she one of ours?"

"Yes. Looks much younger than she is, so we pass her off as fifteen. The johns pay top dollar for her."

"We're going to have to kill Ron," she said.

"I know."

"Where is he?"

"At his office."

"In the executive office suite?"

"Yes. I have a security guard watching him."

"What does the guard know?"

"That Ron's been stealing from the company and he shouldn't be left alone."

"Does he know that Ron will be dead by the end of the day?"

"Yes. He will do the killing for us."

She considered this. "Then we'll have to take care of the guard, too. I don't want him being able to connect this killing to you or me."

"He can be trusted."

"By you. Not me. Once he finishes this job, we must kill him."

"Why?"

"Besides the fact I said so?" she asked.

The look on her face told him he should end his arguing about the guard's life. "I apologize, my lady. It's just been very stressful, and I overreacted. This guard has been a valued employee."

"His value will end today. Where is the girl?"

"Do we have to kill her, too?"

"Of course. She knows he's stealing from me. Once he disappears, she could put two and two together. So where is she?"

"She has disappeared."

"What? How could you let her out of your sight?"

"She left town the day after that video was made. I got her to coax the information out of Ron. She delivered her phone, which held the video. The next day, she was gone."

"When did the guard begin watching Ron?"

"The day after the video was delivered."

"Does Ron suspect you know of his theft?"

"No, my lady, but there's more proof."

Claude handed her several documents. She looked

them over. They were expense reports that Ron had apparently filled out. "These are sham expenditures?"

"Yes, my lady. He has paid for items that are nowhere to be found, paid people who don't exist for services. A variety of thefts such as that."

"He has no idea I am in town?"

"No, my lady."

"You must find that girl and take care of that loose end."

"Certainly, my lady."

She looked up at him. "My regional directors get to call me Circe."

He smiled at her and extended his hand to help her from her seat. "Do you wish to visit Ron now—Circe?"

"Certainly."

3

Circe and Claude walked past Claude's guard who stood outside the door and burst into Ron's office. Ron was startled to see her, and her expression told him she wasn't happy.

"Circe!" he said, doing his best to feign joyous surprise at seeing her. He rose from his seat and walked toward her.

She held out a hand in a stop gesture. "How dare you?"

"What do you mean?"

"You would steal from me and then rise to give me a greeting? A hug perhaps, or even a small kiss?"

"Steal from you? What are you talking about?"

"Claude?" Circe said, continuing to stare with loathing at Ron. "Show him."

Claude held up the flash drive and asked, "You remember that pretty girl from last week? Ericka?"

"What are you talking about?" he asked, but Claude could see he was scared.

"You can end the lying, Ron," Claude said. "I have proof you've been stealing from Circe."

"What kind of proof have you manufactured, Claude? You've wanted my job for a long time now. I guess you've found a way to get it!"

"Not manufactured. Real, and you know it."

Claude pushed the thumb drive into the USB port on Ron's computer. After they watched the incriminating video, Ron said, "I was just bragging to her. Making things up. I wanted to impress her a bit. That's all."

"Impress a whore?" Circe said.

"An impressed woman is more—enthusiastic."

Circe's look of hatred was enough to bring him to silence.

"I have more, Ron," Claude said. "Documents that say you paid people money, but for some reason I couldn't find these people or the product you paid for, no matter how hard I tried."

Panicked, Ron glanced at the door to his office, but Claude, who was younger and stronger, saw the look and tackled Ron before he could reach it.

Circe removed a prepared syringe from her purse and jabbed it into Ron's arm. Within seconds he felt woozy, and the room began to spin. Collapsing to the thick carpet, he tried to speak but couldn't beyond grunts and gurgling. The world had slipped into a haze of confusion.

Claude stuck his head out of the office and signaled the security guard to come in.

Pretending a sudden illness had befallen Ron, the guard, Claude, and Circe whisked him from the office, out of the building, and into the limo.

They told the guard to drive to Ron Widner's address.

After five hours of torture dictated by Circe, Ron took his final breath. The guard had spent the time digging a shallow grave in the garden next to the guest quarters that sat several hundred yards behind the main house on the large estate. After the guard dumped Ron's body into the grave, Claude put a 9 mm to the back of the security guard's head and pulled the trigger, as Circe had instructed. The guard dropped into the grave next to Ron's body. Claude shoveled the dirt over the bodies.

Circe led Claude into one of the bedrooms where they had sex. "I always like to celebrate an employee's promotion to a high-ranking position," she said as she unbuckled his belt.

13

"What do you do with the ladies who are promoted?" he asked.

She shrugged and smiled. "Same thing."

"What if they're not into women?"

"Then they lose the promotion."

He had to hand it to her. She never allowed anything to stop her from getting what she wanted, no matter the cost to others.

He and Circe left the house by seven that morning. Circe would make her flight to Paris via New York after all.

4

Richmond Detective Tony Pantera stood over the dead woman lying in an empty lot. The lot was just within the city limits of Richmond, making this his case and not Henrico County's. Considering the corpse that lay alone begging for justice, he felt the acids in his stomach begin their invasion as if they were at war with his digestive tract.

The victim, currently a Jane Doe, lay sprawled in small patches of weeds that grew like unkempt hair. She was naked except for a thin ankle bracelet. Pantera hoped that would help identify her so her parents could be notified. Or perhaps they had her prints from a prior arrest. She barely looked old enough to drive, if that, much less to have been printed for a previous crime.

Her thin, caramel blond hair lay matted against her scalp. She had used a gold-colored eye shadow that was now smeared in small patches beneath her eyes. She was thin, but not emaciated. She had been dumped there, her legs akimbo, so it was hard to determine how tall she'd been, but Pantera felt she couldn't have been much more than five-two. He guessed she probably weighed between eighty and eighty-five pounds. She was pretty, and her breasts were small, almost pubescent, making Pantera wonder about her age. She looked to be anywhere from twelve to her late teens, but they couldn't be sure until her identity became known. Her pubes were bare, but that didn't mean anything.

The anger over such a tragedy mixed with the acid in his gut, and he shook his head at the senselessness of it all. This was someone's daughter. She should be reminiscing about her prom night or planning an outing with friends, not lying naked in a lot with a dozen people walking around her, trying to find any clue that would tell them the who, what, when, where, and why of this insane reality.

As Pantera turned from the body, he thought of his own daughters, wondering how any parent could survive news such as this. He'd had to tell too many parents of the death of their child, and the thought of having to do it again was almost unbearable. There was never a way to make it sound better. He knew that it was entirely possible that one of her parents had done this, and that was an insanity all its own, but often even those parents were devastated at what they had done.

Pantera's partner, Detective Harry Overmeyer, was approaching as Pantera worked to quell the rising nausea. Harry had been in court, testifying on a case. When Harry had called him to let him know he was finished in court, Pantera was en route to the scene and had told him about the body and its location.

"What do we have so far?" Harry asked.

"Either a very developed child or an older teenager. I'll let you get your own impressions."

Harry walked over to where the girl's body lay, the half-lidded eyes staring at nothing, not bothered by the sun glaring into them.

"Sweet Mother of God," Harry said. He crouched down as Pantera watched him from nearby.

As Pantera had done earlier, Harry pulled an unopened pair of latex gloves out of his pocket tore the plastic wrapping and pulled them on. Then he reached out and tenderly touched the girl's neck. A wide, purple bruise covered her throat. Harry's hand moved gently to the girl's eyelid and raised it as he checked for petechial hemorrhaging, finding what Pantera had earlier. The small red spots were there, meaning it was likely the girl was strangled. That and the bruising to the throat made it more or less certain.

Standing, Harry came back to Pantera. "She looks like a kid with breasts."

"I know."

"How old do you think she is?"

"Good question. Let me go in the middle and say fifteen. You?"

"No idea. She could be anywhere from twelve to twenty. Hard to tell."

Aimee Wells, the new assistant medical examiner, arrived. Pantera had dealt with her before and found her to be competent and detailed. She had worked in the medical examiner's office in Boston. She was a Richmond native who had moved back to her hometown to be closer to her aging mother and her daughter, who was expecting her first child.

She strode up to the body and knelt down to examine her. Pantera came up behind her and said, "How old do you think she is?"

Aimee glanced back at Pantera. Then grasping the girl's jaw, she pulled it open, fighting the *rigor mortis* that was still active. "Her wisdom teeth are coming in, so she's probably in her late teens."

Harry had joined them. "What about time of death?"

"I won't be able to tell you definitively until I run more tests, but based on the level of rigor, I'd say about twelve to fourteen hours. I can give a more precise calculation after the autopsy."

"Thanks, Aimee," Pantera said.

"I take it there was no ID near the body?" Aimee said.

"Nope."

"I'll pass her prints on to you then."

They watched Aimee working on the body, doing preliminary measurements.

"Death lies on her like an untimely frost," Pantera said.

"Huh?" Harry asked, squinting at Pantera.

"It's from Romeo and Juliet. 'Death lies on her like an untimely frost upon the sweetest flower in all the field.' Lord Capulet says it when they find Juliet, thinking she's dead."

"But she was just faking it, right?"

"Yeah."

Harry looked over at the dead girl. "She's not faking it, Tony."

"No, but if her parents loved her at all, they will be devastated."

"What is it with you and Shakespeare?"

Attempting some humor to lighten the mood, Pantera answered, "We were drinking buddies in a previous life."

"Yeah. Let's make some notes and see what we can find out about Juliet, there."

"Juliet," Pantera said. He never liked calling unknown victims John or Jane Doe. It depersonalized them, and he hated that. He would generally give the victim a name he would use, making note of that fact in his notes in case he had to go to court later. Once he knew their real names, he would use that instead of words like *victim* or *casualty*. Looking down at the dead young woman, he said, "I'm sorry, Juliet."

Turning away and pulling out his small notebook for taking notes on cases, he joined Harry and went to work.

5

Arriving at his office, Pantera began transferring his notes into a file on his computer. Using his phone, he'd taken a picture of the woman he called Juliet until they knew her real name. He labeled the file "Juliet" and included the picture. He hoped Aimee could help with her identity.

Harry, who had stopped to pour them some coffee, entered and sat at his desk, facing Pantera.

"Tony, you mind a change of subject?"

"Mind? I'd welcome it," Pantera said, though he continued working.

"I got a call from your ex."

Pantera stopped typing in the middle of a word. "Nancy? You got a phone call from Nancy?"

"Yeah."

"What did she want, and why call you and not me?"

"She asked how I thought you'd feel if she moved back to Richmond."

"Why ask you? She has my number."

"I think she wanted to feel me out first to get an idea how you'd react."

"What did you tell her?"

"I told her she should ask you, but I didn't think it would be a problem, mostly because the girls would be closer. They live over an hour's drive away now."

"Did she ask you not to say anything to me?"

"If she had, I wouldn't be talking to you about it."

"Did she say what she was going to do with the house? Phil was murdered just a few months ago. It seems kind of quick."

"Said she's selling it. Told me it was already on the market, in fact. She said she can't live with the memories it holds."

"Can't blame her there," Pantera said.

A man who had been stalking Pantera had murdered Phil, Nancy's husband. The man had gone to Nancy's and Phil's house in Charlottesville to draw Pantera in. When Harry had arrived, he had shot him, too, nearly killing him.

"Did she say why she didn't want another house in Charlottesville?"

"Nope."

"So why are you telling me this?"

"I guess to give you a heads up. She'll probably call soon. I didn't want you to be blindsided. In fact, I think that's why she called me first, to give you time to think about it before she talked with you."

"Thanks." Pantera took out his phone and opened it.

"What are you doing?" Harry asked.

"Calling her first."

"You want me to leave?"

"No need. It's not like you don't know what we're going to talk about."

After a few rings, Nancy answered. "Hi, Tony."

"Hello, there. Harry tells me you have something you want to talk to me about."

After a brief pause, she said, "Yeah, I guess I do."

"Well?"

"Would you be okay if I moved back home?"

This surprised Pantera. Home? Did she mean move back in with him?

"Home?"

"Sorry. Badly worded. I meant Richmond. That's where I grew up, after all."

Pantera was surprised that he felt relief. Not that long ago, he would have welcomed her with open arms. Even carried her across the threshold as though they were a newly married couple.

"It's a free country, Nance. You can live wherever you want."

"I just want to be sure you wouldn't mind. I don't want you to feel uncomfortable if we see each other more often." She paused. "And I don't want Lisa to feel uncomfortable either."

"Lisa and I are dating, but I'm not sure how serious we are. It's not like I'm buying a ring or anything. She still lives near D.C."

"I understand that, but we will likely see more of each other because we'll both be more involved in raising the girls. Just so you know, they're over the moon about the idea."

Pantera smiled. He'd been working on improving his relationship with his daughters. Apparently, he was succeeding. He'd not been an active father before the divorce, but he purposely made plans with them now and did his best to follow through on his promises to them.

"What about Andrea's girlfriend? I figured she'd be upset they won't be living in the same town."

"They broke up."

"Is Andrea deciding she's straight?"

"Deciding? It doesn't work that way, Tony. It's not a decision; it's the way your heart and mind work."

"Sorry. I guess I meant, is she questioning her sexuality?"

"No. She is who she is. Romantic relationships are no different, no matter what your sexual orientation. Teenagers break up all the time. Being a lesbian doesn't change that."

Pantera was still getting used to the idea his older daughter had come out as a lesbian. She had recently turned sixteen, and while he was fine with it if she really was a lesbian, he still hoped she would decide it was a phase. He wasn't holding his breath, though.

Changing the subject, he said, "There's a house for sale just up the road from my place," he said. "The girls would be within walking distance."

"I'll have to think about that, but I suppose you're okay with the idea?"

"Okay? I'm over the moon, as you say. I'd love to see the girls more, and you and I have managed to remain friends. I can tell you that's not always the case, and I have the arrest records to prove it."

"I'm aware of that. I have an offer on my house, and I countered. My realtor thinks they're very interested."

"Do they know some killings took place there?"

He was greeted with silence. After a moment, she said, "No, and I don't like to think about that, if you don't mind. I nearly had to watch that monster kill our daughter."

"Okay. Do you need me to take the girls while you're searching for a home?"

"It would be less expensive for me if you could."

"Consider it done."

"Okay. I'll be over there Saturday and Sunday looking. I'll bring the girls by around noon Saturday."

"See you then," he said and hung up.

"That sounds like it went well," Harry said.

"It did." He smiled. "The girls are, and I quote, 'over the moon' that they're moving here."

"You're so insecure about that. They love you."

"Yeah, I know, but sometimes they don't like me. Besides, you weren't around when Nancy and I split. They barely wanted to talk to me."

"Quit worrying about it. They're talking to you now."

Pantera turned back to his work, and Harry, who was checking out the missing person reports did the same.

6

Pantera was on his way to work the following morning when his cell rang. The spooky music he had chosen for the Medical Examiner's Office told him it was probably Aimee calling with news of what she'd found out. Tapping his CarPlay screen, he answered.

"Pantera."

"Detective, this is Aimee Wells with the M.E."

"Yes, Aimee. Do you have anything on Juliet?"

"What?"

"Oh, sorry. The Jane Doe. I always give them another name to make it more personal."

"Oh. Okay. Yes, I do have something. Her prints are in the system. I ran them as soon as I got back yesterday after the field work, and the results were waiting for me this morning."

"So who is it?"

"Her name is Miranda Buckhorn, nineteen. She's been arrested for shoplifting and drug possession—coke."

"No solicitation?"

"It didn't pop up, but that doesn't mean she wasn't hooking. It just means she's never been arrested for it."

"Okay. Does the record give an address?"

"Even better. There's a picture of her driver's license."

"Great work, Aimee! Is there an e at the end of her last name?"

"Nope. B-u-c-k-h-o-r-n."

"I'll check it out the moment I'm at my desk."

"There's more," Aimee said.

"Like what?"

"She's had a baby."

This caught Pantera by surprise. "Recently?"

"Well, she was only nineteen, so it couldn't have been that long ago."

"Yes, but can you tell anything? I'm wondering where the baby is now."

"I can't tell how recent, but it wasn't in the past few months, and likely not the past year."

"I have to wonder if there's not a hungry baby out there crying for a mother who will never come home," Pantera said.

"It's possible she gave it up for adoption, but then, there will be records of that if she did."

"Takes a court order to see those."

"Then you have some work to do," Aimee said.

"Yes, I do. Anything else?"

"Not yet. No track marks on the arms or other areas, so if she was doing drugs, she wasn't using a needle."

"Okay," Pantera said. "Keep me posted."

"Of course, I will."

They disconnected, and Pantera wanted to stop the car and do a small dance on the side of the road. He hated the cases with unknown victims. They were much harder to solve.

Booting up his computer as he sat and gulped his third cup of coffee of the day, Pantera punched in the name and began reading the arrest file on Miranda Buckhorn. When he got to the license, he saw immediately it was the same girl.

Staring at her image on the license, he said, "Where's your baby, Miranda?"

Harry walked in with his own coffee and sat. Seeing Pantera's face, he said, "What is it?"

"Her name's Miranda Buckhorn, age nineteen."

"Cool. Aimee find it?"

"Yeah. She's got a record. Shoplifting and possession. And get this. She's also had a baby."

"No shit?"

"No shit."

"Where's the baby now?"

"Good question. I suggest we visit her last known address and see if there's a hungry, wet, poopy baby there crying his or her eyes out."

"Let's go," Harry said, and they left.

About twenty minutes later, they were pulling up in front of the small frame house off Chamberlayne. Getting out of the car, they approached the house. Harry knocked on the front door and waited. They heard footsteps and a woman perhaps in her early forties answered the door.

"Yes?"

"Ms. Buckhorn?"

"No, my name's Collier. Pam Collier."

"Ms. Collier, does a Miranda Buckhorn live here?"

The woman shrugged. "Sometimes."

Pantera asked, "So you do know Miranda Buckhorn?"

"Yes, she's my daughter, but she ain't home much. Mostly, she's out doing God knows what. Why you looking for her? You're cops, right?"

"Yes, ma'am, but we aren't really looking for her."

Before she could reply, they heard a small voice behind Ms. Collier say, "Grandma, can I have a cookie?"

"Is that Miranda's child?"

"Yeah. What of it?"

Harry held out his badge and said, "May we come in for a moment?"

The woman hesitated, and Pantera said, "It's very important. We're not here to arrest anyone, and we're not here to take the child. We're not CPS. We're detectives with RPD."

Ms. Collier sighed and held the door open.

The house was fairly clean, though shabby. The furniture was worn and the walls needed a coat of paint that should have been applied years ago. The smell of cigarettes was in the air, and Pantera noticed the half-full ashtray next to a chair that faced the TV.

"Do you work, Ms. Collier?"

"I do laundry for some folks. They just drop it by and I wash, dry, and fold it. I charge four dollars a pound of laundry. Got a scale in the back. It's accurate, too. You can check it."

"Ms. Collier, we're not here for that either," Harry said.

"Well then, what are you here for?"

"Grandma, can I have a cookie," the child, a girl around two, asked again.

"Yes, honey. The cookie jar is on the table in the kitchen. Just help yourself, but no more than two, okay?"

"Okay." The girl, who Pantera noticed did not look much like Miranda, turned and left the room.

"So, Miranda's name isn't the same as yours. She's married?"

"No. I got married again, but I'm widowed now. Kept the name because it's easier than changing it. I was a Buckhorn when I had Miranda."

"Ms. Collier, I regret to inform you that something has happened with Miranda. She was murdered and her body was found in a vacant lot by the side of the road."

She sat still for a moment before wiping away a tear that had slid silently down her cheek. To Pantera, she seemed to have expected such news and had become resigned to the idea her daughter would die young. "That girl. I told her things would come to no good. She's been wild since she was twelve."

"Did she consider this her home? Her place of residence?"

"I guess so, but she wasn't here much. When she was, she wasn't, you know? She'd sleep all day and go out at night. Didn't like the daytime. Claimed she was secretly a vampire or something. Hated the sun." She looked at the detectives. "I don't mean she really thought she was a vampire, or nothing. She just didn't like the sun. Said it was too hot on her skin, especially in summer."

Pantera looked at Harry and nodded. That part of the mystery was solved.

"And you took care of her daughter?"

"Most of the time. Well, all of the time, really. She mostly would just sit and chat with her when she was here. But that was alright. I'm not the best mom in the world, but she wasn't ready for that stuff. Ready for the sex, of course, but not the responsibility of taking care of a child."

"How old was she when she gave birth?"

"Sixteen. I wish I'd raised her better, but I wasn't ready myself, though I was older. I was nineteen when I had her. Her daddy took off when she was four months old. So I guess he was a worse daddy than I was a mother."

"Ms. Collier, I'm not trying to consider the worst, but do you know if she was hooking?" Pantera asked.

"Like she belonged to a rug makers club. Started in on it early when she was still in high school."

"Do you know who her pimp might have been?"

"No, but whoever it was had money, and lots of it."

"How do you know?"

"Because, he was always giving stuff to Miranda. Expensive stuff. Jewelry, shoes, dresses. Lord, that girl could look like a million bucks when she was dolled up. Funny thing was, she could also pass for a lot younger. She said the men she saw liked that. I think it's disgusting."

Pantera had suspected this when they'd found her and he'd noticed how young she appeared despite evidence she was older.

Miranda's daughter came out of the kitchen and walked over to Harry. "What's your name?"

Harry looked at her and said, "I'm Harry. What's yours?"

"Felicia. I can even spell it."

"Can you now?"

"Yes," Felicia said and proved it. Harry glanced at Pantera, a signal for him to continue the questions with Ms. Collier while he entertained Felicia and was entertained by her.

"Could we go into the kitchen?" Pantera asked, and Ms. Collier, getting the hint, stood.

"Sure. Right in here," she said and led the way.

When they were seated there, Pantera said, "Did Miranda ever mention any names, either of her pimp or one of the men she saw on a more regular basis?"

"No. She told me I was better off not knowing."

"Did she say why she thought your safety might be compromised?"

"Yeah, she said these men were real powerful. She said they could make any of us disappear in an instant, and nobody would ever find us." She hesitated. "I guess they didn't mind if someone found her."

"Yes, ma'am. So you never saw her with any of these men?"

"Well, there was one, but I only got a glimpse of him. He dropped her off one morning just before sunrise. I saw them pull up on the street and I was wondering who it was. Then she got out of the car, and the light inside came on for only as long as the car door was open. I saw him for like two seconds."

"Would you recognize him again if you saw him?"

"Sure," Ms. Collier said. "He looks a lot like

Felicia. I figured he must be her daddy."

"Do you remember what kind of car it was?"

"No. It was still dark, and I had gotten up to start my day. I had a lot of laundry that day, always do on a Saturday morning. Anyway, I wouldn't know a Buick from a Ford. They all look mostly alike to me.

Pantera asked a few more questions but learned nothing new. Finally, he rose and thanked Ms. Collier, saying, "I have to say I noticed you weren't all that upset that your daughter was murdered."

"I've been expecting it for a while, Detective. I guess I sort of made myself get used to the idea. I rarely saw her anyway. Nothing much has changed, really. She just won't walk in the door anymore. Mostly, I'm sad for Felicia. She won't remember her mom at all. First, she didn't see her that much to begin with, and second, she's only three, though a smart three."

"Can we take a look around Miranda's room?"

"Sure. It's this way," Ms. Collier said, and led them down a short hall.

When they entered, Pantera noticed a musty smell because the room had been closed up. They began looking around the room, each starting to one side of the door and moving around the room in opposite directions.

Harry reached the bed in his search and carefully stripped off the covers and sheets. Then he lifted the mattress, checking to see if anything was under there. He found what looked like a diary. "Tony?"

"Yeah?" he asked, looking from the dresser, where he was going through the drawers.

"Jackpot."

"Is that what I think it is?"

"I think so."

Pantera walked over with his phone and snapped a few pictures of the diary as it lay on the box spring mattress. Then he took a video of Harry as he brought out a handkerchief and one of the evidence bags they'd brought with them. Draping the handkerchief over his hand, he carefully placed the diary into the evidence bag. The prints would be able to verify that it was indeed Miranda's diary, though that would likely not be questioned.

Sealing the flap and writing the date, time, and location of where it had been found, Harry said, "You think we'll find anything useful, or just the fantasies and jealousies of a young girl?"

"I don't know, but I hope she named someone who could be her killer. If she included a possible motive, that would be nice, too."

They searched the rest of the room and came up with nothing of consequence. It held nothing more than would be expected in a young girl's bedroom.

They stopped to talk to Ms. Collier on the way out.

"Did you know about this?" Harry asked, holding up the diary.

She looked at it as if they'd found an unusual and mysterious artifact from the moon. "No, I've never seen it before. Is it Miranda's?"

"I would assume so. It was under the mattress."

"No, I never looked under there. To be honest, I was too afraid of what I might find."

As they left the room, Pantera said, "One last thing. Did she have a cell phone?"

"She had one, but she didn't pay for it."

"Who did?"

"She said it was a burner she was given to use."

"Did you know the number?"

"Nope. She wouldn't give it to me."

"Okay, thank you."

When they left the house, Pantera filled Harry in on what he'd found out from his conversation with Ms. Collier in the kitchen.

Harry said, "So, if we find someone who knew Miranda who looks like his gene pool was in charge of creating Felicia, we'll have the child's father."

"Yep. And maybe her killer as well."

"You think he'll come forward and try to get custody of the kid?" Harry asked.

"I doubt it. He never visited her from what we were told, and he has to know if someone does come forward, that person will be suspect number one."

After they pulled away from the house, Pantera said, "I don't understand frightened parents. I can't imagine being afraid to look under one of my daughter's mattresses because I was afraid of what I might find."

"If you suspected one of them was doing drugs, you might. If you were to find drugs, you'd have to arrest her."

"And I would. Not because I'm a mean father, but because a first offense like that would get them into rehab, not jail, unless it was enough to charge with intent."

"See?" Harry said. "Intent to distribute is another matter, and I can assure you that you'd be afraid."

"Not so afraid that I wouldn't look there, especially if I felt I could get her what she needed most, rehab."

"Then again, Miranda didn't turn out as well as Andrea or Beth. There might have been a hundred things Ms. Collier was afraid to find. She said Miranda had been wild since she was twelve. That's a young age to start down that path."

"Yeah, I guess you're right."

"Let's get this diary printed and start our reading assignment," Harry said.

"Let's do it."

When they dusted for prints, they could tell only one person had handled the diary

Two hours later, they were able to open the diary and

read what was there. The early parts were mostly from a much younger version of Miranda. The journal held the typical ramblings of a young teenager. She had apparently had the diary for a long time.

They began to worry that she hadn't written anything in it for years when the handwriting changed suddenly to something more mature. The topics were more mature as well.

She discussed her private sex life, including parties where she would "hook up" with someone. Then she talked about how she was making money by selling her body. This didn't seem to bother her. She claimed not to be like "the street whores," who would sell it to whoever drove by. She considered herself a high-class call girl, bragging that some men would pay over a thousand dollars for one night with her.

She talked about how the more disgusting among them would believe she was only fourteen or fifteen and pay a premium for sex with her. "I was always angry that I was so petite when I was growing up, but I'm taking advantage of that now," she wrote.

Finally, they came to a passage that made them both freeze.

"I gotta see CP for more support money for F."

They stared at the initials. CP. Who could that be? Miranda had apparently wanted to make sure that if her mother found the diary, she would not know the name of Felicia's father. Why? There was so much that was personal in the journal. She would hide this information beyond anything else? Why?

They continued reading and came upon another intriguing sentence. "See you-know-who about payment. He won't like what happens if he doesn't pay what he owes."

"Was she blackmailing someone?" Harry asked.

"Not sure. It could be money she lent someone and

this note is a reminder to collect the debt. Probably is."

"But what if 'you-know-who' didn't want to pay and killed her instead?"

"Then we're in deep shit because there's no clue who 'you-know-who' is."

After finishing the diary, they found no other references to CP or the even more mysterious, 'you-know-who.' They had hoped that at least whoever it was would be named eventually, but it was the only instance of the use of those initials.

Harry asked the question that had plagued them since reading the line about CP. "Why, after all she revealed, would she want to keep the name of Felicia's father a secret? I can understand not naming men when talking about the guys who paid her for sex. She may not have even known their names. But this is the man who got her pregnant."

"Good question. Maybe she's afraid of the guy. Maybe he's an extremely powerful man in the community, or a politician?"

"Could be."

"Then again, she didn't use Felicia's name either, just the initial *F*. It could just be what she did when it came to names. She didn't use any names in the diary except for when she talked about her mom. Even the other person she mentioned was 'you-know-who.' Anyway, we just have to find someone she knew intimately with those initials."

"Yeah. Needle, meet haystack," Harry said.

7

Claude returned to his office after dropping Circe at the airport. He did not know her real name—nobody he knew did. All he knew was that she was powerful in her world. Her interests spread from legitimate financial ventures to the most illegal ones imaginable. For example, Miranda was a girl who often passed for fifteen with customers, who would pay a premium for such girls. He'd heard, though, that Circe had some girls working for her as call girls who were truly that young. Of course, these girls didn't do it because they wanted to. They did it because they were virtual slaves.

Claude had watched as Ron was tortured to death. Circe herself had inflicted much of the pain. It had been something like the ancient idea of dying by a thousand cuts. Circe had watched Claude during this procedure. Her look had its intended effect. Claude knew if he double-crossed her, this would happen to him.

Arriving at his office, Claude leaned back in his chair and looked out the window at the Richmond skyline across the James River. He was in charge now. Circe had already sent an email instructing those in her world that he had been promoted to Senior VP of the Southeastern US operations and that Ron was "no longer with the company."

Now, several days after Circe's visit, he knew he should be happy, but he felt more than a little discomfort with his new position. Screwing up would earn what he now called, "The Ron Treatment."

As the airliner taxied for takeoff, Circe considered the day's events. While Claude had shown himself to be loyal to her, she knew he would bear watching. His promotion was like what the military called a "spot promotion." A need for a higher ranking leader arose, and he was available and high enough in the chain of command to warrant allowing him to be in charge. However, he would hold that position only long enough for her to either decide he was the right person for the job or someone else needed to be moved to Richmond. If the former, he would be allowed to live.

Once they were at cruising altitude, she pulled her laptop from her carry-on and began typing the text of an email to Monique, her executive assistant and someone she had sex with. Monique was young, pretty, capable— and totally devoted to Circe. More than that, she understood they both could have sex with whomever they wanted. Circe didn't love Monique. In fact, Circe recognized she was a narcissist and loved nobody more than herself.

She was careful to word the email in such a way as to appear innocuous, but Monique would understand what wasn't said. For example, "Ron is no longer with the company" meant he was dead. Nobody that high up in the business was allowed to leave alive.

Circe had decided to forego the commercial flight from New York to Paris. She instructed Monique to send her jet over once the maintenance was finished. She would spend a few days in New York, visiting her offices there and enjoying the city. Like many city dwellers, she loved New York. Regardless of one's idea of fun, it was available there, no matter how unique, and her tastes were often bizarre. She pressed send and settled back into her seat, trying to ignore the world around her.

On Saturday, Nancy arrived at Pantera's with Andrea and Beth, who stowed their bags in their respective bedrooms. As a precaution, Pantera now had his home swept monthly for any listening or viewing devices. He'd been the victim of that before, and the girls had been rightfully mortified that they'd been spied on in their bedrooms on one visit. He paid someone he knew in the city's IT department to conduct the sweep and check behind vents, which had been the location of the cameras before.

"Will you be looking into the house down the street?" Pantera asked.

"I'm not sure living a two-minute walk away would be the wisest move for either of us," Nancy said.

Beth said, "We'd love it, but Mom says no."

Nancy looked at Beth and said, "If I want your input, I'll ask for it."

When Nancy had left to begin her house-hunting, the girls went to their rooms and unpacked. A few minutes later, Andrea came out and asked, "Did Mom tell you about me and Dani?"

"Yes. I'm sorry, honey. Are you okay?"

"Yeah. We just—you know—decided to go our separate ways."

"That will happen a lot until you find the person you want to spend your life with. Was there something specific that led to the breakup?"

"Not really. The weird part is I miss her as a friend. We were dating, and now she and I never talk. We were friends before we became a couple. I wish we could just go back to being friends."

"That might be the hardest part of a breakup. Your mother and I were friends before we married. It took a while before we could be friends again, but sharing children sort of forced us to do that."

She gave him a sideways glance.

"What's that supposed to mean?" Pantera asked.

"What?"

36

"That sideways look you gave me, as if I don't know something I should."

"I'm not sure Mom wants to be your friend anymore."

"What? Of course she does."

"No, you don't understand, Dad. Beth and I sort of wonder if she doesn't want to get back with you—you know—romantically."

"I think you're misinterpreting something," he said.

"I don't know. She's very happy to be moving closer to you."

"That's probably because I'll be more available to help out with you two."

"I don't think so. I mentioned that to her when she talked about moving back, and she said she didn't expect you to help out in that way much more than you already do because you're so busy."

Pantera thought about that. The convenience factor really was in his favor. He could see the girls more often and spend more time with them. That was a plus on his side. Nancy never was the kind of mother to want to pawn the kids off so she could go out and have some fun. Still, what Andrea was suggesting was…ridiculous.

Beth entered the room at that moment and said, "Talking about Mom and Dad getting back together?" The question sounded as though the results were a foregone conclusion.

Andrea ignored her and said, "She also mentioned that you said you and Lisa aren't serious."

"Well, we're not. At least not serious enough to be talking about moving in together or something. But we are exclusive."

"She sounded happy about it, Dad," Andrea said.

"Listen, you're just getting the wrong idea about what she's saying. That's all. You're taking it wrong. Maybe it's what you'd like to see happen, so you're letting your imaginations run away with you. She might be lonely. That's easy to see. She loved Phil, and now he's dead. She's sleeping alone now. I can tell you that's a big transition."

"Well, I'm just telling you what I think. You asked why I looked at you like that. I wasn't going to lie."

"And I wouldn't want you to, but you definitely have your wires crossed here."

"I'd love it if you and Mom got back together," Beth offered. "But I still want you to keep seeing Lisa, too."

Andrea laughed. "Yeah, like that's gonna happen."

"Hey, it's my imagination. I can do with it what I want."

"Neither Mom nor Lisa would stand for that," Andrea answered.

"To be honest, neither would I," Pantera said. "Okay, enough of this talk. What do you say we head to the park and grab some lunch after?"

They both thought that was a good idea. As they walked in the park later, Pantera thought about what Andrea had said and worried if she might be right. He preferred to be with Lisa now, and that thought made him consider his feelings for Lisa in a different light as well.

8

Twyla Garrett was worried. Buddy, her ex, had never gone an entire weekend without calling to find out how they were doing, especially the kids. He was a good father. He wanted to spend time with the kids, not shun the responsibility, and on the weekends he didn't have them, he always called. Always.

She'd been slightly worried Saturday afternoon, but that had grown to near panic by Sunday evening. The only thing that would keep him from calling was a tragedy occurring, and she feared the worst, wondering if he'd been in a car wreck. She'd called the local hospitals, but he wasn't there.

He sometimes went fly-fishing up at a place he knew, but then again, he would have called before going there since a phone signal was almost impossible to find once he was up there. She figured maybe he had left early Saturday and planned to call on the way but had been in an accident before he could. Maybe his car was in a deep ditch or down some ravine and nobody even knew he was there.

All of these scenarios whipped through her imagination. The kids, both in their mid-teens, were worried, too. They hadn't said much, but she could see it in their faces. Leanne looked almost desperate to hear from her father by Sunday morning, and Frank was doing his best to remain calm. Still, she could see they were frightened for their father.

Once the kids were off to school on Monday, she called the police to report him missing. They told her she would have to come down to the station and fill out a form. Calling her work to let them know she would be late, she drove to the station.

When she entered, a woman greeted her and asked her business. Then she was directed to an area where she would wait to be seen.

Finally, she was escorted to the detective squad room to be interviewed.

A large man greeted her there.

"Hello, I'm Detective Harry Overmeyer. I understand your husband is missing?"

"My ex-husband."

"Sorry. Your ex-husband is missing?"

"Yes, and so you know, he and I get along well. He's a good father to our kids and has a steady job."

Harry opened a fillable PDF document on his computer and said, "His name?"

"Irwin Jarvis Garrett, but he goes by Buddy."

Harry typed and said, "Date of birth?"

This went on as he completed the basic details about Twyla's ex-husband, including his last address.

"What makes you think he's disappeared?"

"Because he always calls on the weekends when he doesn't have the kids to speak to them. Always. He never fails to do that, no matter what."

"Do you have a recent photo of him?"

"Oh, yes." She fished in her purse for the photo of him taken at their recent July Fourth party and handed it to Harry, who ran the photo through a scanner.

"You mentioned he has a steady job. Where?"

"He's a security guard for Circe Enterprises. They have an office downtown."

She noticed another detective look over at them when she said that, but he went back to whatever he'd been doing. She asked the detective who had looked over, "Do you know something about Circe Enterprises?"

The detective, whose name badge read, "Pantera," looked at her and said, "No, ma'am. I just thought it was an interesting name. Circe is a famous character in Greek mythology. She's a goddess in Homer's *Odyssey*. She's the one who changed Odysseus's men into pigs so he couldn't leave her island."

"Oh," Twyla said.

"Don't mind him. He's a literature nut. Quotes Shakespeare all the time." Harry changed the subject back to the missing person report.

"When was the last time you saw or heard from your ex-husband?" Harry asked.

She thought about the question. "Thursday, I think." Then she said, "No, definitely Thursday. It was the day our daughter was home sick. He called to find out how she was doing."

"He seemed to be okay?"

"Yes."

"Did he seem worried about anything? Preoccupied?"

"No. He was his typical self. He has a hard job, and sometimes the stress can get to him, and he'll drink. Sometimes a lot. That's why we divorced. I just couldn't take watching him drink himself into oblivion."

Harry watched her as she said this. Being a security guard was not that stressful, especially if the place of business was a larger firm. He wondered what else might be happening in the man's life. He also considered the man may have gone on a bender and wasn't communicating with anyone, his ex and his kids included.

"Has he always been a heavy drinker?"

"Not really. He'd have an occasional beer. He started drinking heavily about a year after going to work for Circe Enterprises. That's why I think the stress of that job was too much. Well, I just couldn't handle it

41

anymore. I told him me or the bottle." She looked at her lap. "I guess you can see which one he chose."

"I'm sorry, ma'am. You say you or the bottle. Are you saying he moved on from drinking beer to drinking liquor?"

"Yes. It was like someone flipped a switch or something. He came home all upset one day with a bottle of Jack Daniels. He'd already downed a fair amount of it, and he was stinking drunk."

Pantera had been eavesdropping on the interview and, probably like Harry, wondered what had caused the man to dive off the deep end like that, especially since he'd not been a heavy drinker before. What on earth would cause such a drastic change?

"How long has he worked for Circe Enterprises?" Harry asked.

After a moment to consider, she said, "He started working for them in April three years ago. Whatever happened that made him drink so much happened in September of that year. I filed for divorce that June."

"And you say he is a good father to your children?"

"Oh, yes. A wonderful father. Loves them very much. He even told me he still loves me, and he understands why I divorced him. Said he'd divorce himself if he could."

"Has he ever gone missing before?"

"No. Never. That's why I'm so worried."

"Any idea where he might have gone if he decided to disappear for a while?"

She told Harry about how much he loved to fish and where. "I checked the hospitals, and he's not there."

"The local ones?"

"Yes. Do you think he could be in one out of the Richmond area?"

"I don't know, ma'am. Just something we can check. Have you gone by where he lives?"

"Yes, but he doesn't answer the door. I don't have a key."

"And what's his address?"

She provided it. "If he's there, he might be dead."

"There are a number of reasons he could be there, ma'am. We'll see if we can get inside."

They continued the interview until Harry thought he had enough to begin the search for the missing security guard. The case with Miranda hadn't gone anywhere yet, so he and Pantera could begin this investigation. He hoped to find Irwin "Buddy" Garrett within twenty-four hours. He had probably gone somewhere and passed out, deciding to chuck it all when he woke up. He'd seen it happen before, and he'd see it again.

When Ms. Garrett left, he looked over at Pantera and said, "Want to take a ride over to Circe Enterprises before lunch? Then we can stop by Garrett's to see if he's just sick with the flu?"

"Sure," Pantera said, grabbing his coffee. "But shouldn't we stop at Garrett's first?"

"We would, but Circe Enterprises is on the way to Garrett's place of residence."

Arriving at Circe Enterprises, they entered the building but were stopped by a security guard sitting behind a long counter, blocking further entry.

"Your business?" the man asked, all business himself.

"My name is Detective Harry Overmeyer. I'm with Richmond PD. This is my partner, Detective Pantera. We're investigating a missing person report."

"Oh? Who?"

"You might know him, in fact. He's a security guard here. Buddy Garrett."

The man sat back and nodded, the serious look never changing. "Yeah, I know him. Nice guy, but he doesn't work here anymore."

"Oh? Since when?"

"Since Friday."

"This past Friday?"

"Yep."

"What happened? Was he fired?"

"I don't know. All I know is we received word he was no longer with the company. Not my business to know what happened."

Pantera entered the conversation. "Were you told to make sure he didn't enter the building if he stopped by?"

"Nope. Just told he doesn't work here anymore."

Pantera nodded. It didn't sound as if they were worried he might come in and start trouble. Given Garrett's drinking problem, he wondered about that. Then again, perhaps his bosses didn't know about that problem.

"Can I ask you something else?" Pantera said.

"You can ask whatever you want."

"You ever know him to take a drink?"

The man's demeanor shifted into a toothy grin. "Oh, yeah. Ol' Buddy could put it away. We stopped by a local tavern one night, and he was ripped within an hour."

"Did his bosses know about his drinking? Maybe that was a reason for giving him the boot?"

"Nobody said anything about giving him the boot. He's just not employed here anymore. Coulda quit for all I know. Wouldn't blame him, except the pay here is really good, especially for a guy in his position."

"And what position is that?" Harry asked.

"He was one of Mr. Paulson's right-hand-men."

"Mr. Paulson?"

"Yeah, Claude Paulson. One of the top executives here. In fact, he was put in charge here just last week."

"When last week?"

"Friday."

"The same day that was Mr. Garrett's last day?"

"Yeah."

"So, this Mr. Paulson's right-hand man quits, gets fired, whatever, and Paulson gets promoted the same day?"

"Well, I don't know if he was promoted that day or before that. All I know is the lady who owns the entire business comes in that day, and by the time she leaves, everything's different. No Buddy, no Mr. Widner, and Mr. Paulson's in charge."

"Widner?"

"Yeah, he was the guy who had the job that Mr. Paulson has now."

"So he was fired or quit, too?"

"Yeah, though to be honest, with people that high up and Ms. Circe's being here, I suspect he didn't leave voluntarily. I figured that must be why she was here. To make changes. I hear she lives in Paris, so it must have been a lot happening to bring her here."

"Paris, France?" Pantera asked.

"Yeah."

At that moment, a man stepped over and said, "Gene, what are you telling these men?"

The security guard they'd been talking to looked over his shoulder at the man who'd just asked the question. His eyes widened at the sight of the man in a dark suit standing behind him.

Pantera could see a bulge on the man's chest, suggesting he was carrying.

"Just answering their questions, Mr. Braxton. These are detectives with the Richmond Police."

Mr. Braxton extended his hand. "Leland Braxton. I'm head of security here at Circe. Perhaps you'd like to come with me to my office where you can get answers not colored by gossip and innuendo?"

Pantera glanced at Gene, who sat silently, his face grim, and wondered if the man would be following Buddy Garrett out the door. Braxton did not look pleased that Gene had talked to them at all. While he was being cordial to him and Harry, his anger at Gene was obvious.

"Sure," Harry said, and the two followed Braxton to an office nearby and sat in the lightly padded chairs facing the desk, moving the chairs a short distance away from each other, as Braxton sat in his expensive executive chair.

"What can I do for you fellas?" Braxton asked to begin the conversation.

"We were looking for Buddy Garrett. His ex-wife reported him missing."

"Yes, apparently, he left work early on Friday and called in to tender his resignation."

"You took the call?"

Braxton blinked before answering. "Yes."

"Did he say if he planned on leaving town?"

"No, sir. Just called and said, 'I quit' and when I asked why, he said, 'too much stress.' Then he hung up."

"I take it you are aware Mr. Garrett has a bit of a drinking problem?" Pantera asked.

"Detective, we run a tight ship here. I know everything I possibly can about my security employees. Yes, I knew."

"Did you ever know him to be volatile?"

"Well, any man, pushed to a limit, can get volatile, especially if he drinks."

"So you didn't fire him for his drinking problem?"

"No. I did suggest he attend AA and even offered some counseling the company would pay for, but he said no."

"Did you have any interactions with the woman who is, as Gene put it, 'the lady who owns the entire business' when she was here on Friday?" Harry asked.

Braxton seemed to consider the question.

"It's a simple enough question, Mr. Braxton. Either you did or you didn't," Harry said. Both detectives watched Braxton's face for signs of a lie.

"Well, I guess it depends on what you mean by an interaction. I didn't have a conversation with her, but we did pass each other in the hall, and I greeted her."

"Fair enough. I just thought for a moment you were attempting to be evasive."

"Not at all."

"Do you know why Mr. Paulson was promoted into Mr. Widner's job?" Pantera asked.

Braxton considered this question and said, "I have no idea. I'm not a part of those decisions."

Harry said, "Did Widner quit?"

"Again, I don't know."

"Were you told not to allow Mr. Widner back into the building?" Pantera asked.

"No. Nothing of the sort."

Pantera and Harry had worked out this questioning tactic, where neither would ask more than two questions in a row. It led the person being questioned to possibly get confused, having to turn from one to the other and handle the barrage of questions being thrown at him or her. To Harry and Pantera, it made the person being interrogated look as though he was sitting center court at a professional tennis match while also making the subject slightly uneasy.

"Do you know where either Buddy Garrett or Ron Widner are now?"

"No. Why are you asking me these questions about Mr. Widner? Is he reported missing, too?"

"No. It's just odd that the two men's positions with the company were severed on the same day, especially considering that Mr. Garrett was described as Mr. Paulson's right-hand man. And now Widner's out,

Paulson's promoted, and Garrett's nowhere to be found."

"Have you checked Garrett's home?"

"That's our next stop."

"Then I suggest you go there now. I'm rather busy and don't have any more time for you today."

"Okay," Pantera said. "If we have more questions, we'll be sure to drop by again."

Braxton handed them each his card. "Or maybe you could just email them, and I'll get to them when I can."

"He seemed touchy," Harry said as they left the building.

"Yeah. Like maybe there are some secrets he doesn't want us sniffing around."

"Do you think what that security guard, Gene, was telling us was influenced by gossip or innuendo?"

"Not at all. I feel he was more honest with us than Braxton was."

After lunch, they drove to the home of Buddy Garrett. They knocked but nobody was home as far as they could tell. They went around and looked into the windows and saw nothing. They could even see the bed was made and the breakfast dishes drying in the dish rack, complete with coffee mug. It appeared he hadn't been home in days, but they couldn't tell for sure.

Ms. Garrett had given them the phone number of Buddy's landlord. They called and had the man drive over to let them in for what they called a wellness check. As they waited, Pantera said, "Where's his car?"

"Good question. You think he's hightailed it somewhere?"

"I don't know, but it's not here. Maybe we'll find him dead in the bathroom and his car keys missing."

"Maybe."

When the landlord arrived and they entered the house, they were certain he had not been home in days.

The stench of the garbage in the kitchen wastebasket was apparent from the moment the front door was opened.

They checked the closets and found two empty suitcases and what appeared to be a closet full of his clothes.

"Well, we know he's been gone long enough for the stink of the garbage to take over." Harry said.

"Yeah. But where is he, and why did he leave so suddenly, apparently with only the clothes he was wearing?"

"Tony?"

"Yeah?"

"You have a bad feeling about this, too?"

Pantera nodded. "The worst."

9

Pantera considered the cases facing them. Turning to Harry, who was driving them back to work, he asked, "What do you think about hitting the streets and seeing if we can find a hooker who might know Miranda?"

"Sounds like the thing to do, but they won't be hitting the streets until tonight. You know as well as I do that overtime is off the table. Lieutenant Gariepy passed the word down from on high last week."

"Yeah, and shit rolls downhill. Maybe we could work tonight a few hours and come in late tomorrow? Think he'd go for that?"

"Don't see why not. Where you want to search?"

Pantera considered this. "We can meet at The Watering Hole and go from there. Lots of popular streetwalking in a quarter-mile radius."

"Maybe we could stop in at The Watering Hole after we knock off for the night," Harry said.

"Now you're talking. You think Ashley would be okay with that? I don't want you coming home drunk."

"I always stop at two. You know that."

"Just yanking your matrimony chain."

When they arrived back at the station, they tapped on the doorframe of Lt. Dan Gariepy's open door.

"Come on in. I can share my misery."

Taking a seat, Pantera said, "What's the misery this time?"

"Budget. Why should I be the only one miserable?"

"Yeah, about that," Pantera said, "Harry and I want to come in late tomorrow and work some tonight to balance the hours."

Gariepy tossed his pencil on the desk. "And what happens if a riot starts downtown or something, or something else comes up and I need you before you deign to show up?"

"Then they'll have to okay overtime or we can take the rest of the hours the next day," Harry said. "And you know we'll be in exactly when we say we will."

Gariepy sighed. "How long are we talking?"

"Two hours, tops."

"And why do you need this change in hours?"

Harry said, "We need to talk to some hookers."

"That hard up?" Gariepy asked.

Pantera chuckled. "With Ashley in his bedroom? You kidding?"

"Hey, guys," Harry warned.

Gariepy said, "Is this about the Buckhorn murder?"

"Yes," Pantera answered.

"You know I'd give you overtime if I could."

"We know," Harry said. "But money before lives is the rule of the times."

"Why can't you go talk to some now? There aren't many walking the streets right now, but there are a few."

"Miranda only worked at night. She hated sunlight for some weird reason. She likely didn't know many girls from the day shift," Pantera answered.

Gariepy considered the request and said, "Okay, but be in at ten sharp tomorrow. And if you go over two hours tonight, that's on your own time."

"Got it," Pantera said, and they left the office.

That evening, Harry met Pantera at both men's favorite bar, The Watering Hole. It was owned by Dean Ackerman, who had become one of their best friends. As usual, Pete Bray, Dean's brother-in-law, was in the same seat he'd sat in so often the cushion had reshaped itself into the shape of his backside. Neither detective had ever been inside the bar without Pete's constant presence, other than after he was shot during a robbery attempt a few months before. As soon as Pete had been able to return, he had.

"Hey, you ol' bastard! What's cooking?" Pantera shouted at Dean as they entered. It was the usual greeting from regular customers.

"Well, well. There was some dog shit on the sidewalk outside, and now it's come to life!" Dean answered, which was a new reply.

"Hey, Pete!" Pantera said. "How they hangin'?"

"Softly," he said with a chuckle.

"What you guys been doing?" Dean asked.

"Solving crimes. Or at least trying."

"So, the usual?" Dean said, holding up a bottle of Pantera's favorite whiskey, Writers Tears.

"Not right now," Pantera said. "We're actually on the clock. Maybe when we're done."

"At least have a Coke or something. I gotta make money."

"Okay, a Coke it is," Pantera said.

"Two," Harry added.

The detectives chatted with Pete, and when Dean set the two Cokes on the bar, he said, "So if you're working, does that mean there's been a crime out this way I haven't heard about? Another bodega robbery, maybe?"

"No. Nothing like that. We have to interview some young ladies in the neighborhood."

"Which ones?" Pete asked. His daughter had become mixed up with that business after getting hooked on drugs.

"Whichever ones will talk to us."

Dean laughed. "Hey, you got money, they'll talk."

"And more," Pete added.

"Nothing like that. We have a dead hooker, and we

need to find someone who might have known her."

"Ahh, then you're on a fishing expedition," Dean said. It wasn't a question, but a statement of fact.

"Yeah, and it would be nice if we landed what we're looking for."

"Who's the girl?" Pete asked.

"Name's Miranda Buckhorn, age nineteen," Harry said. "Pretty girl. Hadn't succumbed to the drugs that make you look old before you're thirty."

"Not yet, anyway, huh?" Dean said.

"Yeah, not yet," Pantera answered. Sighing, he downed the rest of his Coke, wishing it had some Writers Tears in it. Thinking of Miranda's body made him numb with regret that the young woman—girl, really—would never see her daughter again. That she'd been murdered and left in an empty lot like litter was what made him determined to solve the case. Someone had to pay for doing that.

He dropped a five on the bar and said, "Keep the change, Dean." Harry rose from his seat and they started for the door.

"Wow! A whole buck just for me!" Dean joked.

"Plus the enormous markup on what amounts to twelve cents in soda," Pantera replied with a chuckle. "See you fellas in a few hours."

They crossed the street and entered the alley that ran through to the next street. Both men were familiar with the alley, especially Pantera, who had been investigating a murder about a year or so ago when he found what had become his favorite bar by walking through the alley from the street where they were headed.

As they exited the alley, they saw four girls wandering along the side of the street near the corner with a traffic light. All four were dressed as if they had a party to go to somewhere and were waiting for their rides. Two wore short red dresses—one sequined, the other looking like imitation red velvet. Neither dress covered much. The other two wore similar "working" clothes. The girls were all of a different ethnic background, as if the pimp had placed them there in case a customer might want his pick of races, which was probably the case. Both men knew who the pimp was, a man who went by the street name of Bam-Bam.

Catching the eye of one of the girls, Pantera motioned for her to step over. Her face told him she knew he was a cop. Harry stepped over to one of the other girls and began a conversation with her.

"Yeah?" the girl said as she approached Pantera. "I know you're a cop, so don't pretend you aren't."

"I won't. In fact, I'm here to ask you a few questions and hoped you could help me out by answering them."

"Depends on the question."

He took out the photo of the deceased Miranda Buckhorn that was taken by the M.E. The girl leaned back in surprise and revulsion.

"What you wanna show me a picture of a dead girl for?"

"I wondered if you'd ever seen her before."

She shook her head. "No."

"Are you sure? You barely looked at the picture."

"I seen enough to know I don't know her. Was she murdered?"

"Yep, and we'd like to make sure you and the other girls who work nights don't join her. It's possible someone is targeting girls like you. After all, you're easy targets and live a dangerous lifestyle."

"It ain't dangerous!"

"Listen, you and I both know what you do for a living. I'm not vice, and neither is my partner over there. We're just looking for whoever did this. Frankly, yes, your lifestyle is dangerous. You climb into cars with strangers without knowing what might happen to you as a result of that one moment. So, if you know who this girl is or have seen her around anywhere before, it would help both of us if you'd tell me."

She stepped closer to look more carefully at the photo but still seemed coiled to run if the need arose. After studying it for a moment, he took out another picture, one Pam Collier, Miranda's mother, had given them when they were there.

She looked at that photo and said, "Why didn't you show me this one first instead of that one of her dead?"

"To let you know how serious the questions were."

She glanced up at him. He'd been watching her eyes as she looked at the photos to see if she registered any recognition. The eyes always told the truth about such things, no matter what the mouth said.

She shook her head. "No. I don't recognize her. Never saw her before."

She was telling the truth.

Because he and Harry were there, looking very much like the cops they were, no customers had stopped to talk to the girls, though a few had slowed down.

Harry, who had identical pictures of Miranda, had finished questioning the first woman he'd spoken to and had moved on to the next. Pantera called out to the remaining hooker and said, "Hey, come over here. I need to talk to you."

She walked over, obviously expecting the request.

"What is it? I ain't got time for chitchat."

"The faster you answer my questions, the sooner you can get back to work," Pantera said. "We're not vice, and I don't care about arresting you for soliciting."

"I figured that when you didn't arrest Charlotte."

Pantera knew Charlotte was not the other girl's real name. "And what name do you go by?"

She smiled. "I'm Dixie." She nodded at the first girl Harry had spoken to and said, "That's Trixie. We do doubles together sometimes." Pantera was only mildly surprised she was soliciting him.

"Yeah, we'll keep that in mind." He held out the first photo. Dixie stepped forward and squinted at it.

"I guess you want to know if I know her?"

"Yes." He watched her eyes.

She studied the photo for a second and Pantera thrust the other picture forward. "This is her when she was alive."

She studied that one as well. A flicker in her eyes suggested maybe she had at least seen her before.

"Nope. I don't know her."

"Okay, you don't know her, but you have seen her, am I right?"

"What makes you think that?"

"Your eyes. They always give you away when you see a picture of someone you recognize."

She huffed out a breath of disgust. "Okay, yeah. I've seen her before, but I have no idea who she is."

"Where did you see her?"

She looked directly into his eyes and said, "In all honesty, I don't remember. It could have been a party or just walkin' down the street. I just know I've seen her face before. And I swear that's the truth."

He locked his eyes on hers to see if she flinched away, but she didn't. Nodding, he said, "Okay, thank you. But do me a favor, will you? If you remember where you saw her, or anything else about her, would you step over to the next street through the alley and go inside The Watering Hole and give the owner or another guy who's always there the message, 'Tell Pantera I remembered.' Would you do that for me? And for yourself?"

"How for myself?"

He explained again how it was possible whoever killed Miranda was out to murder prostitutes.

She thought about it and said, "I ain't going into no courtroom. So if you think I'll be a witness, you can forget about it."

"No, no witness. No courtroom. I just want to find out more about the girl so we can find who did this to her."

"Okay." Her reluctance was palpable, and Pantera hoped she was telling him the truth.

"Thank you."

She returned to the edge of the sidewalk and started smiling at the cars that passed by. Harry joined Pantera.

"What did you find out?" Pantera asked.

"Nothing. Neither girl had ever seen her before."

"The second one I spoke to recognized her, but she couldn't remember from where. I asked her to tell Dean or Pete if she remembered.

They left that area and moved on to another hangout for girls in that line of work. After two hours, all they had was Dixie's revelation that she'd seen her before but couldn't place where.

They returned to The Watering Hole and had a real drink. Pantera told Dean and Pete about the hooker who might come by with a message for him.

"Dixie?" Pete said. "Yeah, I know which one she is. She knows me, too."

Dean said, grinning, "Pete, you been hittin' on the girls again?"

"You know it's not like that. I just give her a ten once in a while to help her buy some food."

Pantera watched this and smiled. Pete was one of the good ones.

After they left the bar, Harry and Pantera stood beside their cars and talked a bit.

"You know, I was thinking," Harry said.

"What about?"

"Miranda had that young girl look. Her mother said she got top dollar for that. Maybe we're barking outside the wrong doghouse. Maybe we should check out places where more affluent customers might be?"

"Not a bad idea, but I'm not sure where those types might hang out looking for prostitutes who can pass for fifteen or younger. It's not like they're in the phone book."

Harry shook his head. "Good point. See you tomorrow."

"Sure thing," Pantera said. "See you then."

Harry smiled. "Ten sharp."

"Yeah."

Pantera went home wondering if they would ever solve the murder of Miranda Buckhorn or the disappearance of Buddy Garrett.

10

On his way to work late the next morning, Pantera phoned Lisa. He should have called her in the past few days but had become too busy, first with his daughters and then with his work.

"Hello, there," he said when she'd picked up.

"Well, he's alive after all."

"Sorry about that. I got busy with my daughters, and then work has been a bear. How you been?"

"Lonely, mostly. If you hadn't called today, I was going to call you this evening."

"Maybe we could get together this weekend if you're free," he offered.

"That sounds good. What do you have in mind?"

"Dinner? Maybe go hear some good blues?" He appreciated that she liked blues music as well. It made choosing the style of music they listened to easy.

"Sounds great to me. Maybe I could come down and we could go to The Camel?" she said, naming a restaurant and bar in Richmond they liked to go to for the very good blues bands that played there every other Friday.

"Eager?"

"Oh, Tony. More than you know," she said.

"Then it's a date."

"You mentioned the girls. How are they doing?"

"I have them every weekend for the time being. Nancy is house-hunting. She wants to move back to Richmond."

"Are the girls okay with that?"

"They love the idea."

"What about Andrea and Dani? Won't they miss each other?"

"They broke up. I'm sure she'll tell you all about it next time she sees you. She spared me the details."

"So you'll still have them this weekend?"

"Yeah, but they can order pizza and watch a movie or something. I'll even let them rent one on TV. They'll be fine with that."

"Sounds fine to me," she said. "I'll get to your place around six."

"See you then," he said. "Love you."

"Love you, too," she said, and they clicked off as Harry was walking through the squad room door.

That afternoon they received a call from Twyla Garrett, asking if they had discovered anything about her ex-husband's disappearance yet. They told her what they'd been able to find out, and she was shocked that Circe's security guard had told them Buddy was no longer with the company.

"He had worked there for eight years! The pay was well above average. It was a stressful job, but he loved doing that kind of work."

"Ms. Garrett, you keep talking about the stress of the job he had. To be honest, being a security guard is usually a boring job. There's rarely anything to do but pass the time. It's not as if the building is in a high-crime area or anything."

"I don't know. I asked him once what was so stressful, and he got angry and said never to ask him again. I figured he just didn't like to talk about his job. He's never been one to do that anyway."

"Did you feel his reaction was strange for him?"

"Yes, but I didn't think much about it after that. He just didn't like to talk about what he had to do for his bosses."

Pantera wondered if sexual harassment was the

reason. Men were rarely the victims, but it did happen. That could explain his refusal to talk about his job and the amount of stress it created. He couldn't imagine anything else that could cause that amount of stress in a security guard's job. Being a cop was much more stressful, but he didn't react in destructive ways to it.

"Ms. Garrett, is it possible your husband was experiencing sexual harassment on the job?"

"What? Buddy?"

"Yes, ma'am. It's been known to happen."

"Not with Buddy. He'd quit if that happened."

"Maybe that's what finally occurred last week? Perhaps he decided the pay wasn't worth it and quit suddenly after taking it as long as he could. That would certainly explain his stress level and anger at being asked about it."

There was silence on the other end, and Pantera waited for her to respond.

"You know, it is kind of weird what happened."

"What do you mean?"

"Well, when he was first hired on, he was paid only a little more than what he had been paid in his last job as a security guard. Then about a week after he came home all upset about the stress of the job, he got a huge raise, nearly double what he'd been making."

"And that didn't make you suspicious?"

"Well, it did, but he seemed okay with doing whatever he was doing for the pay, even if it was stressful, and we were able to pay off all our debts besides the house and his car, which we were still paying for back then."

"Did you suspect he was having sex with someone else?"

"No. If some woman came on to him, he'd just tell her he wasn't interested." She paused. "And even if he was, I don't see why he would get angry about it."

"What if a man was coming on to him?"

She actually laughed. "Are you joking? He's about as much against homosexuals as he would be about having his teeth pulled without being numbed! He loves our kids, but he said if either turned out to be gay, he'd disown them."

Her comment made him think of Andrea and the hatred she would face because she was attracted to other girls and not guys before he moved on. "Then unwanted sexual attention from a man would increase his anger and stress on the job, wouldn't it?"

"Yes, but he'd quit before he took a second comment from him. He'd go to HR at the very least."

Pantera considered this and thought about how HR might do nothing if the harasser was in a high enough position in the company. He considered saying this, but she would only say he would quit immediately if faced with such behavior.

Still, the huge pay increase was telling. It was meant to keep him from saying anything to anyone about whatever it was that was bothering him.

This caused reconsideration about the workplace and how it could have something more to do with his disappearance than they first realized. What if he had decided to accept the problems with the increased pay until he felt he'd had enough and told his harasser—or whoever was the cause of the stress—that he would no longer tolerate it and was going to tell someone outside the building about what was happening?

Pantera also considered that it could be illegal activities that he'd become aware of in his job and was being paid to keep his mouth shut about that. The corporate world held any number of reasons for continued secrecy regarding certain matters.

"Ms. Garrett, I think we're going back out to Circe Enterprises to see what we can find out. I'll let you know when we find anything further."

"Thank you, Detective."

Harry had listened to Pantera's end of the conversation. "So, what's up?" he asked.

Pantera explained what he and Ms. Garrett had discussed, including her comment about Buddy Garrett's feelings about gays.

"Sorry about that, Tony. I know you don't like to hear that stuff, but it's everywhere. Some people prefer to find reasons to hate people instead of letting them live their lives. The biggest problem is many people think that the majority of homosexuals are pedophiles."

"I know, but study after study shows the ratio of heterosexual pedophiles to homosexual pedophiles is eleven to one."

"The people who hate homosexuals don't know that or ignore it."

"Yeah, but they need to know it."

"I agree," said Harry, "but right now we have a case to work. Two of them, actually."

"Wouldn't it be wild if the two cases were connected?" Pantera asked.

"I wouldn't hold my breath."

When they arrived at the Circe building, they entered the large lobby and were once again stopped at the desk by a security guard, this time a different one. In an attempt to grease the wheels as if they were frequent visitors, Harry asked, "So where's Gene?"

The man scowled. "Not here anymore."

"What happened?" Harry asked.

"I don't know. We were just told he was no longer employed here."

Pantera said, "I'm curious. Do you guys have a meeting where those no longer working here are announced or something?"

"No, it's a secure facility, so former employees are

no longer allowed in the facility unless accompanied by someone high enough on the food chain. We get an email every day with names and pictures of both new employees and those no longer working here."

"I see. So, no idea why Gene isn't here?" Pantera wondered about the strength of the security with the security guards so willing to share information.

"Other than I know he didn't quit? No."

Harry asked, "How do you know he didn't quit?"

"Listen, who are you guys? Why all the questions?"

"Sorry," Harry said, "just making conversation."

"Why are you here? You didn't stop by just to chat."

Pantera said, "We'd like to see Mr. Paulson."

"Do you have an appointment?"

"I'm afraid not," Harry said.

"Then you ain't seeing him. Good day." The guard began rearranging the various papers and pencils on the large semi-circular desk.

Pantera said, "We're detectives with the Richmond PD. We really need to talk to Mr. Paulson about an important matter."

"Important?"

"Yes, urgent, in fact."

"And what is this urgent matter you need to speak to him about?"

"Sorry, for his ears only."

"Can't help you."

They were going to have to make the reason more important than it actually was.

Pantera said, "We've uncovered a planned theft of corporate secrets that could result in huge losses to Circe Enterprises. We want to warn him and tell him what he needs to be on the lookout for. Now, if you don't at least call him and let him know we are here, then he'll eventually find out you blocked us and wouldn't even call him to let him decide whether to see us or not. At that point, he'll have someone else to blame. Wanna guess who that will be?"

The guard picked up the phone and dialed a number after looking it up in the staff directory on his computer. After explaining to whoever answered what Pantera and Harry were there for, he waited a moment then said, "Okay. Thank you, Ms. Staples. I'll tell them to have a seat."

Hanging up, he said, "Someone will be down in a few minutes to escort you to his office. You can have a seat over there." He pointed to some chairs to his left that sat against the plate-glass window that faced the street.

A few moments later, an attractive woman in her late thirties to early forties stepped off the elevator. She stopped to speak with the guard before coming over to Pantera and Harry.

"Good morning. My name is Doreen Staples. I'm Mr. Paulson's assistant. Could you follow me, please?"

She turned and started toward the elevators on the right side of the lobby.

As they rode up the elevator, the woman said, "Mr. Paulson can give you eight minutes. He's a very busy man."

Pantera and Harry exchanged a glance. They could be there longer, or Paulson could have them escorted from his office when he discovered there was no planned theft. They would find out what they could in the time they had.

As they were escorted into Mr. Paulson's private office, Pantera nearly fell over.

The man looked like an adult male version of Felicia Buckhorn.

When Pantera looked at Harry, he could see his partner saw the resemblance, too. They had found the first needle. CP was Claude Paulson.

11

Paulson extended a hand and stepped to them. "I don't have much time. I have a meeting in a few minutes, and there are a few things I have to do before it begins. You mentioned something about someone planning some kind of corporate theft?"

Pantera said, "About that. We apologize, but we needed to get in to see you, and that seemed the easiest way to accomplish that. The truth is that an employee of yours has gone missing, and we could use some information about what he did here."

Paulson flushed with anger. "Which employee?"

"Mr. Irwin Garrett. He goes by Buddy."

Pantera noticed a momentary shift in the man's eyes before Paulson said, "It's a large company, detectives. I don't know everyone here. I'm afraid I can't help you."

"We were told you did know him," Pantera said. "He was described as a 'right-hand man' to you."

Paulson's eyes flitted between the two detectives. "Who told you that?"

"One of your other security guards."

Paulson blew out a breath in disgust. "And which one would that be?"

"We only know him as Gene."

"Well, this 'Gene' is making things up to sound as if he knows more than he does about the business here. It's typical of people in the more blue-collar jobs in a company. They start bragging that they know a lot more than they do. Makes them look important. I'll be sure to find out who this 'Gene' is and have Leland Braxton, my head of security, have a talk with him about telling lies, especially to the cops. Now, if you'll excuse me, I have a meeting to prepare for."

"Actually, he was fired after talking with us."

"Good. Was there anything else?"

Harry asked, "Would it be possible to see Garrett's personnel file?"

"Those are confidential. You'll need a court order to do that."

Pantera shrugged. "Have it your way, then," he said. "We'll return with a search warrant."

"Fine. When you do, ask to speak to someone in HR. I don't have time for such trivialities."

Thirty seconds later, they were being escorted down to the lobby by a fuming Doreen Staples.

"Did you know Buddy Garrett?" Harry asked her as they descended.

"Why would I?"

"Just wondering."

"I think you need to get all your information on any employees from HR."

"It doesn't bother you that he's missing?"

She turned to the detectives. "No, what bothers me is how you've implied that we're hiding something."

Harry shrugged. "Well, we're just going by what we were told."

"Well, you won't be going by what I tell you because that will be nothing." At that moment, the elevator doors opened. She stepped out with them and escorted them to the security desk. "Good bye," she said before turning back to stride back to the elevators.

As they walked to their car, Pantera said, "Can you believe our luck? Did you notice that Felicia Buckhorn is a two-year-old female version of Claude Paulson, better known as 'CP'?"

"Yeah. I guess that's how you find needles in haystacks, just chance upon them without trying."

"When do we tell Pam Collier?"

"Soon. She can get an order for a paternity test, and Mr. Paulson can find himself financially responsible for his illegitimate daughter."

"I know looks aren't a sure thing, but I've never seen a kid resemble a parent more," Harry said.

"I just hope our luck holds."

Once they were in the car, Pantera said, "By the way, methinks Circe Enterprises has something to hide beyond the paternity of little girls. Something big, in fact."

"And methinks you are right. Do you believe what he said about blue-collar workers?"

"Sometimes that happens. Not in this case, though. Gene appeared to know exactly what was going on there. Anyway, why say Garrett had any kind of special relationship with the top boss? If he was going to lie in order to brag, he'd say he himself was the right-hand man for Paulson."

"And why isn't Braxton the 'right-hand man'? He's head of security."

"Good question."

"Maybe Gene was talking about more like doing the dirty work."

"Dirty work? For a security guard?"

"Hey, I'm just grasping at straws here," Harry said.

"We could ask Gene about what he meant, but he's not there anymore. We don't even have a last name."

"Yeah, another needle. Maybe we'll run into him at Walmart this weekend or something."

"I don't shop at Walmart. Maybe we could find out where he lives from his personnel file."

"I thought we were only planning to look at Garrett's."

Pantera smiled at Harry. "I guess that depends on the wording of the search warrant. What do you say we go write one up to search the personnel files of – quote – any employees who have left the company in the past three months?"

"Sounds great to me."

"Then step on it. My money's on the idea Paulson just told us a huge pack of lies."

"Same here. The question is, why?"

"Gotta be hiding something big," Pantera said.

An hour later, they had finished the warrant and only needed a judge's signature. Pantera called one of the court clerks he knew and asked him to try to speed the process a bit.

They had their warrant by three o'clock that afternoon after a phone call from the judge, who wanted to be sure looking at the files was necessary in advancing their case.

"Let's roll," Pantera said, and they left for Circe Enterprises, with a stop at the judge's office for his signature on the way there.

Entering the lobby, they encountered the same guard who'd been there before. Presenting the warrant, Pantera said, "Which way to your HR Department?"

The man studied the warrant as if he couldn't understand what it said. "What is this?"

"It's a search warrant. It allows us to look at the personnel files of any employee of Circe Enterprises who ended his or her employment in the past three months, whether voluntarily or involuntarily."

The guard looked at Pantera. "What do you want me to do with it?"

"As I said, show us the way to your HR, or Human Resources, Department."

Sighing heavily, the guard checked the directory on his computer, lifted the receiver of the phone on his desk, and punched in three numbers. After a moment, he was connected and told whoever had answered that they needed to come to the front lobby security desk. Then pointing at the chairs, he said, "You know the drill."

After nearly fifteen minutes, a man walked to the desk from the elevator. As he approached, the guard said, "These are two detectives from Richmond PD. They apparently have a warrant to look at some files. Could you escort them to HR?"

Three minutes later, they were sitting at the desk of the director of personnel, Lakesha Franklin. Her look as they sat told them she was unhappy about their visit.

"What's this all about?" she asked.

Pantera handed her the warrant and said, "We have this search warrant to search the files indicated."

"That's a bit vague, isn't it? All personnel files of those who left the company in the past three months?"

"Maybe, but it's what the judge signed off on."

"Why don't you just tell me the names of the people whose files you want to see?"

Harry answered, "Because, we aren't sure which files we need to see exactly."

"Okay. I guess we can't say no, can we?"

"Not without being held in contempt of court," Pantera said.

Sighing in obvious exasperation and a desire to get this over with, she clicked her computer.

"Good. Only six files here that match your criteria. Do you need hard copies?"

"Yes, please," Pantera said.

She clicked her keyboard and a printer that sat behind her began spitting out pages. Pantera counted as the printer worked. The six files amounted to thirty-seven pages.

She escorted them to a conference room and said, "You aren't allowed to take these with you. You must review them here and return all thirty-seven pages to me. Also, no pictures."

"What if we need hard copies?" Harry asked.

"Then get your judge to sign another order allowing you to have them. This is only to search them," she said, holding up her copy of the search warrant. "And that's all I'm going to let you do. Search through them."

"We are going to need addresses of some of these people," Pantera said.

She stepped into a nearby office and returned with a single sheet of stationery with the company's letterhead. "Then use this. I'll need to see it before you can leave. Don't write anything on anything else. You got that?"

"Yes, ma'am," Harry said, with some sarcasm.

She squinted at him. "Well, if you're gonna get sarcastic with me," she said and stopped a young woman who was walking down the hallway past the door. "Connie? Would you sit with these gentlemen while they conduct their business and make sure they only write on the stationery and that's all? No pictures. If they try to defy you, come get me."

"Sure, Ms. Franklin."

When the personnel director had left, Harry looked at Connie and said, "Must be fun working for her."

"She's not so bad. At least she keeps her hands to herself."

The first pages of the stack were about an employee who had retired from their bookkeeping department two months ago. They saw nothing they needed from this file and set it aside.

The next file was for Eugene Crawford, who worked in security. Harry copied down his phone number and address, smiling at Pantera.

The next few pages in the stack involved an employee who had resigned a month ago. He had worked in a department called "Acquisitions." Pantera wondered if this was about acquiring some sort of goods the company sold or acquiring other companies.

They set those pages aside and moved on to the next pages, which were about Irvin Garrett. They looked these pages over with great care. He'd apparently received several promotions during his tenure, the first not long after he started with Circe. Paulson had signed off personally on three of his five promotions, which were a lot for having only worked for the company for eight years. This seemed to lend the truth to Gene's statement that Garrett was a "right-hand man" to Paulson.

Pantera wrote copious notes about Garrett before they moved to the next set of papers in the stack.

The name at the top of the first page made both men sit back in shock: Miranda Buckhorn.

The detectives slowly turned their heads to register the amazement of the other. Miranda Buckhorn was an employee of Circe Enterprises?

Sitting forward, they both read the details of her employment. She was listed as a "special details assistant" to Paulson. The same thought went through both of them. Miranda was a hooker by her own mother's admission. A party girl extraordinaire. The inner workings of Circe Enterprises were, as they'd seen, private. They seemed to be a holding company for several other businesses. Was prostitution one of them?

Pantera noticed there were almost no details in her file other than her age, phone number, next of kin, and address, which matched the one they had.

When they looked at the next page, it was for a woman named Ericka Oliver, age twenty, who was also listed as a "special details assistant" to Paulson. Again, the details contained only her age, a phone number, and an address. The entry for next of kin said *none*. Pantera jotted that information down and looked at Harry. Did those job titles mean hooker? That they were both employed in the same capacity led to the hope she might know something about Miranda that would help.

"Are you thinking what I'm thinking?" Harry asked.

"Pretty sure. We'll compare notes in the car."

They finished up and returned the papers to Ms. Franklin.

"Let me see what you got there," she said, indicating the letterhead.

"We'd prefer you not see what information we deemed important," Pantera said, nodding at Connie, who had escorted them from the conference room. "She'll vouch that we didn't write on anything else or take any pictures."

Lakesha frowned and looked at Connie. "Well?"

"All they did was write on the letterhead."

Lakesha glared and said, "Okay, fair enough. Connie, would you escort these men to the front entrance?"

"Yes, Ms. Franklin."

When they were outside the building, Pantera said, "I think the term 'special details assistant' is a euphemism of sorts for prostitute."

"I think you're right."

Pantera checked his watch. "It's nearly time to knock off. We need to get back to the station and organize these notes. Tomorrow morning, we can drop in on our good buddy Gene."

When Pantera arrived home, he put on some jazzy blues and fixed himself a Writers Tears on the rocks. The information on the two cases was coming at them quickly, but neither he nor Harry could make out what it all meant.

He recalled the joke that the two cases might be connected.

It wasn't a joke anymore.

Claude Paulson worked late that night. As he left the office and headed for his car, he noticed there were only a few cars besides his in the employee lot. These would mostly belong to the security guards and custodial staff. He froze as he climbed into his car, wanting to kick himself.

He noticed the red Mustang parked near one corner of the lot. He recognized it as belonging to Buddy Garrett. Taking out his phone, he called Braxton.

"Damn it! Buddy's car is in the employee lot! We need to get rid of it. Tonight! I figured you would have handled that!"

"I'm sorry, sir. I didn't think about it."

"Then what are we paying you for? Get it done before sunrise!"

"Yes, sir," Braxton said, not mentioning that Paulson hadn't thought of it either.

12

That Saturday, Nancy dropped the girls off. She looked as though she'd had little sleep. "You okay?" Pantera asked.

"Yeah, just tired. I'm working to finish a project before my last day at work."

"When will that be?"

"On the 15th of next month. The house sold, and the sale closes the day after that. I'll rent an apartment after that if I need to."

"You'll find a place," Pantera said. "You want some coffee?"

"I'd love some." She hesitated and Pantera could tell she had to talk to him about something important. "Tony, the girls will be starting school soon, and I don't want to move them out of their old school into a new one after it starts."

"I agree."

"Good. Because they might have to live with you for a while at the start of the school year. Even if I find a place, I'll be back and forth until the middle of September when my job ends there. I've had some job interviews on Zoom, but there's already one that wants to meet me in person. I'll need to leave work early one day for that and drive back after it. They'll be fine for days like that, but once school starts, my life will be crazy until I'm settled in Richmond and start whatever new job I get. Even if we find a house, it won't close for several weeks, at least."

"That's not a problem. They can stay here."

"Thank you, Tony. You're a prince."

"Nah, Just a dad."

"You've become a better one since—" She let the rest of the sentence hang in the air, not wanting to say *the divorce.*

"Thank you for noticing."

The girls came into the kitchen where Pantera and Nancy were talking.

"What are y'all talking about?" Beth asked.

"I didn't want to bring it up until I talked to your father, but you'll be staying with him for the first couple of weeks of school."

Beth grinned at her father. "Really? Cool!"

"I'm glad you're happy about that," Pantera said. He looked at Andrea, who seemed preoccupied.

"What's up with you?" Pantera asked.

"Nothing."

"You're not looking forward to staying with me?"

"It's not that." She sighed and said, "I'm going to lie down for a while."

After she'd left the room, Pantera asked, "Do you know what's wrong?"

Nancy looked at Beth. "Beth, could you go unpack or something?"

"I know what you're going to talk about," she protested.

"Be that as it may, I want to discuss it with your father in private." Beth huffed, more disappointed than angry. "Okay." She gave her father a peck on the cheek and said, "I'm glad we're going to be staying with you when school starts."

"Me, too," Pantera said.

When she'd left, Nancy said, "Dani called Andrea last night. She wants to get back together."

"Oh. How does Andrea feel about that?"

"I think she's conflicted. I'm sure she still has some feelings for Dani, but she's also moving away. It was why she looked forward to the move. Get a fresh start somewhere else. That sort of thing. Now, though, she feels like she can't begin seeing Dani again if she wanted to, which I'm not sure she does. It's a confusing time for her. Sixteen isn't an easy age."

"I remember. Heartbreak on every corner, it seems."

"Yes, and I think she just realized that while most of her friends in Charlottesville know about her sexuality, she'll have to deal with that all over again. Some kids are fine with it, but others can be just as hurtful as adults, even worse."

"She's a strong girl. She'll handle it. She's always been an 'if you don't like it, lump it' kind of person."

Nancy gave a weak smile. "I hope you're right."

Pantera decided it was time to change the subject. "How's the house-hunting going?"

"Not bad. I have a few I'm interested in. I'll look at them again today and decide which one I want to make an offer on."

"Far from here?"

"No, not really. The farthest one is maybe a twenty minute drive."

"The closest?"

"Actually, I guess I should talk to you about that. I thought about the one down the street and really like it. I just don't know if it's wise to live that close to you."

"I thought about that, too. I wasn't sure if we should live that close together, but it's not as if we'll be seeing a lot of each other, really. You'll have your life, and I'll have mine. We'll just be within easy walking distance."

She gave him a wistful look. "I guess you're right."

"It will be fine wherever you decide to live. I'm looking forward to seeing the girls more often."

At that moment, the doorbell rang. They heard Beth answer the door, with a, "Hey, Lisa!"

Pantera and Nancy joined the two in the living room. Lisa was carrying a picnic basket. "I made the executive decision that we are all going on a picnic today."

Nancy said, "I'm envious, but I guess that's life." She looked at Pantera. "I'll see you tomorrow evening."

"Sure thing," he answered.

Nancy left, and it occurred to Pantera that she seemed disappointed that Lisa arrived when she did. When he was cleaning up before the picnic, he found her coffee cup nearly full, and what the girls had said ran through his mind. Was she enjoying his company now? She had mentioned how much better of a father he was now. Was she thinking maybe he would return to being a good husband as well? He wasn't sure how he felt about that.

At the picnic, the girls decided to play Frisbee golf in the park, choosing trees and other natural landmarks as the "hole." While they were playing their game, he and Lisa talked.

"How's the job?" she asked.

"Killing me."

"Tough case?"

"Yes and no. On the one hand, we've found out quite a bit we didn't know at the start, and it appears the murder of Miranda Buckhorn may have had some connections with Circe Enterprises, though we're not sure the extent. It's just odd. A top security guard there disappeared the same day she was killed, and the new chief executive of the office is likely the father of Miranda's little girl."

"That is weird."

"Yeah, but in reality, we don't know anything. We have our suspicions, but that's all."

"If she was killed because of something to do with Circe Enterprises, what do you think was the reason?"

"Beats me. I mean the head guy might be the father of the child and would be subject to support payments, but it's not as if Miranda was living an elegant lifestyle and needed the money to support her daughter in that manner. Even then, I'm not sure Claude Paulson, the chief executive, would do something like kill her over support for the kid."

"How old did you say Miranda was?"

"Nineteen."

"And her daughter is two?"

"Yes."

"That means she got pregnant when she was either sixteen or just turned seventeen."

"Yeah, so he's a bit of a perv, too. Not surprised."

"That's statutory rape, isn't it?" Lisa asked.

"Yeah, but it's rarely charged. It's a class one misdemeanor in Virginia when the female is at least fifteen. Probably the most he'd have to do is pay a fine."

"Is he married?"

"We don't know. I guess we should ask him." He paused. "If he will let us back in his office."

"It's that hard to get in to see him?"

"They don't let anyone in the building without an escort, and getting up to see him is more than difficult. We might have to follow him after work one evening and talk to him wherever he lands."

"Did you piss him off?"

"You could say that." Pantera told her about their ruse to get in to see him.

"Tony, you're investigating a murder. You have to be allowed to speak to the people who could give you information."

"That's true, but if we force the issue, he'll lawyer up. We need his cooperation, even if it's reluctant."

"What about the security guard? Is his disappearance your case, too?"

"Yeah. Strangely, that's how we discovered Miranda's connections to Circe. We were going through the personnel files of the employees who had either quit or been fired in the past few months, and lo and behold, there's a file with her name on it. She was listed as a 'special details assistant' to Paulson, along with another young woman, who is twenty."

"Did you find anything else incriminating?"

"No. We just looked through some rather sparse documents that were printed out for us to look at. The head of the HR department wasn't too happy about that, either. She—" He stopped suddenly, his mouth agape at what he'd just thought of.

"What?"

"She didn't give us Widner's file."

"Who's Widner?"

A look of disturbed wonder was frozen on his face as he looked at Lisa. "He's the guy who was in charge before Paulson took over. He left the same day Miranda was murdered and Garrett disappeared."

"I take it Garrett was the security guard?"

He nodded. "We specifically asked for all personnel files for those who had worked for the company in the past several months but were no longer there. We had a search warrant giving us permission to do so."

"Then the personnel director withheld a file."

"At least one. I'm left wondering if there were others she didn't share."

He took out his cell and dialed Harry. When he answered, Pantera said, "I have a question about our search of personnel records, and I feel kind of stupid for not having the same question when we were looking at the files."

"What is it?" Harry asked. "You sound kinda pissed."

"I am. Both at myself and Ms. Lakesha Franklin."

"What about me? You mad at me, too?"

"Actually, yes. You should have thought of it too."

"Thought of what? Come on, Tony. I got burgers on the grill."

"Think about it, Harry. Are we aware of an employee who used to work there, but doesn't anymore, whose file was not shared with us?"

After a moment, Harry said, "Holy shit. Widner."

"Yeah. Widner. Why didn't she give us his file? The warrant didn't specify 'no executives' or anything like that. We should have been given his file, too."

"I take it we're going back on Monday, then?"

"You bet your burgers we are. And I plan to ream out one Lakesha Franklin for withholding the file, and I hope everyone in that section hears me."

13

When Pantera arrived at work, he found Harry sipping his coffee and poring over the notes from their search of the personnel files. He looked up when Pantera entered. "How could we have missed that?"

"Easy. First, we weren't thinking about Widner. Second, we were really only looking for information on Buddy Garrett and Gene Crawford. It was luck they included files from the two girls. Not considering Widner in the search of records was a mistake. The only reason I can think of to withhold his file is that there was something they didn't want us to see in there."

"So when do we go back and look at Widner's file?"

"As soon as we've talked to Gene."

"Really? You want to talk to him first? I think we should get to Circe first thing. Find out what they're hiding from us."

"No, I think we should talk to Gene first. He no longer works there, and having been fired, which I think is safe to assume since he didn't seem ready to quit when we saw him, he might be willing to dish as much dirt as he can. Who knows? That dirt could help us understand information in Widner's file."

When they arrived at the address for Gene Crawford and knocked on the front door, which had no doorbell, an older man answered.

"Can I help you?" he said.

"We're looking for Gene Crawford. Does he live here?" Pantera asked.

"Sure does. I'm his daddy. Just here for a visit. I

live in Baltimore. Leavin' tomorrow on the train to go back home. A good son, Gene. Not like my other boy, Ray. That boy never calls, never writes. Nothin'. Gene? He's a good son."

"Is he here?"

"Where's my manners? Yeah, he's here. Y'all come on in. Do you know Gene from work, or something?"

"In a manner of speaking," Pantera said.

"Course, he don't work there no more. They fired him. Damn, ungrateful people. Told him to get his stuff and leave."

The old man turned to holler down the hallway. "Gene?! You got some men here to see you!" Then turning to the detectives, he said, "He'll be right out. Can I get y'all some coffee?"

At that moment, Gene came into the room, a puzzled expression on his face. When he saw Pantera and Harry, he scowled. "What the—! What are you guys doin' here? Come to apologize for getting me canned?"

Gene's father said, "These are the men got you fired?" His demeanor had changed entirely. He looked ready to beat the two detectives with a baseball bat.

"I'll handle it, Papa. Why don't you go drink your coffee?" The father left, grumbling. Turning to Pantera, Gene said, "I repeat, what are you two doing here?"

"At the moment, we're wondering why you blame us for being fired. We didn't do anything."

"You asked me those questions. I was just trying to make conversation, but my boss didn't like it."

"He didn't like that you were talking to us?" Pantera said.

"Not at all. Said you were looking to find out stuff about the company that you didn't need to know, and I was obliging you. He said it showed I lacked an understanding of what security was."

"Mr. Crawford, we're very sorry. We had no idea

you would be fired for answering some rather harmless questions," Pantera said.

"Well, I was. I have some savings, but that won't last more than a few months, but I'll find another job. It was just a shock to see you guys in my living room after what happened. Apology accepted, but now, I'll ask a third time, but that's my limit. What are you two doing here?" A sudden thought hit him. "And how did you find out where I live?"

Harry spoke for the first time. "Mr. Crawford, we're investigating a murder and a disappearance, and we think they are somehow linked."

"Who was murdered, and who disappeared?"

"A girl named Miranda Buckhorn. The man who disappeared was Buddy Garrett," Pantera answered.

"Buddy ain't disappeared," Gene said.

"He hasn't?" Harry asked. "Then where is he?"

"I don't know, but he's still around. I saw his car in the lot when I left. I remember because it was in the employee parking lot, and I thought they would have taken his card that opened the gate to get in there when he left. Damn sure took mine!"

"What kind of car did he drive?"

"A Ford Mustang. Cherry red. He loved that car. Can't blame him, though. It's a nice set of wheels. Cleanest car I ever saw. If it's there, he's there." Gene seemed to calm a bit. He didn't seem as angry.

Pantera gave Harry a puzzled look. What would Garrett be doing at the office after not bothering to contact his ex or his kids? On the other hand, this news could point to possible foul play. If Garrett was dead, he wouldn't have retrieved his car.

"And you're sure he was in your words, 'Paulson's right-hand man'?"

"Yeah. Whenever you saw Paulson walking around the building, Buddy was his escort of sorts. Buddy would run errands for him. Even pick up the guy's dry cleaning. That kind of thing."

"And you saw Buddy's car in the employee lot the day you were canned?"

"Yeah."

"Okay, we'll check into all that," Pantera said. "What we'd like to ask you now is what you know about the company you worked for."

"Nothing much, really. They were a business, but it was always kind of secret what they did. My friends pretty well figured they had a lot of government contracts on some sort of secret shit, so what they did was not for public consumption. It's not like they got a lot of customer visits."

"Then why is a security guard posted at the entrance to the building if there aren't people visiting the building?" Harry asked.

"For that very reason. They didn't want people visiting or roaming the halls or anything like that. People from the outside were literally escorted everywhere they went inside the building, as if there were secrets there that they needed to prevent anyone from seeing. We were there to stop anyone who came in that didn't work there and find out why they were there. If it was legitimate, we had to call someone from the department they needed to visit to get an escort. That was a big rule. No free roamers in the building."

"That does sound secretive," Harry said.

"Do you remember anything about Garrett's last day there? Anything unusual happen?" Pantera asked.

"Oh, yeah. Something real unusual."

"What?"

"The big cheese came in."

"The 'big cheese'?" Pantera asked.

"Yeah. The boss. The lady who owns the place. I was floored. She lives in Paris, and had only been in the building one other time a couple of years ago for a board meeting. Well, there wasn't any board meeting the other day, and she comes in like she owns the place—oh, wait. She does. Anyway, she strolls in with Mr. Paulson on her heels. He looked like a scared rabbit. I figured she was going to fire him, but it turned out she was promoting him. That certainly was a surprise because he sure looked scared out of his mind."

"What's this woman's name? The 'head cheese' as you say?"

"She just goes by Circe. You know, like Sting or something. A one-word name. That's why it's called Circe Enterprises. She owns the whole thing."

"Was Ron Widner at work that day?"

"I guess so."

"Since Paulson has his job now, I guess he'll be moving into Widner's office." Pantera said.

"Hell if I know. I don't know that much, really."

Pantera said, "Is there anything you can tell us about Ron Widner?"

"Not really. He never said one word to me."

"You say that Paulson looked frightened when he came in with Circe. How did Circe look?"

"Like she wanted to kill someone. I remember the other time I saw her, when she came to the board meeting, she was all smiles. Not this time. She was loaded for bear. I remember thinking how glad I was that I wasn't in Paulson's shoes, because I had the idea from his expression that she was pissed at him. Turns out, it must have been Widner."

"And she was mad enough to can him," Harry said.

"Yeah. I don't know how it all went down. I'm just telling you what I saw when they came in. She was pissed, he was scared, and I was relieved it wasn't me."

"And you have no idea what Circe Enterprises does as their business?"

"No. Maybe a lot of things. I guess Enterprises covers a lot of shit."

Pantera took out his wallet and pulled out the photograph of Miranda Buckhorn her mother had given them. Passing it to Gene, he said, "Do you recognize this woman?" Pantera watched his eyes and saw the recognition.

Gene stared at it for several seconds before handing it back. "I'm not sure. Maybe I saw her around some, but that's all."

Gene's father reappeared from the kitchen. "You fellas ain't left yet?"

"We were just going," Pantera said.

"Calm down, Papa. They're not at fault, really. It's just how Circe operates. Too secretive by far."

As they walked to the car, Harry said, "I have to say I agree with our pal Gene. Circe is much too secretive. Makes me wonder what the Hell is going on there. Seems like there's plenty of money in whatever they're doing, but I'd just like to know what that is."

"I agree, and it definitely warrants a deeper look. I don't trust any business that is so secretive visitors have to be escorted everywhere to make sure they don't see anything. Makes it look like everything they do is illegal in some way."

"Yeah."

"Did you notice Gene's recognition of the photo?"

"Yes, and it made me wonder why he took several seconds to answer. I think he knows her more than having just 'seen her around' before."

"Maybe he had to come up with a good answer."

"You think Gene killed her?"

"Basically, I think anyone who knew her at all killed her until they're proven not to have done it."

"Even her little girl?"

"Harry?"

"Yeah?"
"Don't be a smart ass."

After the detectives left, Gene went to his bedroom and lay down, staring at the ceiling. He thought about Miranda. He knew her better than he'd admitted, but he didn't want to tell them. He didn't want the detectives looking into anything. He especially didn't want them finding out anything about his relationship with Miranda. That could lead to real problems.

Then he thought about the envelope that he'd been entrusted with. After a moment, he rose and pulled the envelope from where it lay beneath his mattress. Buddy Garrett had given it to him with the instructions that it should not be opened unless something happened to Buddy. Now, Gene was unsure what to do. He wondered if Buddy was dead, but he'd seen the car in the lot the day he'd left Circe for the last time. That meant Buddy was alive, didn't it?

Staring at the envelope, he tapped it twice and placed it back in its hiding spot, still unsure what to do with it. He'd thought of giving it to the detectives, but he'd decided not to. They would open it regardless if Buddy was alive or dead to help them with the case. However, Buddy had been adamant about keeping it sealed unless something bad happened to him. Gene had figured "something bad" involved Buddy's death.

"This has some dangerous information in it," Buddy had said. "You don't want to know what any of it is unless something happens to me. Then, you're free to open it up and read what's in here. But not before. You got that?"

Gene had asked why he didn't give it to his ex or someone else, and Buddy's answer had provided a good enough reason for that.

Gene had reluctantly agreed to keep the envelope,

but only because Buddy was so desperate for someone to have it. Buddy's final words on the matter had been, "If you open it, your life will be in danger, so don't unless something happens to me. If I die of some kind of natural cause, you might just want to destroy the envelope without opening it. It's that dangerous."

14

Walking into the building, Pantera and Harry walked to the security guard at the desk, the same one they spoke to the last time they were there.

Heaving a deep sigh, the guard said, "What is it this time, detectives?"

"Seems your director of personnel left a file out of the mix the other day, and we're here to see it," Harry said.

"And how do you know she left one out?"

"Easy. We know he was fired by Circe just a few days ago."

"It's possible his file wasn't transferred to the termination/resignation files."

"Funny, all the other files for people who left Circe that day were. To be honest, we're getting tired of coming out here," Pantera said.

"I'll call personnel. You can have a seat over—" the guard said, but Pantera and Harry were already headed to the chairs they'd occupied twice before.

Over the next half hour, Pantera stepped up to the desk twice to ask if perhaps someone else could escort them, but all the guard did was point at the chairs in reply.

"They think we're going to get tired and leave," Harry said.

"Then they don't know us very well."

Pantera watched the guard who, after a while, lifted the receiver of his desk phone and punched a few numbers, speaking to someone for about ten seconds. Three minutes later, Connie, the same young woman who'd been assigned to watch them before, showed up. Smiling, as if Ms. Franklin hadn't made them wait on purpose, she said, "This way, gentlemen." They followed her to Lakesha Franklin's office.

Her executive assistant told them Ms. Franklin was busy on the phone when they arrived, so they waited again in two more uncomfortable chairs. Ten minutes later, Ms. Franklin came out to escort them into her office.

"Can't even walk from one room to the next without an escort," Harry joked.

"Security," Pantera answered.

As they sat, Ms. Franklin said, "We take security seriously here at Circe. Other companies could learn a thing or two from us on that front."

Pantera said, "Yes, well, it seems you took it a bit too seriously when we were here before."

"Care to explain what you mean?"

Harry, who had moved his chair five or six feet away from Pantera, said, "There's a file you didn't give us."

Lakesha looked at Harry. "Oh?" Which one?"

Pantera said, "Ron Widner."

Turning to Pantera she said, "I wasn't aware you were interested in executives."

Harry said, "The warrant didn't make that distinction." Her gaze shifted to Harry.

Pantera added, "So why did you?"

They watched with some amusement as the director turned her head from side to side as if watching a tennis match.

"Could you move your chair closer to your partner's?" she said to Harry, obviously irritated.

"I like it here."

She frowned and said, "Let me print that out for you."

"Along with any other files you may have conveniently left out," Pantera replied.

She gazed at him and said, "I didn't conveniently leave it out. I told you that—"

"Yes, we heard you," Harry said.

"We just don't believe you," Pantera said.

This time, she didn't look at them as they spoke, choosing instead to look at neither of them.

She opened a file on her computer and typed in an inquiry. The computer screen glowed on her face as the document opened on the screen.

"You're going to be disappointed," she said. "Nothing nefarious here."

"We'd like to see it anyway," Pantera said.

She punched some keys and the printer spit the pages out.

"Another thing," Harry said.

"And what would that be?" she asked.

"Those personnel files seemed rather—I don't know—sparse. There weren't many pages in any of them. One man had worked here for years, but had only three pages of documents."

"We keep the barest of files on our employees."

"A security-conscious place like this? I'd think there'd be reams of pages on every person working here."

"No. If the files are hacked, then certain information, such as job descriptions and security clearances, could be used against us by anyone who wanted that kind of information to try to get through our tight security here."

"How secure of you." Pantera changed the subject since this one was getting nobody anywhere. "Shall we peruse what you have for us in the same conference room?"

"Yes," she said and dialed a number on her phone.

After a moment, she said, "Connie? Could you come here and escort the detectives to the same conference room they used the other day?" As she hung up, Pantera and Harry could hear Connie saying, "Yes, ma'am," but Ms. Franklin didn't wait for the response, anticipating the obvious answer.

Connie appeared at the door, and Harry and Pantera rose and followed her. As they left the office, Ms. Franklin said to Connie, "Stay with them, same instructions as before."

"Yes, Ms. Franklin," Connie answered and led them to the conference room.

As they looked through the five pages of Ron Widner's file, they found that Lakesha Franklin had been correct. There was nothing in the file that could help them other than the reason for termination: embezzlement.

When they returned to Lakesha Franklin's office, Pantera said, "Widner was fired for embezzlement. I assume he's being prosecuted for that?"

"I have no idea. That would be up to Mr. Paulson."

"Is it possible we can speak to him?"

"How would I know? I'm not his secretary."

Pantera said, "I guess what I'm saying is, could we be escorted to his office so we can speak to his executive assistant and try to get in to see him today? We're growing tired of sitting at the security desk and waiting."

She smiled at this statement. "I guess there's no harm in trying, but I have to warn you—he's a busy man."

"So are we," Harry said.

Connie escorted them to where Paulson's office had been, but he and his assistant were no longer there. The offices had obviously been emptied of the various materials necessary for the job. Only bare bookcases, empty desks, and other signs of abandonment remained.

"Where did they move to?" Pantera asked, wondering if Lakesha knew Paulson would no longer be in that office.

"I have no idea," Connie answered, the look on her face showing she was telling the truth.

Pantera said, "Do you mind taking us to someone who would know where he's located now? Other than your boss, that is."

His words seemed to sting. "Oh, I'm sure Ms. Franklin didn't know about this. She wouldn't have sent you here if she did."

As Harry outright laughed at the statement, Pantera shook his head. "How long have you worked here, Connie?"

"Three months."

"I hate to break it to you, dear, but your boss is a class-A 'Boss from Hell.' She doesn't care about you or any of the other employees here. Like many people, she's out for herself, which includes keeping us from speaking to the top boss in this building so she doesn't have to explain to him why she let us waltz into his offices in the middle of the day, unannounced."

Harry added, "Yes, you should watch your back because, honestly, she will stab you there if it would help her. You're basically nothing but potential road kill to her."

Connie looked upset at this, so Pantera added, "Just don't cross her, and you should be okay, but if another job comes along with similar pay and advancement opportunities, I'd take it."

"Umm, okay." She looked as though she were a child and someone had just popped her favorite balloon.

"So, how about it? Is there someone who might know where Paulson's office has been moved to?"

"Not that I know of."

They stood in thought a moment until Harry said,

"Maybe he moved into Widner's old office. I'd think the head man would have the nicest office in the building. Paulson's head honcho now, so maybe he's there."

"Do you know where that is?" Pantera asked.

"Not exactly, but I know it's on the top floor in what's called the executive suite of offices."

"Would you take us there? You can tell Ms. Franklin we asked someone where to find Paulson before you could stop us so you don't get blamed for anything."

She took a deep breath and said, "Sure." They went to the elevator, and when they stepped off, it was easy to see where Paulson had re-located to. His executive assistant, Doreen Staples was arranging books on a bookshelf. They could hear Paulson from inside the nearby office, apparently telling some people where he wanted the desk moved as they arranged the furniture.

Harry and Pantera thanked Connie, suggesting she return to personnel. As she stepped back onto the elevator, Pantera and Harry stepped down the hallway into Paulson's new office.

"Well, we meet again!" Pantera exclaimed as he entered.

"What the Hell are you doing here?" Paulson demanded.

"Our jobs," Pantera responded.

"And how does that concern me?"

Harry said, "It's beginning to look as though it concerns you quite a bit—unless you could clear a few things up for us."

"I'm a little busy here."

Pantera said, "What a coincidence. So are we."

Paulson looked around at the mess that moving in created and said, "How long will this take?"

"Maybe five minutes," Pantera said, choosing a small number without knowing the actual answer since it would depend on where Paulson's answers took them.

"Follow me," Paulson nearly grunted and led them to an empty office down the hall.

"Now, what do you want?" Paulson said, taking a seat behind the desk.

Pantera and Harry took the seats across from him, Harry again moving to one corner of the desk and Pantera to the other. "Has Ron Widner been arrested for embezzlement?" Pantera asked.

Paulson was clearly taken aback by the question. "What?"

"Easy question," Harry said. "One of those yes or no kind."

"And we'd like an answer," Pantera said, "and not next week."

When Paulson didn't reply for a moment, Harry said, "Yes or no, Paulson?"

"No."

"And why not? Isn't Circe Enterprises interested in assuring that other employees know that stealing from the company will be prosecuted?" Harry asked.

"Of course, we are."

"Then why no arrest?" Pantera asked.

"Madame Circe chose not to pursue the matter. She'd rather it remain our secret. How did you find out?"

"We saw his personnel file," Harry said.

"You did? Who gave you permission to look at those?"

"A circuit court judge," Pantera said.

"Judge Malcolm, I believe," Harry said. Again, the detectives watched as Paulson grew almost dizzy shifting his gaze back and forth, causing him to feel overwhelmed and surrounded.

"Yes. A little thing called a warrant."

"Then you actually went to get one?"

"Yes," Harry said. "Did you think we wouldn't?"

Pantera said, "After all, you suggested it. Did you think we were too lazy for that, or something?"

"We were wanting to keep the theft in-house," Paulson said. "Madame Circe won't be happy if this gets in the news."

"Sorry, Paulson, but she's not my boss, and frankly, I couldn't care less if she gets pissed. In fact, I'd love to see her get pissed enough to come back here. I'd enjoy asking her a few questions," Harry said.

"That's the second time you've called your boss 'Madame Circe.' Is that what she's called?" Pantera asked.

"That's what she prefers to be called when referred to in the third person."

"Do you know her last name?" Harry asked.

"No. I don't know anyone who does."

"Odd for someone so high up as to own a big multi-billion dollar company like this," Pantera said. "Is Circe her real name, or does she just use it because of the company's name?"

"I have no idea," Paulson said. "Listen, we've been here at least five minutes. I told you we weren't pursuing an embezzlement charge against Mr. Widner. That should be enough. We have our reasons for not filing charges."

"You mean that you're trying to hide something?"

"No. Who suggested that we were trying to hide anything?"

Pantera stood. He was ready to go because it was obvious that Paulson wasn't going to share anything of value with them. Harry stood with him, and they looked down at Paulson.

Pantera gazed into Paulson's eyes, holding them there, and said, "A few things, Paulson. We smell something fishy going on here at Circe Enterprises.

We're not sure what it is—yet—but we're going to find out. We've got several firings and/or resignations that happened on the same day a young woman was found dead in a vacant lot on the outskirts of town. And it turns out this dead woman, like the missing security guard we can't seem to find, had some kind of job here, even though we are told by the girl's own mother that she was a prostitute, and that's how she earned her living. The mother never even mentioned Circe Enterprises, and she would have if she'd known her daughter was employed here in some capacity. Furthermore, said murdered girl had a connection to you as well. First she is listed in her personnel file as being some kind of special assistant to you. Not only that, but her daughter looks a lot like you, which places you squarely in the 'person of interest' file. Finally, the missing guard who no longer works here must have been back recently because a friend spotted the missing guard's car in the employee parking lot after he was no longer an employee. So there's a lot for us to look into, and in the coming days and weeks, we're going to be so far up your and the company's individual asses, you'll need a colonoscopy prep and a crowbar to get us out."

"You don't have anything, detective."

"You're right. We don't have proof of anything, but believe me, if you or anyone in this company is involved in any way with the death of the girl, we're going to find out. We're also going to find the missing security guard that you claimed not to know, but at least one person said you knew well. That in itself is more than enough suspicion to make us want to bed down here for a few weeks until we figure everything out—or discover there's nothing there to find. We may not have the proof yet, but that doesn't mean we won't find it."

"Go ahead and waste your time. I don't care. You'll never find anything incriminating on me or Circe

Enterprises!" Paulson was practically shouting now.

"Just because it's well-hidden doesn't mean it's not there. And if it is there, no matter how well hidden it might be, we'll find it, so you needn't worry about that." Turning he started to leave the office with Harry behind him, but he stopped and turned back to Paulson. "Or maybe you should worry about that. I guess that depends on if you know you're guilty of something that could send you to prison."

They left the office and headed to the elevator. By the time it arrived, Paulson still had not come out.

15

Pantera drove to the entrance for the employee parking lot and parked. They surveyed the cars beyond the fence but saw no Ford Mustangs, especially not a cherry red one. "I guess Garrett's not here today."

"If he was here the other day," Harry said.

"True. It may have been just his car was here. That, of course, would raise a lot more questions, such as if his car was here but he wasn't, where was he?"

"I'm beginning to believe that wherever he was, he's still there."

"And if that's the case, who moved his car?"

"Good question."

"I'm starting to have a theory."

"Okay, what?"

"We have to make a few assumptions. First, assume that Claude Paulson is CP from Miranda's diary, and the father of Felicia Buckhorn."

"Not a difficult assumption to make."

"Agreed. Now, let's assume that Paulson does not want to pay for the upbringing of a child. I saw a ring on his left hand indicating he's married, so add to that reluctance the idea his wife wouldn't be in favor of that either. Of course, she knows nothing of the child Paulson fathered with a hooker who for some strange reason is employed as a 'special assistant' to him at Circe."

"I'm following."

"Miranda, as stated in her diary, goes to see Paulson, demanding money and perhaps more, such as letting the wife in on what's going on."

"I doubt Paulson would appreciate the idea."

"He'd hate it. Now, assume Paulson truly does have a close working relationship with the now missing Buddy Garrett, the combination security guard/owner of a cherry red Mustang that was seen here in the lot after his employment ended but is no longer here."

"Okay. I think I see where you're going with this," Harry said as the climbed into the car for the ride back to the detective squad.

"Paulson either kills Miranda himself with his bare hands—I noticed he probably works out somewhere—or he gets our pal Buddy to do it. In either case, he gets Buddy to dispose of the body, having him use a company car for the purpose or getting a rental using a corporate account."

"Sounds reasonable so far."

"When Buddy returns a few days later, he meets Paulson outside the gates of the employee lot. Once there Paulson lets him into the lot to get his car. Buddy Garrett then hightails it, following the orders from his boss to leave town for a few weeks until things die down."

"What does Buddy Garrett use to pay for this trip?"

"The cash Paulson likely paid him to handle whatever needed handling."

"So in your scenario, Garrett is still alive."

"And lying on a beach somewhere in Florida living the good life."

"How does Circe showing up suddenly figure into this?" Harry asked.

"She doesn't. She's gotten wind that Widner is stealing from her company and shows up without much notice to fire him and replace him with Paulson, since he's next on the hierarchy of the company's Richmond location."

"So why is Paulson described as scared shitless

CHARLES TABB

when she shows up? Wouldn't she have informed him of what was going down? Why look like he's the one who might be fired?"

"Not sure. Maybe he's the one who's been embezzling and has managed to pin it on Widner and now he's nervous he'll be found out. Or perhaps he's scared that in all this inter-office intrigue, the murder of Miranda will come to light at the wrong moment and start causing fingers to be pointed his way, or Circe's arrival throws some kind of wrench in his gears for handling the situation."

"Maybe he missed meeting Garrett at the gate because of her sudden appearance," Harry offered. "He could be frightened that now Garrett will show up and cause trouble."

"Could be. It's plausible and explains a lot."

"It does feel weird that she would fly all the way from Paris to fire a guy. She could do that over the phone," Harry said.

"Maybe she had plans to come to the states anyway and just made a short detour."

"And why Richmond for a headquarters for a worldwide corporation? It's not like making it Tappahannock, but it's not Philadelphia, DC, or New York either."

"Maybe we could do some research on the company. Find out why they're so secretive. I find it odd that two young women were on the company's books as employees with the same title. I have to wonder how many other employees who are listed as a 'special assistant to Mr. Paulson' we might find if we had full access to the personnel files of current employees," Pantera said.

"I don't see how we get a judge to okay that."

"Me neither." Pantera drove for a minute before saying, "Let's take a detour. Maybe two."

"Where to?"

"Let's tell Pam Collier what we learned about her daughter's employment. Then we can stop in to see Twyla Garrett and ask about that Mustang and Buddy's relationship with Paulson."

Harry gave a thumbs-up, and Pantera turned left at the next intersection.

Pam Collier, looking as though she could use a good night's sleep, greeted them.

"Good day, Ms. Collier," Pantera said. "We just have a few questions we want to ask you because of some information about your daughter that has come to light."

"Sure. Have a seat. Don't be too loud, though. Felicia's napping."

They sat on the sofa and she took her chair. Pulling a pack of cigarettes from the pocket of her housedress, she withdrew one and lit it. "I hope you don't mind if I smoke. It calms my nerves."

Pantera said, "No, go right ahead." He hated cigarette smoke since quitting himself, but it was her house.

She blew out a stream of smoke and said, "Okay, go ahead."

"Did your daughter ever mention Circe Enterprises?"

Her brow furrowed in thought. "No, who are they?"

"It seems it's a company she was listed as having worked for."

Her head pulled back in surprise. "You mean she was getting a regular paycheck from them?"

"I'm not sure about that. We just found out in a separate investigation that she was employed there until recently."

"How recently?"

Harry checked his notes. "Until a few days before her death."

"If she was making money at a regular job, it's news to me. How could she keep a job like that working as a hooker?"

"About that," Pantera said. "We've not found any records of her ever being arrested for prostitution. That's unusual considering you implied she'd been doing it for a while."

"She always told me she had what she called 'high-class clients' for customers. She didn't do her work on street corners."

"Yes, ma'am. You see, we're wondering if her job with Circe Enterprises wasn't as a call girl of some kind."

"Does this Circe Enterprises have a lot of money?"

"Yes, ma'am. I'd say so."

"I guess that would explain the high-class clients."

"Yes, ma'am. Also, did you ever hear her mention a man named Claude Paulson?"

"No. I never heard of him. Is he her pimp?"

"He might be, but we aren't sure at this point. However, we do have some information about him you might can use."

"What's that?"

"It's possible he's Felicia's father."

"Really?" Her eyes widened in surprise.

"Yes," Harry said. He took out his phone and punched a few buttons, bringing up a picture of Paulson that he'd secretly snapped when Pantera was talking to him earlier. He held the phone out to Ms. Collier.

"Oh, my Lord! She looks just like him!"

"We thought so, too," Harry said.

"If he's the father, he should help out with the cost of raising her, shouldn't he?"

"I imagine a court would see it that way, but I'm

not a lawyer. You might consider seeing one. A court could order a paternity test, and if it turns out he's her natural father, he could be ordered to pay child support," Pantera said.

"Does he have a lot of money?"

"I'd say so, yes," Pantera answered, "though if he's responsible for her death, he likely won't be earning much in the future."

"I wish she'd had her own phone in her name," Harry said. "If she had, we could trace what numbers she called, which ones called her, and any texts that were sent or received."

"Can't you do that now?"

"Not without knowing the number or at least knowing who purchased the phone for her."

"She refused to give me the number. Said the person who gave it to her told her never to give it out unless he said she could."

Pantera rubbed his chin. "I guess it was for her clients' use only."

Harry said, "Maybe there's another way." Pantera nodded, having already thought of that.

They thanked Pam Collier and left. On the drive to Twyla Garrett's house, Pantera said, "I know what you're thinking about the phone number. It would be very likely that Paulson has it. In fact, he may have been the one to give it to her if 'special assistant' means a prostitute in a call girl service that he runs."

"Yep."

"The problem is, how do we convince a judge to allow us to get his call records or find out what phones he purchased? We have no reason to look into that beyond suspicion. You can hold suspicion in one hand and doubt in the other, and they both weigh the same. Nothing. On cop shows on TV, getting a warrant is as easy as falling off a log. In reality, not so much."

"Yeah, I know."

They arrived at Twyla Garrett's house and were invited in.

"Any news on Buddy?"

Pantera said, "No, ma'am. There is something that's puzzling us, though, and we thought maybe you could answer a few questions so we can get a better handle on some things."

"Okay."

"Is it possible Buddy got involved in some kind of illegal activity?"

"Buddy? No. He'd never do anything illegal."

"Not even if his life or the life of you or his kids were at stake?"

"What have you found out? Are we in danger?"

"No, ma'am," Pantera said. "We're just considering all possibilities."

"Now that, I don't know. I guess he could get involved in something if there was some kind of threat to his family. Even after we divorced, he was awfully protective. Always wanted to know where we were and what we were doing. It wasn't like some ex-husbands keeping tabs on their ex-wives. Nothing like that. He just told me to be extra careful. I could tell he was worried about me and the kids."

"Yes, ma'am," Pantera said.

Harry asked, "What about his car? What can you tell us?"

"That Mustang? Lord, he loves that car! Have you found it?"

"No, ma'am, but it was in the employee lot at Circe after he was no longer officially employed there."

"How do you know it was there?"

"Another employee reported seeing it there."

"After Buddy wasn't working there anymore?"

"Yes, ma'am," Harry said.

"Well, he wouldn't have just left it there. That I can tell you. Have you looked to see if it's still there?"

"Yes, ma'am. It was gone."

"Then Buddy's definitely alive. He won't let anyone else drive that car. Too afraid someone will wreck it."

"Yes, ma'am," Pantera said. "Tell me, how close was his working relationship with Mr. Claude Paulson?"

"I don't know. I've heard him mention the name, but that's all. Isn't he one of the big chiefs at the company?"

He ignored her question. "In what context did he mention Mr. Paulson?"

"Nothing much, really. Just that he could be difficult to work for."

Pantera glanced at Harry. This could mean they had a fairly close working relationship, giving more credence to their belief Paulson was lying.

"Have you ever met Claude Paulson?" Harry asked.

"No. At least I don't think so. I did go to a Christmas party once that the company rented a ballroom in the Richmond Convention Center's lower level for, so I guess I could have met him without remembering it." She mused for a moment and added, "That was—what?—three Christmases ago."

"That's about all for now, I guess," Pantera said. "If we think of anything else, we'll let you know."

"Thank you, detective. And when you find him, tell him I'm royally pissed."

"We'll do that," Harry said. They left and headed for the station to complete the paperwork on the day's visits.

16

When Natalie Oliver's phone rang, she almost ignored it. Checking caller ID, she saw it was Gene Crawford. Natalie, who had used the name Ericka in Richmond, had run away from her job at Circe as a high-priced call-girl. She had become a liability to her so-called boss, otherwise known as a pimp in lower-class circles. His method of handling liabilities could be painful at best and deadly at worst.

She hesitated before answering Gene's call. She liked Gene, but to be honest, she wasn't up to talking right now. Her head felt ready to disintegrate.

Realizing that he'd just call again later if she didn't answer, she pressed the answer button and said, "Hey, Gene. Whatcha want?"

"Are you in town?"

"No, I split."

"Where are you?"

"You won't tell anyone, especially Paulson?"

"Of course not."

"I'm in Roanoke. Got a job at a diner here."

"Then you haven't heard?"

"Heard what?"

"Miranda was murdered."

She sat up too fast and her head swam. "What?!"

"You heard right. She was murdered last week. I didn't hear from you, so I assumed you hadn't heard."

"No. I don't read the papers or anything."

"Yeah, she's dead. Are you still…working?" he asked, wanting to change the subject from discussing Miranda's death.

"Hooking? No. I'm waitressing." She felt the tears spilling over her eyelids. "What happened?"

"You mean with Miranda?"

"Of course with Miranda! What else?"

"Not sure. She was found dumped in an empty lot."

"Oh, Jesus!" She clutched a stuffed teddy bear to her chest, one she'd had since childhood. "I can't believe it." She'd been very close to Miranda.

"There's more."

"What?" She wasn't sure she could handle more bad news.

"Buddy's missing."

"Missing?"

"Yeah. He disappeared the same day Miranda was killed."

"Holy shit, Gene! What's going on there?"

"I don't know."

"Can't you just, you know, ask around? See what anyone knows?"

"Can't. I got fired."

Natalie was silent for a moment. "What happened?"

"These detectives came in and I was talking to them about some stuff that's happened in the company. Nothing drastic, just basic informational stuff. Next thing I know, Braxton, who had walked up behind me when we were talking, calls me into his office and reams me out, telling me they don't have room for a security guard who doesn't understand the concept of keeping things secure."

"What kind of stuff were you telling the cops?"

"Well, they were asking about Buddy, and I told them he didn't work there anymore. That surprised them, so they started asking more questions, like about his drinking habits."

"Why would they want to know that?"

"Hell if I know. They were asking what seemed to

me to be harmless questions. It wasn't like it could cost Buddy his job at Circe. Anyway, they asked about that, and then I was just saying he was Paulson's right-hand man and how Widner must have been fired the same day Buddy must have quit."

"Widner's gone?!"

"Oh, yeah. Forgot to mention that. The head lady herself came in and must have sent him packing. Next thing I know, Paulson's got Widner's old job, and the cops are there looking for Buddy, who's disappeared entirely. His wife reported him missing. It's all a big sack of shit here."

"Jeez!" Ericka said. "I heard 'her royal highness' lives in Paris. Something bad must have happened to bring her all the way to Richmond. What are you gonna do now?"

"See if I can get work as a security guard somewhere else, I guess."

"Jeez, Gene. I'm sorry." Ericka could tell there was something else on Gene's mind. "Is something else bothering you? You kinda sound like someone who's not done with the important news."

Gene heaved a sigh and said, "Yeah, I guess you could say that."

"So what is it? Spill."

"Well, about a year ago, Buddy left me something he said was important." He paused, trying to decide if he wanted to share this information with Ericka. He'd called mostly to tell her about it, but now he was having second thoughts.

"What, Gene? Come on, man."

"He left me an envelope."

"A what?"

"An envelope."

"What's so important about that?"

"He said he needed me to hold onto it, and if

something happened to him to open it, but not before."

"Okay, Gene, you're scaring me. Do you think something happened to Buddy?"

"That's just it. I'm not sure. It's not like someone found his body. He's just, you know, missing. He might have decided to leave town like you did."

"Holy shit! Are you going to open it?"

"I don't know. That's just it. He was really serious about me not opening it until I knew something had happened to him."

"Why wouldn't he give something like that to his ex? They're still kinda close."

"I asked him that, and he said she might open it early to find out what's in it that's so mysterious. He said he could trust me not to do that."

"Oh, wow. What are you gonna do?"

"That's the question of the hour. Maybe of the month or year."

"Will you call me and tell me about it if you do open it? You got me curious now."

"I don't know. It depends on what's in there. Knowing Buddy, it could be a joke just to rattle me."

"Yeah, he always was a practical joker. Maybe you should open it for that reason only."

"I'm not sure. I think he would have asked me about it later if he wanted me to open it, but it's true. He knew he could trust me not to open it until I'm supposed to. And the way he put it to me was 'in case something happens to me.' He didn't say it like in case he keeled over from a heart attack or died in a car wreck or something. He really looked kind of scared when he gave it to me and warned me that knowing what was in it could even put me in danger."

"Shit," Ericka said. "That's creepy. I know some bad shit was going on at Circe. That's why I left."

"You mean other than the prostitution ring being

run out of there?"

"Yeah. Other bad shit."

"What kind of bad shit?"

"I don't know exactly. Just a feeling I got, vibes people gave off, and like I said, I'm not talking bad shit like Paulson and his girls. I mean really bad shit."

"Ericka?"

"Yeah?"

"You don't think they'd do something like kill Buddy, do you?"

"I don't know, Gene. Maybe they would. Frankly, I wouldn't put anything past Paulson. He's definitely a guy who takes and does what he wants and doesn't care." Her tone suggested that an experience with Paulson haunted her.

"Yeah," Gene said, hoping he had done the right thing by telling Ericka about the envelope. He'd hoped she would help him with the decision of whether or not to open it, but she hadn't really.

"Listen, Gene, I gotta go. Let me know if something happens, okay?"

"Sure. Later, girl. Take care."

"You too."

"Talk to you soon," he said.

17

The next day, Pantera sat at his desk, thinking about the two cases they were working and how odd it was they were connected through Circe Enterprises. He opened Google on his computer and searched for the company. The company's website claimed it was the parent company for a variety of businesses that were involved in everything from finance to wholesale distribution. Pantera wondered if perhaps they were also involved in illegal business ventures, such as drugs and prostitution. Their slogan, "If you need it, we have it!" made him wonder as well. Wholesale distribution could mean a lot of things, depending on how you look at it.

When Harry walked in, Pantera waved him over. "Look at this," he said, and Harry bent to the screen and looked at a picture of men in suits sitting at a large conference table. The man at the head of the table was listed in the photo description as Ron Widner. The man to his right was Claude Paulson. A woman stood at one side of the table next to a whiteboard. She was pointing at various line and bar graphs and speaking to the half dozen men, who appeared rapt. She was identified simply as "Circe, President and CEO."

"Circe?" Harry said. "No last name?"

"Nope. I've looked for where she's mentioned on the site, and she's always just Circe."

"Like Cher, Madonna, or Sting. Funny. They're famous enough to have one name. I've never heard of Circe before."

"Other than in literature, neither have I," Pantera said. "But she apparently goes by just the one name."

"I'm sure some searching will connect her with a last name."

"I've tried that, though I've not delved into it far. So far, only the one word, much like the sorceress in *The Odyssey*."

"I doubt her parents named her Circe. We need her real name."

"Agreed. There's only one other mention of her on Google, and that after pages and pages about the character in literature. The other link took me to a brief write-up on the company's website, but basically, all it says is she founded the company sixteen years ago and remains its largest shareholder with 50.5% and lives in Paris."

"France?"

Pantera nodded. "What do you think of when you find someone who owns over fifty-percent of a large corporation's stock?"

"Mountains of money."

"Okay. Then what?"

"More mountains of money."

"Think about the person, not the wealth. What does it say about a person who does that?"

"I've never known anyone who had. They may own the largest share, but not over half. It's practically unheard of. This woman might be the richest person on Earth, but we haven't heard of her."

"That goes along with the point I'm making. Think about it. What is the most important thing to a person like that, other than the money?"

Harry considered the question. Then his face lit up. "Ahh. Control. If they own over half the stock, no other stockholders can override any decisions."

"Yep. A control freak. It's all about being in control."

"Any other big stockholders?" Harry asked.

"I don't know. I've not delved deep enough."

"Well, then, start delving, my friend." Harry pointed at Pantera's computer screen. "She's quite a looker. Who knows? If she's ever in town, you could take her to dinner."

"First, I have no interest in someone that controlling. Second, I'm already knee-deep in a relationship, with another one threatening."

"Oh?"

"Yeah. The girls tell me Nancy wants to get back with me."

Harry was silent before saying, "And how do you feel about that?"

"Conflicted, Dr. Overmeyer." He stood to get himself another cup of coffee. "That's just the kind of question a shrink would ask."

"It's a valid question."

"I know. But the possible answers all scare the hell out of me." He stood. "I need more coffee."

Pantera started toward the small lounge down the hall, and Harry said, "Get me one, too?"

"Sure."

When he returned with the coffee, Pantera said, "Maybe we could get one of our cyber geeks on this. See if they can find anything on this Circe."

"Why are you so interested in her? She lives in Paris. You think she has anything to do with Buddy Garrett's disappearance or Miranda's death?"

"I just think it's odd she flew all the way here for one day, and when she leaves, there's a new boss in the local executive's seat, and the old boss has been canned. Why would she do that? Why not just call Widner on the phone and fire him that way? She's the one with over fifty percent of the company's stock. She can pretty well do it however she wants, and in the corporate world, firing people face-to-face isn't always necessary."

"Maybe she didn't fire him. Maybe she transferred him to another city."

"Then why would Paulson appear frightened when he and the head lady walked through the doors. He obviously knew something, and whatever it was scared him. Besides, if Widner was transferred, his personnel file wouldn't have been in the former employees' files."

"Good point."

"And what the hell happened to Widner? We haven't even barked up that tree yet. I mean, did he move away? Is he moping and drunk all day at home? We should check him out, ask him what he knows."

"My guess is when we find him, he won't be saying much. When it comes to information, that place is like the CIA. Secrets on top of secrets, and under that, you find more secrets."

"Hey, someone finds shit out, but usually it's the people who know which person and what questions to ask."

"And you think Widner might talk about Circe?"

"Yep. Both the company and the woman."

"We have his address in our notes," Harry said.

"Then what are we waiting for? An invitation?"

Thirty minutes later, they were pulling into the driveway of Widner's magnificent home. The grounds alone looked more like a small park than a lawn. They came to a security gate, but no security guard was inside. The gate was open, so they drove through and up to the mansion.

"I didn't know anyone owned a parcel this large in Richmond just for a house. Property is at a premium, and in this neighborhood, just enough land to set my house on would cost three times what my house is worth," Harry said.

"Welcome to Buckingham Palace of Richmond," Pantera answered.

116

"Yeah, right."

"No, seriously," Pantera answered and pointed at a large, ornate sign near the main entrance to the house. It read, "Welcome to Buckingham Palace of Richmond" in gold lettering that was recessed into the metal sign.

"A bit ostentatious, don't you think?" Harry said.

"That's what the extremely wealthy are."

Winding to the palatial home, they found a late-model Chevrolet parked outside. Harry said, "The butler's car, I suppose."

"Not Widner's, I assure you."

At the door, they found an intercom with two buttons, marked *Talk* and *Call*. Pantera pressed Call and waited. When there was no response, he pressed it again, holding it longer this time.

A man's voice said, "Yes? Yes? What is it?"

Pressing and holding Talk, Pantera said, "Sir, my name is Detective Tony Pantera. I'm with Richmond PD. My partner and I would like a word with Mr. Ron Widner. It's rather important."

After a brief pause, the man said, "Mr. Widner is not here. Good day."

Pantera pressed the call button again. The man was back on. "What? I told you Mr. Widner's not here."

"Yes, but you see, if he's not here, then we need to find out where he is."

"He's in Bermuda."

"Bermuda?"

"Are you deaf? Yes. Ber-mu-da," the man on the other end said, pronouncing each syllable carefully. "Now, be gone."

Pantera pressed the call button again. Within two seconds, the man was back on.

"I said he's in Bermuda. Now go away! I have work to do here!"

"What kind of work?" Pantera asked.

"I'm closing up the house for the season. I was told Mr. Widner would not be back for months, and I have to be in Chicago for a wedding tomorrow."

"Sir, if you could just open the door and talk to us for ten minutes, I promise we will leave you to your work."

A half-minute later, the door latch sounded and the door opened as if it, too, were in a hurry.

A short, stout man with thinning gray hair and large muttonchop sideburns that looked like brushes on his cheeks stood there, peering at them through small wireframe glasses.

"Yes? Yes? What do you have to ask me?"

"Sir, did Mr. Widner say exactly when he would return? The exact date?"

"Not that I know of."

"Why did he go to Bermuda?"

The man looked nonplussed for a moment before saying, "He decided to chuck it all and leave for an extended vacation."

"You said you were told Mr. Widner would not be back for months. Does this mean Mr. Widner did not tell you?"

The man again looked confused. "No, it was someone who worked at Circe Enterprises."

Pantera said, "You're not making complete sense. Start from the beginning and explain what happened."

The man took a deep breath and said, "Mr. Widner left for work as usual. That afternoon, I received a call that he was going to Bermuda. No return date. I asked the woman, 'what about his job?' and she said he had quit."

"When was the last time you spoke to him?"

"His last day as he left for work. The woman I spoke with told me that he'd decided to chuck it all— quit his job and go on a long vacation, starting in

Bermuda and wending his way through the various island nations of the world and that it could be months before he arrived back in Richmond."

"So a woman who works at Circe Enterprises told you this?" Harry asked.

The man looked at Harry as if he had not noticed him before. "And who are you?" the man said.

"I'm Detective Harry Overmeyer. I'm Detective Pantera's partner.

The man nodded. "Well, good for you. Yes! I said that. Again, are you hard of hearing?"

"No, sir, just asking for verification of the information."

The man looked at the ground and shook his head in frustration. Looking back at Pantera and Harry, he said, "The lady told me he was leaving for an indeterminate length of time. As far as I know, he's in Bermuda and has been there for several days now. I have nothing more to tell you because I don't know any more than that."

"And he never even came by for luggage or to pack for this long trip?" Pantera asked.

"I have no idea. I had other things to do and wasn't home until nine that evening. He could have come home and packed, I suppose."

"Are his suitcases missing?"

"I don't know. Why would I care about that?"

"Would you mind checking?" Pantera asked.

"Would it get you to leave and let me get on with my work?"

"Of course," Pantera said.

Huffing, the man turned and said, "Follow me."

Soon they were in a large, very tidy bedroom. The man went to the large, walk-in closet and entered, the detectives following. Four suitcases of varying sizes were along one wall. "His best Louis Vuitton cases are missing," the man said.

Harry said, "He has two sets of suitcases?"

"Yes. These are his Samsonite luggage for domestic trips. He always takes the Louis Vuitton when going abroad."

Harry shook his head. "The super wealthy."

"About the secretary," Pantera said, "did you recognize her voice?"

"I've never met her or spoken to her before."

"Never?" Harry asked.

"I don't usually deal with those in Mr. Widner's employ. I just take care of his house and deal with the people who maintain the grounds and such."

"How old did the secretary sound to you?"

"I don't know. She wasn't a child or anything. At least in her thirties, I'd say, maybe as old as her fifties or sixties. A woman."

"Can we get your name and address, please? Just for the record," Pantera asked.

"Reginald Hallwater. I live in the quarters in back."

"We didn't see any separate quarters," Harry said.

"It's about a hundred yards from the house. I have a golf cart to get me back and forth. Now, will you be needing me for anything else? I really must get busy."

"So you're going to Chicago?"

"That's what I said, isn't it? I have to finish this and find a place for my cat to stay before my flight this evening."

"Your cat?"

"Yes! Mr. Whiskers! He can't just live here alone. Someone has to feed him, at least until I return."

"But you've had several days to find a place for the cat," Harry said.

"Yes, I have, and so far, nobody wants the creature. He's mean as a devil from Hell. Well, with anyone besides me, of course."

Pantera said, "There are plenty of places to leave a

cat. Vets have kennels for dogs and cats, as well as lots of privately owned kennels."

"A kennel?!" Reginald's expressions suggested they had offered to shoot Mr. Whiskers.

"Sorry, just trying to help."

"Are we done now?" Reginald asked.

"Yes, we are. When will you be back from Chicago?"

"On Tuesday of next week. Now, if you will kindly follow me, please." He led them to the front door. As he abruptly closed it behind them, he said, "Good day, gentlemen!"

As they drove away, they discussed what they'd discovered. Widner's sudden disappearance created more questions than answers, and they weren't even sure he'd left town. The Bermuda story didn't seem likely. Of course, being fired could have led him to leave the country, but they were skeptical.

After the detectives left, Reginald, whose last name was actually Widner, wiped his brow with a handkerchief. He knew exactly where his son Ron was, and he also knew he might be blamed for his death if they found his body, or rather the bodies. The people his son had worked for would make sure of that. He knew Circe was a powerful woman, and Claude Paulson was dangerous as well.

Nobody knew Reginald was Ron's father, at least nobody in the Eastern US. They had worked out that arrangement years ago when Reginald needed a place to stay and something to keep him busy. Ron had offered to allow him to live in the servant's quarters and enjoy the good life if he would become Ron's butler. That would allow him to remain busy, taking on a simple and usually stress-free job, and his son would support him.

Now, though, things were different. He had risen to go to the bathroom in the night when he'd heard voices in the woods not far from his quarters. Looking through his window, he saw them dump Ron's body into a freshly dug grave. Then he watched as Claude Paulson stepped up behind the man who had tossed the body into the grave, and shoot him in the head. Reginald heard the thump of the silenced pistol and flinched, nearly falling over from the shock.

After Paulson and the woman he recognized from photos as Circe had left, he had gone to the graveside of his son and the unknown man and wondered what to do. If he turned the true killers in, he could likely face the same fate. It wasn't as if nobody else at Circe Enterprises was capable of such an act.

Reginald needed to get as far away from Richmond as he could. He would keep quiet about the bodies and what he'd seen, at least until he was long gone from here.

18

Circe was ready to leave New York for home. She loved New York, but Paris had a certain flavor that no other city in the world had. If she was away for more than a few weeks, it beckoned her the way some of the expensive whores she'd known beckoned rich customers. She'd known a few whores who were not so expensive, but she also knew that escape from that degrading life was possible. She'd made the escape herself.

Nobody knew her past. Only Monique, the only lover she could handle on a fulltime basis, knew her surname. However, not even Monique knew where she came from, and nobody she knew besides Monique knew her real name, Yvette, that her prostitute mother had given her.

She had canceled her flight home to stay in New York for a few days, and that had turned into a full week. She had shopped, eaten at the city's finest restaurants, seen a few plays, both on and off Broadway, and had enjoyed sexual liaisons with several men and women, even joining a couple she met at a pub on 2nd Avenue. But the fun was over now, and she was returning to Paris, this time on her private jet, which she'd had sent from Paris to pick her up. It had been costly, but she was rich enough that spending that much for her comfort was like some people buying a fast-food hamburger and fries just to enjoy some greasy food. She was a billionaire several times over, and spending a million dollars, one-thousandth of a billion, was like some clerk in a store having a thousand dollars to blow and spending a dollar. The math was the same.

Now, she leaned back as the Learjet soared above the clouds and thought of her past and how far she had come from her humble beginning.

Her mother was a prostitute in a brothel in New Orleans in the early 1970s. Circe had seen the movie *Pretty Baby*, but other than the location, her life was far different. She'd never posed nude as a child, nor had she become a child prostitute where horrible men bid on being her first. Her first time was not so elegant. She'd been raped at age eleven by one of her mother's regulars, and her mother had killed him for what he'd done. A certain high-ranking official with the New Orleans Police Department had received a lifetime of free visits to the brothel for ignoring the killing. Yvette eventually took a different name to fully dispose of her past.

She was a lover of classical Greek mythology, and the character of Circe, the sorceress who was the child of Helios, the Sun God, and the ocean nymph, Perse, intrigued her from the start, perhaps because she was the result of a symbolic joining of the sun and the sea. She loved how Circe had turned Odysseus's crew into pigs, which in many ways was appropriate, so he would have to remain on her island and be her prisoner and lover. The idea of her having that power over men intrigued her, and the thoughts of that power and what that afforded her had resulted in her first sexual feelings as she daydreamed about having such supremacy over the world of men.

So she took the name of Circe as her own and when she moved from New Orleans forever, swearing never to return, she would only tell a very select few her real name, and those were always women, and then only those she would trust with her life.

She had survived at first by turning tricks and had eventually become what in common parlance was called a "madam." She used only the most beautiful women as her ladies, coaxing them into the business with lies about how much money they could make just for giving men and occasional women a few moments of pleasure. Yes, they could make money, but nowhere near what they made for Circe.

She had also learned her lesson well from her mother and the man who ran the brothel where she worked. Offer free sex to a few select men, and in a few cases select women, and the law turned a blind eye to what was happening under everyone's noses. At one point, she realized her business was servicing the city's entire town council, as well as the chief of police and the district attorney. She would pay the girls what they were due and was happy to do so.

She managed to make over $600,000 in two years, which she turned into nearly two million by the end of three. She made some wise investments with some of the money, and set up a illegal drug operation with the rest.

Within two more years, she had over ten million.

With that, she did what the money people always said to do: diversify. She expanded her business interests, started Circe Enterprises, and by the end of last year, she was worth nearly four billion in US dollars.

Her early life had been hard, but she'd learned much from those hardships.

The exhaustion from the trip and New York parties set in, and she moved to the bed that took up most of the rear of the jet. She napped for a few hours, and when she woke, they were less than an hour from the coast of her beloved France.

When they landed, Monique was waiting for her.

"Good morning!" she said, approaching Circe, waiting to be kissed.

Circe pecked her on the lips. "Let's go. I have much to tell you."

Once the luggage was loaded into the trunk of the limo, the women climbed into the back seat. After a more passionate embrace, Circe sat back and watched through the window as they approached the city from the northeast, the Eiffel coming into view.

Their penthouse apartment was between the Arc de Triomphe and the tower, and she never tired of the view, mostly because such beautiful views were nonexistent when she was a child. The window of the one-room apartment where she and her mother had lived looked out onto a crumbling concrete block wall where rats scurried in and out of the hollows, sometimes making their way into the apartment where either she or her mother would chase them out with a broom.

Monique allowed Circe to watch for a moment before asking, "So what did you need to tell me?"

Circe checked the barrier between them and the driver to ensure it was closed tightly to prevent him from hearing what she said.

"I had to get rid of Ron Widner."

"Oh?"

"Yes. He was stealing from me. Probably used it to pay for that mansion he lived in."

"Where is he now?"

"Where nobody will ever think to look. Buried on his own property."

"Who's in charge of the East Coast now?" Monique asked.

"Claude Paulson."

"Claude? That bastard?"

"I had no choice. He was available, and on such short notice, I couldn't find anyone else. Besides, he was next in line and may have decided to double-cross me somehow if I placed someone else in the position."

"How do you know Ron was stealing?"

"Paulson showed me proof."

"I bet he was happy to do that."

"I'm sure he was, especially since he had to know it saved his life. One thing about Claude, though. He won't do something stupid to mess up the good thing he now has. Ron was a fool."

"I guess they're wrong," Monique said.

"About what?"

She turned to Circe and smiled. "There's no honor among thieves after all."

19

The day after the visit to the Widner home, Pantera couldn't help but wonder where the investigation would lead. It felt mired in a stack of suspicions without any proof. They had no idea where Widner had gone. If he'd flown anywhere, he'd traveled with a fake passport. They had managed to get a search warrant the previous afternoon to find out if anyone with the last name of Widner had flown to Bermuda in the days since Widner's last day at Circe. It was an easy computer search once they had the warrant, and none of the airlines that flew out of Richmond showed anyone named Widner flying anywhere from there. The man had basically disappeared.

Harry had a call into US Customs and Border Patrol in Washington to see if they could trace whether Widner had even left the country. A passport use search was underway but they wouldn't hear anything on that front for days, perhaps weeks, considering that their request was not deemed to be urgent. They suspected he was still in the country, but an answer from Customs would provide proof.

After lunch, Harry asked, "Maybe we could talk to some of the people who saw him leave the building."

"I called about that, figuring our visits were becoming more unwelcome every day. I managed to speak to his executive assistant." Pantera shuffled through his notes, searching for the woman's name. "Rose Tipton. She said she was running an errand when he left."

"Did she say what kind of errand?"

"Nope. Just said when Paulson came in with Circe, the lady told her to take some papers to personnel."

"How convenient," Harry said.

"Yeah, I thought that, too."

"Did you ask her if she phoned Reginald?"

"Yes, and she says she didn't."

"Could have been someone else," Harry suggested.

"Could have been, but very doubtful. I'm starting to wonder if our buddy Reg wasn't telling us some lies. Either that, or Ms. Tipton is, but I don't see why she would."

"Why would Reginald lie?"

"Maybe he was involved in some way in whatever happened to Widner. Ms. Tipton did verify that Reginald was the caretaker, though, so he was telling the truth about that. Even described him, so it wasn't an impostor either."

"Those sideburns pretty well nail him," Harry said.

"Yep."

"Someone had to see Widner leaving, though. Maybe our pal, Gene?"

"We could ask him. When we talked before, we weren't looking for Widner, but now I'm wondering where he went."

"I think we should pay Gene a visit," Harry said.

"Yeah. Maybe he can explain why we can't find any of the people whose employment with Circe ended that day other than a dead Miranda Buckhorn."

They drove to Gene's home but he wasn't there. His father must have either returned to his home in Baltimore or was out somewhere himself. Pantera left a card wedged between the door and the door jamb, asking Gene to give them a call.

"What now?" Harry asked.

"I'd like to say we knock off early and grab a drink or three at the Watering Hole, but we can't."

"True. So my question stands unanswered."

"What was the name of the young girl who left Circe a few weeks before Miranda was killed?"

Harry took out his small notebook and flipped to the pages from the day they searched the files. "Ericka, with a 'ck,' last name Oliver, age twenty."

"Maybe we can find her. Get a take on some things." Pantera took out his phone and googled "Ericka Oliver, Richmond." There were no hits. "Hmm. Nothing. And with the uncommon spelling, you'd think we'd have found something online. I recall there was no mention of next of kin in the file. What's her address?"

Harry checked his notes. "Ledbetter Place Townhomes. 12C."

"Nice digs," Pantera said.

"Maybe we go talk to her and find out a little more about Circe Enterprises and Claude Paulson."

"Let's do it," Harry said.

Twenty minutes later, they pulled up at the gate for Ledbetter Place. As they approached the gatehouse, they were surprised to see the guard had a familiar face.

"Can I help you guys with something?" the guard asked, not looking up as he set a soda can on a small desk behind him.

"Hello there, Gene," Pantera said.

Gene's reaction was more than they expected. His eyes bulged as he gaped at them.

"Are you guys following me or something?"

Pantera said, "No, we were looking for you and you weren't home, so we said to ourselves, now where might Gene be? And Harry over here says, 'maybe he's working at the entrance gate for Ledbetter Place.' So I said, 'then let's check it out,' and now here we are."

Gene's confusion was almost comical. "What?"

"No, we're looking for a young girl who worked at Circe but quit or was fired a few weeks before Garrett disappeared. Her file says she lived in a townhouse here."

"You mean Ericka?"

"So you know her?"

Gene looked as though he may have said more than he should, but it was too late now. "Yeah. I know her."

"Do you know if she's home?" Pantera asked.

"She doesn't live here anymore."

"Where does she live?"

Gene looked around, as if waiting for someone to spring from the lush foliage nearby and attack him. "I don't know."

"Then how do you know she doesn't live here?"

"She left town, but that's all I know about it. She wouldn't tell me where she is now."

"You spoke to her?"

Gene sighed. "Yeah, I spoke to her. On the phone."

Pantera smiled. "Then you have her number." It wasn't a question.

"Come on, man. Why you want to talk to her? She doesn't know anything."

"Now, how might we find out if she knows anything or not?" Turning to Harry, he said, "You have any ideas on that, partner? I mean, if we only had her phone number, we could verify for ourselves that she doesn't know anything helpful."

"I agree. Too bad we don't have her number," Harry answered, smiling.

Pantera turned back to Gene and looked at him, eyebrows raised.

Gene heaved another sigh and said, "Okay. I'll give you her number, but you can't tell her I gave it to you."

"We'll just say we got it from some employee at Circe."

He recited the number to Pantera, who wrote it down.

Turning back to Gene, Pantera said, "While we have you here, we were wondering if you know of anyone who saw Ron Widner leave the building the day he was canned."

Gene thought for a moment and said, "No. Not that I heard about, but then people leave the building all the time. I'm not sure anyone would notice."

"You were at the entrance desk that day. You didn't see him? If he was fired, wouldn't security escort him out?"

"Yeah, unless Paulson and Circe did."

"So he wasn't with them when they left the building?"

Gene's jaw dropped. "I never saw them leave."

Pantera noticed the fear or worry in Gene's eyes.

"I take it there are other exits," Pantera said. "They didn't just camp there on some sofas."

"Yeah, but it's a very secure building. There's only one other, but it's at the loading dock."

"Isn't that a fire hazard?"

"The loading dock and the front entrance are actually the most convenient places to exit," Gene explained. "And the front has five sets of double-doors. Plenty to handle the number of people in the building. It's not like we have a bunch of customers visiting."

"So either they come out where the security desk is or they leave through the loading dock exit?" Pantera asked.

"Yeah, but there'd be no reason for them to go out that way. It doesn't make sense."

"Well, you said yourself they didn't leave through the main exit," Harry said.

Pantera asked, "Who would be watching that exit?"

"Nobody, really. It's locked against anyone coming in that way unless something is being brought into the building from a truck, which doesn't happen that often.

It's not like Circe gets product deliveries, or anything. It's mostly for stuff like new furniture or bulk office supplies. That kind of thing."

"Why would there be an unattended entrance and exit in such a secure building?" Harry asked.

"Because it's locked down tight to prevent anyone coming in that way. You have to have a special security card to unlock the doors, and there's like a ten-digit number you have to punch in to open them even after the card's been scanned. Leaving the building that way would also require getting through the padlocked gate to get to your car. It would only be convenient if there was a fire."

"Why would they use that exit?" Pantera asked.

"I don't know. It makes no sense."

"Are there security cameras that watch those doors?"

"Of course."

Pantera looked over at Harry. "I think we have another search warrant to write up and get signed."

20

As Pantera and Harry were sitting at their desks to compose the new search warrant, Reginald Widner was sitting in his hotel room in Atlanta, hoping he was doing the right thing. He wanted his son's body to be found. He would never testify to what he saw, but at least his son would get a proper burial. He'd never done much for him, but he could do this.

He opened his laptop and signed on to the hotel's internet. Then he began to type. They would be able to trace where it came from, of course. By then, he would be long gone with a new identity under the name Elliot Parks. It was something he had asked Ron to set up for him several years ago, hoping he would never have to use it, but now it became a necessity. Once this task was complete, he would drive to another hotel in the car rented under the name Elliot Parks, check in there for one night, and get a cab to the airport tomorrow morning. He had reservations on a flight to Los Angeles. From there, he would fly to Honolulu. Who knew where he'd go from there. He hoped that and the new identity would be enough to allow him never to be seen again by anyone he knew.

He typed his message before taking out Pantera's card and entering the detective's email address. He gave the email the subject line "Urgent message about Ron Widner from Reginald Hallwater." He sat for a moment, prayed he was doing the right thing, and pressed send.

Seconds later, Pantera's phone dinged, but he was too busy with the warrant to look.

"You get a message from someone?" Harry asked.

"Yeah, an email, but I don't want to leave this for now. It can wait."

Pantera bent toward the computer screen and typed while Harry went to get them some coffee.

To increase the chances a judge would sign the warrant, Pantera wrote that a missing person hadn't been seen leaving the building by its one and only public entrance. The details of how and when he left, whom he left with, and if he ever returned through the same entrance and exit at the loading dock were important. Still, it would take some convincing to get a judge to sign off on such a search.

They typically could ask to see the footage of a business's security cameras, but they knew attempting that with Circe Enterprises would be a waste of time.

"Why don't you give Ericka Oliver a call while I finish the warrant?" Pantera said.

"Sure thing. What's the number?"

Pantera took out his small notebook, opened it to the page with Ericka's number, and tossed it to Harry.

Harry dialed the number, but Ericka didn't answer. "No answer," he said. "You think she's monitoring her calls?"

"People with less reason to do that often do."

"Can't make her answer."

"Nope. Maybe she'll answer if we call enough."

"Doubt it, but it's worth a try."

"Should we work up a warrant to search her whereabouts through the number?" Pantera asked.

"Not a bad idea. We can find out which towers are getting her signal. It would let us know the area where she lives, at least."

"Why don't you start on that one, and I'll finish this one." Pantera returned to his work.

After completing the search warrant requests, they left to find a sympathetic judge. Halfway to the courthouse, Harry said, "You ever check that email?"

"Naw. Slipped my mind."

"Jeez, Tony. Sometimes I will email you on a Saturday morning about something for Monday, and you'll get to work without ever seeing it."

"I figure if it's that important, people can call."

"That's true, but what if they don't have your phone number, just your email?"

"Then it can wait. People who are important enough to have my attention at a moment's notice have my phone number."

Harry shrugged. "Maybe you won the Publisher's Clearing House Sweepstakes."

"Gotta enter to win that."

"Yeah, but who knows? It could actually be important," Harry said as Pantera pulled into the parking lot of the courthouse.

Putting the car in park, Pantera glared at Harry before fumbling his phone from his pocket. Glancing at the screen, he said, "Holy shit!"

"What is it?"

"An email from Reginald Hallwater."

"What does he say?"

Pantera read the email aloud.

Good day, Detective Pantera. I have thought and thought about our meeting and feel I must confess a few things. First, my name is not Reginald Hallwater. I won't tell you what it is, but I was close to Ronald. He was like a son to me. I apologize, but I lied to you when I told you he was in Bermuda. The truth is he never left the country at all. I'm fairly certain you have figured that out by now, or at least you were well on your way to doing so. You struck me as very competent and thorough. The truth is that he never left the state or the city. He never even left his estate.

You see, Ronald has been murdered. Not by me, of course. I would never do such a thing. I am not a violent man. I'm not an innocent, but I have never harmed another human being, at least physically, other than some fist fights I had when I was young. It was my fear that I would be charged with murder that caused me to lie to you. Please forgive me that act of self-preservation. I am atoning for that now to some extent. The truth is that I witnessed Ronald's unceremonious burial. Those responsible did not see me. I am certain if they had I would be dead as well.

They also killed another man who was with them, possibly to ensure nobody ever found out what happened. I'm not sure why and honestly don't care. After they had dumped Ronald's body in the shallow grave, they shot the man who dropped him in the hole dug in the soft dirt of the garden, not far from my own quarters. Then the killers covered the bodies with the dirt and left, leaving me with the horrible memory of what I witnessed.

You will find the bodies of Ronald and the other man together in a single, shallow grave in the soft earth about twenty yards from where I stayed. I mentioned the quarters where I was living, and that was the truth. There is a garden of sorts there, which is where they buried Ron and the other man. I could give more details, but the bodies should be easy enough to find now that you know they are there. Get one of your cadaver dogs to sniff them out.

Again, my apologies for misleading you. Do not try to find me. I've taken drastic steps to ensure you never will, and believe me, you'll only be wasting your time. Besides, while I know who it was that killed Ronald and that man, I would die before testifying, whether by my own hand or someone else's is immaterial. Suffice it to say, I would never take the stand, nor will I tell you their identities, something I hope to use to hopefully spare my life if I'm ever found by them.

I bid you and your partner adieu and mountains of luck. You will need it.

The fictional Reginald Hallwater

"Holy shit," Harry said.

"I guess it's true that we need to see that footage after all for more important reasons. The tone of the email is one of fear. I think it's obvious who killed Ron Widner. The last known people to see him alive were Paulson and Circe whatever-her-last-name-is."

"I think it's time we paid Mr. Paulson another visit," Harry said.

"First, we need to see that security footage."

21

Pantera called and requested a cadaver dog to search the Widner property, concentrating on the garden next to the quarters located behind the main house. Then he and Harry found a judge to sign off on the search warrant.

Arriving at Circe Enterprises, they walked around the building, searching for the loading dock area. When they found it, they were blocked from approaching it by a locked gate. The gate had a keypad locking mechanism as well as a chain and padlock, making it difficult for anyone to get onto the property from there.

They walked through the main entrance and presented their warrant. The guard, whom they had never seen before, glanced at it and tossed it back on the desk he sat behind as if dismissing it.

"What's this?" the guard, whose name tag read *Diggs*, asked, his tone both bored and confrontational.

Pantera said, "It's called a search warrant. You've heard of those, right?"

"Yeah. What are you looking for?"

Pantera picked up the warrant again and held it out so the guard could read it. "Funny thing about search warrants," he said, "they always list exactly what we are looking for. Since you're a little slow on the whole reading thing, I'll tell you." He looked at the warrant as if he didn't know what it said. "Hmmm. Seems we need to see security video footage of your loading dock area from one day last week."

"What day last week?"

"Wednesday."

"Ain't gonna happen," Diggs said, smiling.

Harry said, "Perhaps you don't understand how this works. This document is legal. It isn't a matter of whether or not you want to show us the video. Not doing so would land a lot of people, including you, in front of a very angry judge."

"No, you're the one who doesn't understand," Diggs said. "Security video ain't kept forever. It's on a loop that records over the footage from the same day last week. We only keep it if something happened during the last seven days, like a break-in or something like that. Today's Thursday, and since you said you needed footage from last Wednesday, it's gone. Erased yesterday."

Pantera felt a strong desire to see if he could shove the guard's smirk down his throat. He exchanged a glance with Harry and said, "Then we need to talk to Braxton."

"Head of security?"

"Yeah, congratulations on knowing your boss."

Diggs said, "What? You think he can magically bring the video back?"

"What we think doesn't matter, at least not to you. Pick up the phone and dial whatever you have to dial to get him out here."

Diggs heaved an angry sigh and placed the call. "Is Mr. Braxton around?" He listened and answered, "Two cops out here need to speak to him." Diggs waited again before saying, "How do I know? All I know is they're cops who want to see something we don't have, and now they want to talk to Mr. Braxton about it." After a moment, he said, "Okay, I'll have them wait."

Hanging up, he pointed at the chairs the detectives were all too familiar with. "Plant it over there. He'll be with you when he can."

Pantera considered just walking past the desk to go

to Braxton's office but decided against it since it probably wouldn't work anyway and would just cause them to wait longer.

They sat in the uncomfortable chairs and waited. Twenty minutes later, Pantera approached Diggs again and said, "Any idea what the holdup is? Is he dealing with some security breach or something?"

"First, if he was, I wouldn't tell you about it. Second, who knows what's keeping him? He could be taking a shit for all I know. Just sit down over there and he'll be here when it suits him."

Pantera rejoined Harry and fumed. As they waited, Pantera received a call from Detective Matt Stovall.

"They're here," Stovall said. "Just like your email said they would be."

"Two men?"

"Yeah. And we have an ID on the other guy, a fellow named Garrett. Irwin Garrett. That's according to his DL, and the photo matches the deceased."

"How'd they die?" Pantera asked.

"Well, that's up to the ME, but Garrett has a bullet hole in the back of his head, so I'd say that's what killed him if I had to guess. No telling about Widner. He was tortured, though."

"Jeez," Pantera said. "Thanks for handling this."

"Don't mention it. Not every day we have a double homicide like this, especially involving torture."

"What makes you say he was tortured?"

"Well, I could begin with the broken bones, but I'd say the freshly severed fingers and the fact his balls and his tongue have been cut off kinda nails it."

"Good Lord."

"Yeah. My guess is wherever this torture happened would be quite a mess unless they covered everything with plastic sheeting first."

Pantera sighed and said, "Okay, keep me posted."

After he'd told Harry what was found at the Widner home, Harry said, "Oh, my God. What would he have to do to suffer that?"

"Who knows? The broken bones don't really suggest anything specific, but the fingers suggest maybe he was stealing from someone. The amputated tongue suggests he talked too much. The balls? Maybe he was fucking around with the wrong person."

"At least we found Garrett," Harry said.

"Yeah, and now we have to break that bad news to his ex. She seemed like she probably still loved him."

They sat in silence, contemplating what lay ahead for them in the investigation, considering the odd turn it had just taken. After another twenty minutes, they saw Braxton approaching the security desk. Pantera and Harry stood and walked over. Nobody offered to shake hands.

"What now?" Braxton asked.

"We need to talk to you about some security footage that I've been told has been erased," Pantera said.

"Why do you think I would know something about it?"

"We don't. That's why we need to talk to you."

"So talk."

"We'd prefer to do this in your office."

"And I'd prefer we talk out here."

Pantera looked at Harry and back at Braxton. "Fine," he said. Then raising his voice to ensure anyone within fifty yards could hear them, he said, "I need to talk to you about the murder of Ronald Widner."

Braxton went pale and did his best to maintain some composure.

"Fine. We'll talk in my office."

They followed Braxton to his office and sat across from him.

"Okay, tell me what's going on."

"We just found Widner's body. There was another body found with his, one of your security guards, Buddy Garrett."

"I don't understand. Did they kill each other?"

"No. They were both killed and buried together."

"Where?"

"We're not saying yet," Pantera said and changed the subject. "Is it true you only have security surveillance for no more than the last seven days?"

"Yes. We only keep it if something has happened that would entail viewing the footage."

"Would Ron Widner leaving by the loading dock exit be unusual?"

"Yes."

"Well, that's how he left the last time anyone saw him alive."

"You mean the day he was fired?"

"Yeah. And here's another thing: Paulson and the lady named Circe left through that exit as well," Pantera said.

"And it's very likely they were with Widner when he left through this inconvenient exit," Pantera added.

"You think they killed Mr. Widner?" Braxton said, almost laughing. "That's insane."

Pantera ignored the question. "If his leaving by the loading dock entrance was unusual, why would the footage be discarded?"

"Because it would have nothing to do with anything regarding the company's security. By unusual, I meant only those things that appeared to be a threat. Just because Widner left the building through the loading dock entrance with our company's founder and Paulson does not mean there was any kind of security breach or a threat of any kind. Quite the contrary, actually. It's the opposite of a sign of danger that the founder of the company and another executive was with him."

"So whoever watches the security camera feed wouldn't do anything to save that footage?"

"No. The truth is unless something drastic happens, we typically don't even check the footage. It's not really monitored by anyone. It just records and we check it if we have a reason to."

Pantera and Harry exchanged looks. Harry said, "That doesn't sound much like the overzealous security of Circe Enterprises."

"We don't waste man hours having someone sit and watch a camera feed. There are alarms in place if someone tries to breach the building's security."

Pantera said, "Fine. We need to see how someone would go from Widner's office to the loading dock exit."

Braxton stood and said, "Follow me."

They walked to the bank of elevators and rode to the floor where Widner's office, now Paulson's, had been. As they came to the hallway leading to the door to Paulson's office, Braxton pointed. "That was Widner's office. To leave by the loading dock, he would have come down this hallway and turned right, going in this direction," he said, pointing down the hallway in front of them.

Leading them about fifteen feet down that hallway to another elevator, he said, "This elevator is for executives only. It goes all the way down to the basement floor, which is where the loading dock is."

"Let's see it," Pantera said.

Braxton flashed a key card in front of a scanner, and the elevator door opened immediately. "This elevator was installed for the convenience of the top executives to be able to move about the building quickly. It is rarely used for emergency exits, though, since getting through the locked gate at the entrance to the loading dock area can take time, and it's not exactly convenient to the employee parking lot. Still, being able to get to the basement from here is basically for added security to protect the executives. If it is taken to another floor, the car automatically returns to this floor to prevent having to wait for the elevator car to arrive in case of a problem."

"What kind of problem?" Harry asked.

"Everyone is susceptible to the equivalent of a home invasion these days, Detective. It happens at schools and smaller businesses on a regular basis now. What's to prevent it from happening in larger corporate buildings?"

Harry nodded. The violence ordinary citizens were exposed to had grown at an alarming rate.

They stepped onto the elevator and Braxton pressed the button marked *B*. The elevator descended in silence, the doors opening onto an empty warehouse space below the main building. The doors to the loading dock lay about forty feet in front of them.

"Could you open the doors?" Pantera said.

Braxton took out his key card again and strode over to the scanner. After scanning the card, he checked his phone and punched in a ten-digit number he found there on a keypad. "Extra precaution," Braxton said. "It's a double-lock mechanism that takes both a key card and the proper number sequence on the keypad to open the doors. The number sequence changes once a week, and we receive it by encoded text."

As the doors automatically slid open along a track, Pantera again wondered what was so secretive about the work Circe Enterprises did that required such security, but he didn't ask because he knew he would be rebuffed, and though he didn't like it, Braxton would be completely within his rights to refuse to answer the question.

"How often does the company use the loading

dock?" Pantera asked.

"Not often. We're not in the business of buying and selling merchandise except in special circumstances."

"What kind of special circumstances?" Harry asked.

Braxton looked at him coldly and said, "Special ones."

"So it's entirely likely nobody ever noticed they left through this exit?" Pantera said.

"That's almost a certainty since nobody monitors the cameras."

Pantera said, "Excuse us a second." They stepped far enough away to avoid being overheard.

"What do you think?" Pantera asked.

"I think it's odd that the security here is so heavy, but they don't monitor the security cameras."

"Me, too. You think he's lying?"

Harry glanced at Braxton and said, "Hard to say, but I've never seen a building with tight security that doesn't have someone monitoring the security cameras."

Pantera nodded and began walking over to Braxton. "We want to see where you would view any footage if something odd did happen."

"Why would you want to do that?"

"Just for our report. Being thorough."

Braxton nodded and said, "This way."

They returned to the elevator and had to wait as it descended from its permanent spot above them. Soon, they entered the security suite where Braxton's office was. Braxton stopped at his executive assistant's desk. "Any calls for me while I was out?" he asked.

The assistant, Ms. Kensington according to her desk nameplate, looked surprised at the question before she said, "Yes. Mr. Raintree called and asked you to call him immediately about an urgent matter."

Braxton turned to Pantera. "This won't take long. Just have a seat, and Ms. Kensington will get you something to drink."

Turning abruptly, Braxton disappeared into his office. Ms. Kensington looked at the detectives. "Shall I get you something to drink?"

"None for me," Harry said.

"I think I'd like a coffee. Two sugars and light on the cream," Pantera said.

"Certainly," she said and went to get the coffee.

The moment the door to his office was closed, Braxton went to his desk phone. Dialing an extension, he waited. Braxton had a signal with Ms. Kensington for whenever he needed some private moments in his office when he was with someone. He would enter her office and ask if he'd had any calls. She would reply by saying a fictitious Mr. Raintree had requested an urgent call back as soon as he came in. They rarely used the signal, but it came in handy when it was needed.

When the man answered the call, Braxton said, "Empty the room. I want nobody in there monitoring until I call you back."

"Yes, sir," came the reply.

Braxton hung up and dialed another extension.

"What is it?" Paulson said when he finally answered.

"Those detectives are back," Braxton answered.

"What do they want?"

"They say they found the bodies of Widner and Garrett." The silence on the other end of the line told Braxton how bad this news was. After a moment when no reply came, he said, "Mr. Paulson?"

"I'm here. They're here now?"

"Yes, sir. They seem to think it has something to do with his job. They apparently discovered that Widner left with you and the queen," he said, using a common term for Circe. He paused before adding, "Is there something I should do?"

"No."

"You had me get rid of Garrett's car," he reminded Paulson. "That puts me in the middle of this."

"Here's the official story. We don't know what happened. He'd been fired, and he left. Buddy Garrett, who was in the room when Circe fired Widner, was angry over the sudden firing and quit immediately when Widner was canned. They were apparently lovers. Ron didn't want to leave by the main entrance, so he and Garrett left by way of the loading dock."

"They know you and the queen didn't leave by the front entrance either."

There was a pause, then Paulson said, "Okay. The bitch and I followed them to make sure they really left."

"Yes, sir. What do you want me to do with the detectives? I can't exactly volunteer that information without any knowledge of what happened."

"Are they waiting to come into your office?"

"Yes, but I have to take them to the video room first."

"Alright. Once you're all back in your office, tell them maybe I can help with what happened and call me. You can put me on speaker, and I'll tell them what I just told you. We'll feed them a load of bullshit and you can send them on their way. We can't have them snooping about. Too many activities we would rather they not discover."

"I understand, sir," Braxton said.

"Fine. Now, do your job and get them the hell out of this building."

"Yes, sir." Paulson disconnected the call abruptly, and Braxton sat in his chair, considering his next move.

He'd known about the killings, of course. His knowledge could land him in jail if the truth that he knew came out. But it would land him in the grave if he said anything to the detectives or anyone else.

148

Paulson was guilty of murder or at least conspiracy to commit murder. Now, Braxton knew the head of the company, the woman known as Circe, was just as guilty. If he found evidence that she'd taken part in the murders, his job wouldn't be worth a nickel.

His life would be worth even less.

22

Ericka had received several calls from numbers in Richmond she didn't recognize, but she'd ignored them. There was nobody there she wanted to talk to or hear from. Besides, it was probably the police. Gene had texted that they were looking for her, and within a half hour, the calls from Richmond had begun.

She dialed Gene and waited while the call went through, but in the end, it went to voice mail.

"Hey, Gene. It's Ericka. Give me a call."

Hanging up, she grabbed a beer from her refrigerator. Her life had become fucked up since going to work at Circe. She'd seen it as an easy moneymaker. That was true as far as the money went. She'd been rolling in it. Ledbetter Place was no slum. Rent there had been nearly three grand a month, and she had one of the less expensive apartments in the complex.

Now, she worked as a waitress, often dealing with drunk or angry customers. She worked the 5-11 shift at a cheap, twenty-four-hour diner. It was tempting to return to the life of a prostitute, but if she did, it would not be anywhere near the money she'd raked in at Circe. She couldn't return to Circe because that would probably get her killed.

The "entertainment" department at Circe had been Paulson's idea. He'd taken advantage of his position and had sex with all the girls he'd hired to be call girls whenever he wanted, and since he'd not paid for his pleasure, it was more like rape than consensual sex. He was nothing more than a luxury pimp who arranged special entertainment for rich clients.

She'd been allowed to keep half her earnings, but the job itself was degrading. Despite the money, she'd never met another of the girls who didn't consider her life as being one big ride on the depression freeway.

At least now she earned an honest living that, while stressful, wasn't dangerous. The news that Miranda had been killed was a shock. She knew she could have come to the same end, especially after helping Paulson get a confession from Widner about stealing from the company. She'd had a few customers at Circe who liked it rough, and she'd been kicked, punched, whipped, and strangled to the point of nearly passing out more than once. In that life, she had to take whatever was dished out. In the diner job, she could at least walk out if things got worse than she was willing to handle.

She had tried texting Buddy, but there had been no response. She was worried about him. The firing of Widner was a danger sign, and she wondered if Buddy had decided enough was enough and split.

But if that were the case, why didn't he reply to her text? She'd had sex with Buddy on several occasions. These were freebies, but she didn't see him as a customer so much as a friend with benefits kind of thing. She never reached climax when working, though she'd developed a good fake orgasm from hours of watching porn when alone, so what she considered "real sex" with another person was nice when it was available.

She'd even dated Gene for a while until his jealousy started showing. Sometimes, he scared her, and she often felt Richmond was too close. This made her think of Miranda again, and she pushed the thought away as too painful.

She'd known Buddy was scared, but he'd never told her anything about why. He didn't have to say it was because of his work. She knew that Paulson was capable of anything, and Buddy was his hand-picked security guard. This told her Buddy knew where the bodies were buried, both literally and figuratively. That was enough to scare anyone in Buddy's position.

Now, she wondered if Paulson had finally decided to get rid of the person who knew those things. She also wondered if he'd killed Miranda. Had she seen or heard something incriminating? She doubted it. Besides, she felt she might know who her killer was and why.

She decided to text Gene since he didn't answer her call. Her anxiety was such that she needed to know she had told him what she intended to. She was afraid of him, but knowing what might have happened to Buddy was important.

Gene, open the envelope. Even if Buddy's alive, he's missing, and that qualifies as "something happening" to him.

If Gene turned up dead, she would disappear to some state out west like California, as far from Virginia as she could get. Then she wondered if that would be far enough. She might be afraid of Gene, but she was terrified of Paulson.

She finished her beer and rose to shower and get ready for work. It was already a long day, and the end of her upcoming shift couldn't arrive fast enough.

As she showered, she reconsidered becoming a hooker, maybe free agent one, if there was such a thing. She could be her own pimp. That she'd been a high-priced call girl in Richmond might help her get clients if she could figure out where to advertise herself. It wasn't as if she could run an ad in the paper: HIGH-PRICED CALL GIRL FOR DISCREET DATES. JUST CALL…. What she did know was standing on street corners hoping for a john to come along wasn't for her.

She would consider her options tomorrow. Maybe

an idea would occur. She was still young and attractive, and waitressing for a crappy diner wasn't her future. Besides, the money was better if she sold her time to men and even sometimes women. That happened far more often with rich women than most people realized.

23

Braxton stepped out of his office. Pantera and Harry were seated in the outer office, waiting. Braxton smiled as best he could and said, "I guess you want to see the video room now?"

"That would be nice," Harry said.

"Follow me," Braxton said and walked out the door to the hallway beyond. Two minutes later, they were in an area that held six video monitors. Nobody else was there. The monitors were each presenting images from different areas of the building, with the picture switching every few seconds to another area.

"Because each camera is recording non-stop, we see no reason to have anyone monitoring the images," Braxton said. "It's not as if anyone can just walk in off the street and saunter through the building. As you've seen, we screen every person entering and don't allow them free access to anything."

"What if someone tries to break in through the loading dock entrance?" Pantera asked.

"If whoever it is has a key card, then it's not breaking in, is it? And if whoever is trying to enter through there does not have a card and attempts to break in, an alarm will sound at the security desk at the entrance. Someone is always manning that desk."

"And what if it's at night?"

"As I said, someone is always manning that desk, 24/7. Each guard at that desk works a four-hour shift at the desk and four hours walking the hallways and checking on things."

"When do they eat?" Harry asked.

"Between the four-hour shifts. We have a break room for them."

"What if the guy at the desk needs to use the bathroom?" Harry asked.

"He radios another guard to come watch the desk."

Pantera said, "We need to talk to Paulson."

"I think it might be easier if you come to my office and I phone him," Braxton said, happy he could make it appear he was openly helping them for a change.

When they were seated in his office, he dialed Paulson's extension. Doreen answered. "Mr. Paulson's office."

Braxton put the phone on speaker and said, "Hey, Doreen. Leland here. I need to speak to Mr. Paulson. It's important."

"Okay, Leland. Hold on a second. I'll see if he has a moment."

They were put on hold for a few seconds, and Paulson came on the line. "Yes, Leland? Doreen says it's urgent."

"Yes, sir. I have the two detectives, Pantera and Overmeyer here with me. They need to talk to you, and I figured it would be easier if I called to avoid having them possibly overstay their welcome." Braxton glanced at the detectives and winked as if he was just juicing Paulson up to take the call.

"Well, thanks for that. What do they want?"

Pantera spoke up, not sure he entirely trusted this call. Braxton was acting like a good buddy to them, which was totally out of character for him.

"Mr. Paulson, it has come to our attention that you may have been one of the last people to see Buddy Garrett alive."

"What?! Buddy's dead?!"

"Yes, and so is Ron Widner."

"Oh, my God!"

"Yes. It seems you were with Circe when she fired Widner. Buddy was there, wasn't he?"

"Yes. I guess I should come clean to you guys since Buddy and Ron are dead."

"That would be nice," Pantera said.

"I didn't want to say anything because Buddy and Widner were lovers. I didn't want to admit I knew Buddy because I didn't want you to start asking questions I would be uncomfortable answering, but you're right. He was my personal security guard. I knew he and Ron Widner were secretly lovers, and I wanted Buddy to see that Ron was a man who could not be trusted. He had stolen a great deal of money from the firm, and I had proof."

"What kind of proof?" Harry asked.

"Documents, charges on the books that were doing nothing more than putting cash into Ron's pockets. I contacted Circe about it, and she came here specifically to fire Ron."

"How did you know they were lovers?"

"I caught them together one time. It wasn't a pleasant scene. I was going to fire Buddy, but Ron said he'd fire me if I did."

"Okay, go on," Pantera said.

"Well, when Circe fired Ron, I guess Buddy felt he had to back him up the way Ron had backed him up. He quit, too. Ron didn't take it well, of course, and said he wanted to leave the building through the loading dock. Circe and I escorted them down since we were confiscating their key cards. Once we were down there, Circe saw no reason to go back into the building and, well, she invited me to have dinner with her. We left together, and I didn't return to work until the next day."

"Do you have an intimate relationship with Circe?" Harry asked.

"Let's just say I didn't say no."

"Fair enough," Pantera said.

"I suppose you understand why I wasn't forthcoming before?"

If Pantera took him at his word, he could understand, but he wasn't sure he wasn't being lied to. And if he were, this one was a whopper. Still, it was a believable whopper. It fit with everything they knew, other than the part about Widner and Garrett being lovers.

"I guess that answers our questions for now. But why were you so reluctant to have us discover that Widner and Garrett were lovers? That's not exactly all that rare, you know."

"Corporate reputation. I didn't want it out that our local CEO was having an affair with one of the male security guards. Bad press is deadly in our business, and Circe made me swear not to tell anyone. In fact, I'd appreciate it if that could be kept under wraps. If it gets out, Circe will know it was from me, and I'll be searching for a new job."

Pantera looked at Harry, who shrugged.

"I guess that's all for now, Mr. Paulson," Pantera said. "We appreciate your help, even if it was delayed."

After disconnecting the call, Braxton was silent for a few seconds before saying, "Is that all for today?"

"I guess so," Pantera said. "Would it be possible to speak to any security guards who were friends with Buddy Garrett?"

"You think one of them killed him?"

"No, we just have a few questions to ask them."

"Such as?"

Pantera glare was similar to Braxton's scowl at Harry earlier when asked about special circumstances. "Questions."

"Well, I'm not sure if any of them were particular friends of his."

"How would we know if we don't speak to them?" Harry said.

"Fine."

Braxton made a call to one of the guards. When the guard showed up, Braxton said, "These two men are detectives with Richmond PD. Take them to the security conference room and answer their questions to the best of your ability."

"Yes, sir," the guard said and indicated the open door he'd walked through. "This way, gentlemen."

After they left, Braxton called Paulson and filled him in on what was happening.

"What will the guard tell them?" Paulson asked.

"Nothing important. I used the key phrase 'to the best of your ability.' They know that means tell them nothing."

"Good," Paulson said. "Let me know when they're gone."

"Yes, sir." Braxton hung up and radioed the guard at the desk.

"Yes, sir?"

"Donnelly, have Lexington relieve you at the desk and come to my office. The detectives want to ask some questions, and I want you to answer them to the best of your ability."

"I understand, sir."

"Good. Be here as soon as you can. I imagine they will be done with Morton quickly when they discover he can't tell them anything of value."

When Donnelly entered Braxton's office, Braxton said, "If they ask you if you think Buddy Garrett was gay, tell them you suspected as much. That you'd caught him coming out of a bathroom stall with a low-level male employee."

"Yes, sir," Donnelly said, wondering what was going on but knowing he had to do what Braxton said.

Just over an hour later, Pantera and Harry left the building, more confused about what had led to the deaths of Widner and Garrett than ever. One of the guards, the one who'd been at the front desk named Donnelly, had said he'd caught Garrett in the men's room with another male employee but had kept his mouth shut to allow Buddy to keep his job.

"What now?" Harry asked.

"We go see Buddy Garrett's ex-wife to let her know about Buddy's death."

"When do you think we'll hear from the cell company about Ericka Oliver?"

"Soon, I hope. We need to find out where she is. I'd love to get a look at her call list and texts."

"Do you believe that about Buddy Garrett and Ron Widner?" Harry asked.

"Not sure. On the one hand, it provides a fairly believable story that seems to exonerate Paulson and fit with his desire not to tell us anything, but on the other, it seems—I don't know—unreal."

When they arrived at Twyla Garrett's, they strode to the front door, unwilling to speak to her about this but knowing they had no choice.

She greeted them with a smile as she opened the door to their knock. "Hello, detectives. Come on in." She stood aside to allow them to enter. "Excuse the mess. I haven't had time for housework much lately. I've had to take on extra hours at work. Have a seat."

She sat in a chair near the sofa where they sat and pulled out a cigarette, lighting it. "I know. Nasty habit, but my nerves are all wrung out from worrying about Buddy. Have you found out anything?"

Their sad expressions signaled the bad news. Pantera said, "Ms. Garrett, I'm afraid you won't be seeing him again. His body was discovered in a shallow grave this afternoon."

Twyla's face paled as her eyes filled, the first tears sliding slowly down her cheeks. She didn't move, as if she had turned into a statue of a woman smoking a cigarette. "What?" Her voice squeaked as though it was difficult to get the air past her throat.

"We're very sorry, Ms. Garrett," Harry said. "We'd give anything to have better news."

Her cigarette dropped from her limp fingers as she moaned the wordless sounds of loss and pain. The moan became a long, fraught scream of "NO!"

Burying her face into her hands, she wept, wailing her anger and misery to the otherwise silent room and the two detectives.

Harry reached down and retrieved the lit cigarette as Pantera moved to help her from the chair so she could lie down. As he helped her up, she began pounding his chest with her fists, yelling, "You're lying! You're lying!" before collapsing into his arms.

Helping her to the sofa so she could lie down, they stood there for the next ten minutes or so as she wailed and wept, punctuating her sobs with questions about what she would do now and how she would tell their children that their father was dead.

When she had regained her composure enough to communicate with them, Pantera asked, "Ms. Garrett, this might be even more difficult, but is it possible that Buddy was gay?"

Her look of shock froze them all. "Buddy?"

"Yes, ma'am. It seems there might be some evidence that he was having an affair with a man, perhaps even more than one."

She shook her head. "Whoever is saying that is lying. Buddy wasn't one of those gay basher types. He believed people should live and let live, but—" She shook her head again. "No way. He definitely liked women."

"There's not even a slight chance he was at least bisexual?"

"None. Absolutely not." She sat up again and lit another cigarette. "Neither of us have problems with gays. My brother is gay, and Buddy didn't have a problem with him at all. I remember when I told him, his response was like that didn't matter at all. I even once asked Buddy in a joking way if he might ever cheat on me with my brother since Clint is so good looking. He laughed and said, 'he's not my type,' and grabbed his own crotch with a smile, meaning my brother didn't have the right equipment. He even added, 'now if you had a sister.' We were just, you know, joking around. Buddy would not have cheated on me with anyone."

"I'm sorry. We had to ask," Pantera said.

"Who's saying that about him?"

"I can't tell you. There's no sense in stirring up a hornet's nest over this."

Twyla Garrett started crying again, and Pantera asked, "Is there a friend or relative nearby who could come over?"

"Barbara. She's a friend. Told me if I needed her to let her know," she said between sobs.

"Do you have her number?"

"Yes. It's on a list of numbers under the magnet on the fridge."

Harry went into the kitchen and found the number. Using Ms. Garrett's house phone, he dialed. When Barbara answered, he said, "This is Detective Harry Overmeyer with Richmond PD. I'm at Twyla Garrett's house. She said you had offered to come over if she needed anything. I think she needs a friend right now."

"Oh, dear. Is it Buddy?"

"Yes, ma'am. I'm afraid so."

"Oh, my. Yes, I will be there in ten minutes." Harry could hear the deep sadness in her voice.

When Barbara arrived, Harry let her in and she went straight to Twyla and held her. When they separated from their hug of shared misery, Pantera said, "Ma'am, could I get your last name?"

"Shields. Barbara Shields."

"Ms. Shields, did Buddy ever say anything to you that suggested his life might be in danger?"

"No. We rarely spoke to each other, really. Just casual conversation. I knew him fairly well, but I can't say we were friends exactly. He was just the husband of my best friend."

Pantera looked at Harry, who nodded.

"Thank you for coming over, Ms. Shields. If you'll excuse us, we have to get back to work."

"Find out who killed Buddy!" Twyla nearly shouted.

"We will do everything in our power to do just that," Pantera answered.

The detectives left the house and drove to the Widner home, saying little. Being the bearer of the worst news possible was part of the job, and they both hated it.

24

When they arrived at Widner's, they drove around to where Reginald Hallwater had lived. The crime scene investigators were well involved with their work in the garden nearby. Pantera and Harry were greeted by Detective Stovall.

"About time you guys showed up. I was just handling things 'til you got here, you know. And I don't mind handing it off to you, believe me." He looked around the crime scene, the beautiful landscaping marred by the crime scene tape and two dead bodies lying near a hole in the ground.

"You'll have your notes to us by tomorrow?" Pantera asked.

"Yeah. First thing."

"Thanks," Pantera said.

Harry and Pantera walked over to the bodies and found Amos Jackson, the chief medical examiner, stooped over the bodies of the two dead men. Amos was a large man who had once played linebacker for the New Orleans Saints. He'd not been good enough to last in that role, so he had finished his medical degree and become chief medical examiner in his hometown of Richmond. Pantera would have asked why Amos was on this job and not Aimee Wells, but he knew such a case with two victims would be claimed by Amos, who sometimes enjoyed the spotlight that a double homicide would provide.

"Hey, Amos. Whatcha got?" Pantera asked.

Amos turned and grinned, his white teeth stark behind his brown skin. "Detective Tony Pantera, as I live and breathe! And Detective Overmeyer!" he said. "What took you so long?"

"We had a few things we had to do first. I figured the bodies weren't going anywhere."

"Well, other than the morgue, no. I was just about to load 'em up and take them in without you seeing them in their final habitat."

"Glad we could get here in time," Pantera said and squatted beside Amos. "What do you have?"

"This one here," Amos said, pointing at Widner, "was tortured, and we're not talking being forced to listen to bad music. Whoever killed him wanted it to be slow and painful."

Pointing at Garrett, he said, "This one, though, was quick. There's a gunshot wound in the back of the head, which probably killed him instantly. I'm wondering if he was a security guard who came upon the scene and surprised the killer."

"No," Pantera said. "He worked at the other victim's place of employment. In fact, the tortured guy's his boss."

Amos turned his head to look at Pantera. "The guy was here with a security guard from where he worked?"

"Yep."

Amos pointed at the .32 caliber pistol strapped to Buddy Garrett's hip. "Then why is that still holstered? You'd think he'd at least have it out if someone was torturing his boss."

"Not if he was part of the crew that did the torturing," Harry offered.

"Then why was he killed, too?" Amos asked.

"Good question," Pantera said. "But as they say, 'dead men tell no tales.'"

Amos nodded, still squatting over the dead men. "You're right about that. Death's the surest way to buy silence."

Harry said, "I don't suppose anyone found a shell casing, did they?"

"Not that I know of," Amos said. "You'll have to check with the crime scene techs."

Turning Garrett's head to the side, Pantera examined the area around the bullet hole. "It looks like there might be powder burns. Be sure to check."

"Gee, I never would've thought to do that," Amos said with humorous sarcasm.

Standing, Pantera said, "I think I'll be stopping by The Watering Hole later to try and forget this entire day."

"You and me both," Harry said. Looking at Amos, he said, "Want to join us?"

"I'll have to take a rain check. Doris has reservations at The Camel for tonight."

"Have fun. I think I need a quieter atmosphere tonight," Pantera said.

"That's true," Amos said. The Camel doesn't qualify as quiet under any circumstances, but especially on Friday nights."

"Maybe we can go there together when I'm in a more festive mood," Pantera said.

"I'll count on it," Amos said and stood, "So, can I take the bodies in now?"

Pantera turned to one of the crime scene techs. "You guys through with the bodies?"

"Yeah," the tech answered. "We put what we found on them over there," he added, pointing to a folding table that had been set up nearby.

Turning to Amos, Pantera said, "They're all yours."

Amos turned to a couple of men waiting nearby. "Load 'em up, fellas," Amos said. Looking at Pantera and Harry, he said, "I'll catch you guys later."

"Yeah. Later, Amos," Pantera said.

"Later," Harry added.

The detectives went to the table and examined what was there. Nearly all of the bagged evidence had come from the dead bodies. A couple of cell phones, wallets, keys, and some other items that would have been in their pockets but were mostly worthless in the investigation were bagged and tagged and waiting to be more closely examined. Both wallets contained cash, ruling out robbery as a motive, though neither detective thought that would be the case anyway.

"Other than the phones, I don't think we can get much from this," Harry said.

"We may not get much from the phones."

"Do you think Miranda's murder had something to do with this?"

"I have no idea. The truth is it could be totally unconnected to anything having to do with Circe Enterprises."

"Or it could have everything to do with it."

"Yeah, or it could," Pantera said. "We're doing a great job of figuring this out, eh?"

"In other words, we don't know much at all, which lends the truth to what you say."

"I think we both know who killed Widner and Garrett."

"Circe and Paulson?"

"That's who my money is on. While Paulson's story can't be easily disproved, I don't believe it, exactly."

"What about the other guard who said he caught Buddy and another man coming out of the same bathroom stall?"

"That doesn't mean they were having sex. It could have been a conversation they wanted to keep private. Or maybe Buddy liked to do a few lines of coke and that was his supplier."

"I guess that's as possible as the two of them having

sex in a bathroom stall, though that wouldn't be my first choice for a location. Beyond that, except for them being the last people to see the two dead men alive as far as we know, what else do we have?"

"Jack shit," Pantera answered. "Like I said, we're really tearing it up, aren't we?"

"But I'm still wondering about the torture. I mean, why torture the guy? Severed fingers, missing tongue and balls. Sounds like something you'd read in *The Godfather*."

"Well, there's a reason Mario Puzo included details like that in his book. They happen. But like I said before, the tongue suggests he said something he shouldn't have. The fingers might mean he stole something. The balls might be because he put his dick where it didn't belong."

"Or maybe that was just part of humiliating him, not to mention the pain of having them cut off while he was alive," Harry said.

"And Paulson told us he had stolen from the company. I doubt he thought we'd find that interesting in the effort to solve Widner's murder."

"There has to be a motive."

"Want to know my theory?" Pantera said.

"Sure."

"Circe shows up at the office, and she and Paulson leave with Widner, probably taking Garrett as a driver and assistant of some sort. They drive here, torture Widner for their own reasons, and bury him in the freshly dug earth of the garden, meaning the digging wasn't as difficult. That was likely done by Garrett anyway since I don't see Circe or Paulson doing the manual labor. Digging up dirt that had already been turned and the tree roots removed would be easier and faster anyway."

"How would Miranda fit into all this?"

"Beats me. Maybe she didn't have anything to do with this murder at all. Or perhaps she knew more than they wanted her to know."

At that moment, a tech walked up to them. "Detectives?"

"Yeah?"

"We finally managed to get the door open. Very secure place they got here."

"Thanks," Pantera said. Looking at Harry, he said, "Shall we take a stroll through the rest of the house ol' Reg wouldn't let us explore?"

"Sounds like a winner to me."

The home held little of use for them until they arrived in the basement. That room looked like the torture chamber it had become. Long-dried blood was everywhere. The crime scene techs took over, collecting samples and taking pictures while Pantera and Harry watched from nearby.

The most intriguing thing about the area was a pile of ashes in the middle of the floor that appeared to have once been wet. Smoke had stained the overhead ceiling.

"What do you suppose that used to be?" Harry asked.

"Beats me, but maybe we'll know in a few days."

They stepped closer to the ashes and saw a bit of fabric had not fully burned.

"Looks like clothing of some sort," Pantera said.

"Yeah. What do you think it means?"

"No idea, really, but since there's so much blood it suggests maybe some kind of coveralls, probably a light cotton, to keep the mess from getting on them."

The crime scene techs continued collecting the evidence while Pantera and Harry watched and wondered where this all would lead.

Two hours later, they were seated at their desks. Harry went for coffee for the two of them while Pantera opened a recently delivered file that contained Ericka Oliver's cell phone records.

"She lives near Roanoke," Pantera said. "Her real name is Natalie. Natalie Oliver."

"Anything interesting in her call log?"

"That's what I'm searching for right now."

"What about her texts?"

"I have a link to her texts. I'll go through them when I'm done here."

"Any numbers she calls regularly?"

"A few. We'll check those out later."

He opened his computer and entered the data for locating and reading Ericka's texts and began to go through them. Most of them were innocuous, either to friends where she was talking about where to meet up, or to her mother. Then a recent one caught his eye.

"Uh-huh. This is interesting," Pantera said.

"What?"

"Seems she's been texting with Gene. At least someone she calls Gene, and the conversation suggests it's our Gene."

"What do they say?"

Pantera smiled. "A lot."

25

Harry peered over Pantera's shoulder as they reviewed Ericka Oliver's texts, Harry said, "What do you think she means when she says, 'Open the envelope. Even if Buddy's alive, he's missing, and that qualifies as something happening to him'? What envelope do you think she's talking about?"

"It sounds like Gene has an envelope with instructions to open it if something happens to Buddy."

"I guess we have to pay our friend Gene another visit."

"Yep."

Harry checked the time. "You think Gariepy will okay the overtime? It's ten minutes to quitting time."

"I don't know, but even if he doesn't, I'm for going there now and finding out what this is all about."

They strode to Lt. Gariepy's office door and knocked.

"Come in, fellas!" Gariepy called.

Pantera closed the door behind them and said, "Lieutenant, we need to get approval for OT."

"Again?" Gariepy said, not looking up from the paperwork strewn on his desk.

"Of course."

"Denied."

"You don't even want to know what it's about?"

"Doesn't matter. Childers said no OT, so no OT."

"I swear, that ass wipe would prefer a crime wave to granting a few hours overtime."

"Like him or not, he's still Chief of Detectives, and his reasoning doesn't concern us."

"Like him?" Pantera said and turned to Harry. "Since when does anyone like Childers?"

Harry shrugged. "Beats me. The only ones who claim to need to kiss his ass."

Gariepy looked up from his paperwork. "Guys, have you ever heard the phrase 'to get along, go along'?"

"Yeah. Heard it," Pantera said. "But it was created by guys like Childers to prevent anyone from questioning stupid decisions."

"Be that as it may, you'd be wise—and a lot happier—if you exercised that idea once in a while."

"Do I ever do anything I shouldn't to buck the system?" Pantera said, adding, "Don't answer that" when Gariepy looked at him.

"I don't need to." Gariepy said. "No overtime, Tony. Childers would have my hide."

"He'd likely make a suit out of it and wear it to a press conference," Pantera shot back.

"You're probably right, and I don't want to be his next suit, so go home."

"How about we do another tradeoff? We work two extra today and leave two hours early tomorrow?"

Gariepy looked from Pantera to Harry. "Okay, but only one of you. The other has to go home. You two can decide which one. The other one has to take off two hours early tomorrow." He turned back to his paperwork before adding, "You usually come in late when we make these little deals."

"I figure we'll want to get to work on what we have tomorrow after the visit that warrants the OT."

"Break in the case?"

"Could be," Pantera said. To Harry, he said, "So, flip you for who gets to go see our favorite security guard and ask why he never mentioned the envelope."

Gariepy looked up again from his paperwork. "What envelope?"

171

"Hey, you had your chance to find out why we were asking about overtime, but you weren't interested," Pantera said, closing the door behind them as they left.

Taking out a coin, Pantera said, "Heads or tails?"

Harry said, "You can go. Just give me a call when you get a look at the envelope's contents. I'll meet you at The Watering Hole. Or have you forgotten you need some time away from all this and a little drink to help you forget?"

Pantera smiled at his partner. "I'll let you know when I'm headed that way."

Gene sat on his sofa after arriving home from work and stared at the message from Ericka. She was right. Disappearing did qualify as something happening to Buddy. He just hadn't looked at it like that. Buddy had seemed to think his life was in danger, and now Gene felt foolish for not realizing he should have opened the envelope days ago. He wondered if he hadn't because he didn't want to see what was in there.

Going to his bedroom, he fished the envelope from its hiding place under his mattress. Sitting on the bed, he did his best to calm his rushing heartbeat, trying to breathe deeply and slowly. What was in the envelope scared him even though he had no idea what it might be, only that Buddy had warned it was bad shit. Taking one last deep breath, he wedged a finger into the opening at the top of the flap and pulled, tearing the paper.

What he found inside was a long letter addressed "To Whoever I Chose to Keep This."

As Gene read the letter, his stomach tightened with each sentence. It detailed the terrible things Buddy had been more or less forced to do by Paulson. These tasks included the murder and disposing of bodies. Paulson was evidently using Buddy as a hit man and general situation handler.

Near the end of the letter, Buddy had typed, "Paulson told me I must do these things, or he will get someone else to do it for him after killing me and my family."

He had included details of several illegal tasks, including one murder, saying he included the details to make his story verifiable. Still, even Gene recognized that there was zero in the letter that would prove Paulson had told him to do any of it. There was only Buddy's assertion that he had.

Still, Gene believed every word of the letter. It was no surprise that Paulson would do such horrible things. Convincing the police and a jury he was capable of this, however, would be a different matter. Paulson would deny everything, of course. All Gene had was the knowledge of what had happened. Whether or not he believed the details didn't matter. Only what could be proved did, and so far the details proved just one thing: Buddy was the person who had committed these crimes.

Even a halfway decent lawyer could have the letter laughed out of court.

Maybe Buddy had left town, figuring he was about to be arrested. Maybe he wasn't missing but in hiding.

He put the letter back in the envelope and replaced it under the mattress. He needed to decide what to do next while also considering the high bar of "beyond a reasonable doubt." Besides, if he became involved, his own criminal acts could be discovered, and that was something he wanted to avoid at all costs.

Grabbing a beer from the refrigerator, he sat at his kitchen table and considered his options. When he'd made up his mind, he rose to retrieve the letter. Using his phone to take a picture of one page, he started an email to Paulson at his company email address.

Paulson, this page is from a long, detailed letter my

friend Buddy Garrett left with me in case something happened to him. You will notice you are heavily mentioned on this page, and it's not the only page where that happens. Apparently, you forced Buddy to commit a series of crimes on your behalf.

I want $20,000 in bills no larger than a 20 to keep my mouth shut about the existence of this letter. Call me.

He added his name and phone number, figuring Paulson would be able to figure out who was emailing him easily enough and deciding that didn't matter. Paulson would tell no one about the blackmail. He would call to talk about what was in the letter. He could claim the letter itself was a hoax. No actual proof existed that Buddy had told the truth, but it would cause Paulson problems he didn't want at the very least. It was at least worth the effort. He was familiar with blackmail, both as perpetrator and victim. If it worked, Paulson would likely offer half, and the dickering would begin.

Attaching the picture of the last page of the letter with the threat to kill Buddy's family, he closed his eyes and breathed deeply for nearly ten minutes in an effort to get his heart to slow down before finally pressing SEND.

After hiding the letter again, he texted Ericka.

Call me ASAP.

While waiting for Ericka's call, he opened another beer and sat in his living room, looking out at the street. He felt his heart sink when he saw Detective Pantera's car pull into his driveway and the detective climb out. Just as Pantera approached his door, Gene's cell rang. Looking at the screen, he felt his heart skip. It wasn't Ericka. It was Paulson. He'd have to wait, and as Gene turned his phone off to avoid having it ring from

Ericka's call, it occurred to him that making Paulson sweat a bit might be beneficial in the long run.

Going to the door, he opened it to find Pantera with his fist raised to knock.

"Expecting me?" Pantera said.

"Nope. Saw you through the window. I was just having a beer and unwinding from the day."

"Mind if I come in?"

Gene glanced around the room before letting Pantera inside.

"So, how's the job at Ledbetter Place working out?" Pantera asked.

"It's a job," Gene said. "Pay isn't as good as Circe, but it'll do."

"Great," Pantera said as he sat in a chair in the living room without being invited to sit. "Heard from Ericka Oliver lately? We'd really like to speak to her sometime in the next few days."

"Ericka? No. Sorry. It's not like we're best friends or anything. We're just…acquaintances."

"Really?"

"Yeah."

"You had us thinking the two of you were good friends."

"Not really." Gene thought for a moment and said, "Well, maybe more than acquaintances, but not much more."

Pantera nodded before shocking Gene with his next question. "So, did you open the envelope?" He hoped his voice didn't give away the lie.

Gene froze, staring at Pantera. "What envelope?"

"The one that concerns Buddy Garrett."

"I don't know what you're talking about."

"Come on, Gene. The look on your face when I asked about it told me you know damn well what I'm talking about."

"No. I didn't open it," Gene said. Denying it had ever existed would be fruitless. They obviously knew about it, just not its contents. "How did you find out about it?"

"We couldn't get any information from you about Ericka's whereabouts, so we got a warrant to see her cell phone records. That includes texts."

"When did you get them?"

"This afternoon. Now, where's the envelope?"

"I decided to burn it."

Pantera stared at him a moment, not believing him.

"Fine, Gene," Pantera said. "Have it your way. That's the way you want to play it, that's up to you. We'll be back. Don't destroy that envelope or its contents."

"I told you. I burned it already."

Pantera stood and said, "Yeah, and I went on a date with Jennifer Aniston last night." As he stood in the open doorway to leave, he said, "I was hoping you wouldn't be a hindrance to the investigation, Gene. I guess I misjudged you."

"Just exercising my rights as a citizen."

"Yeah. Have fun with that," Pantera said and left.

As soon as Pantera had pulled out of the driveway, Gene retrieved the letter. He couldn't destroy it—it was worth too much money—but he could hide it somewhere other than his home. He started to call his cousin Andre but decided against it. Pantera would see the time showing he called right after Pantera left and get a warrant to search Andre's house.

Stuffing the letter into a new envelope and sealing it, Gene waited ten minutes before leaving and driving to Andre's. Once there, he gave the envelope to his cousin with strict instructions to hide it somewhere and not open it. He could trust Andre to do as he was asked, especially after telling Andre that if the envelope was still sealed when Gene came to retrieve it, Andre would become $500 richer sometime next week. He figured $19,500 for him and $500 for Andre, once he got paid by Paulson.

26

After his call to Gene went unanswered, Paulson stared at what Gene had sent him, thinking about how he would handle the situation. The single page sent contained a detailed description of the murder of a man in Philadelphia who had been blackmailing Paulson. Of course, some letter or other document Garrett had passed on to Gene meant nothing in court, but the fact the victim had ties to Paulson, along with the possibility that the information the man had possessed might still be out there somewhere, could cause scrutiny from the police when Paulson wanted it least. Such scrutiny would surely cause Circe to fire him, maybe worse. Or he could end up disappearing the way Widner had. This would have to be handled, but now he was unsure who could handle it for him.

Paulson had threatened Garrett's family to force him to do his bidding, regardless of the illegality. Garrett had been a reluctant executioner, but he knew his family's safety was in danger if he failed. Now, he wondered if killing him had been a mistake, though he'd had no choice. That had been Circe's idea. She'd insisted on it, in fact, and Paulson knew better than to disagree with something she had decided was necessary.

He needed another private security guard willing to do anything to protect his family. Opening the personnel files on his computer, he began a search using the terms "male," "married," and "children," limiting the search to those employed for at least one year to eliminate job hoppers. Beyond that, he knew the $30,000 per year raise would help convince him. His job was to make sure the man had no choice but to accept the offer that wasn't an offer at all. Not accepting it would mean death to the man. Accepting it could mean death to him and his family. At least accepting could mean everyone lived.

After twenty minutes, he had his choice. Ray Foster was thirty-five, married, and the father of three children, all under the age of twelve. A note on Ray's file mentioned he had an extensive juvenile record but had a clean record since becoming an adult, though Circe was supposed to be unable to access that information. They had their sources, however, and that Ray had been in trouble repeatedly while a teenager would help. The important part of his past record was that Ray had the capacity to commit crimes. He would just need the proper incentive.

Paulson checked Ray's schedule and found he was off that day. That was perfect. He would need to speak with him without anyone else knowing in case he turned down the offer, which wasn't likely given the repercussions of refusing.

He walked to his car, climbed in, and pulled out his cell, punching in Ray Foster's phone number that he'd taken from the file. After a few rings, Ray answered.

"Hello?"

"Ray Foster?" Paulson asked.

"Yes."

"This is Claude Paulson, CEO at Circe Enterprises, Richmond."

Paulson could almost hear the man begin to sweat.

"Uhh, yeah. Okay. Is there a problem?"

"Not exactly. I was just needing to speak to you in private. And by private, I mean that nobody can know we talked, not even your wife."

"Okay. Go ahead."

"I'd rather not discuss this on the phone. It's that sensitive. Can we meet?"

"Sure, I guess. When?"

"There's a Publix about a quarter mile from your home. Be standing at the southeast corner of the building in about twenty minutes. I'll pick you up there."

"Umm, do we really need the cloak and dagger stuff?"

"Are you questioning my judgment?"

"No, sir. I'm just, well, surprised by it all. This sounds really serious, and I can't figure out why you need to talk to me about it."

"You will when we meet. Again, don't tell anyone it's me. Just tell your wife if she's there that you have to run somewhere. Make something up, but for her own safety, she can't know you're talking to me. Understood?"

"Yes, sir."

Paulson disconnected without saying goodbye and drove to the Publix.

When he arrived, Ray Foster was waiting, pacing back and forth.

As he climbed in, Ray said, "My wife is at work today, and the kids are at camp, so nobody knows about this."

"Excellent."

Thirty minutes later, Paulson pulled over on a gravel country road in nearby Goochland County. The road was rarely traveled and would be where Ray Foster's body would be found if he turned down the offer. Paulson could see Ray's anxiety growing as they left the city, obviously heading for a rural area. Paulson was sure Ray was wondering why they needed such an out-of-the-way place to talk and that the true reason may have occurred to him. The growing confusion was evidence he had no idea why his life might be in danger.

When Paulson pulled over, he turned to Ray and said, "I need a personal security guard."

Mild shock crossed the man's features. "You brought me all the way out here to ask me to be your security guard?"

"Yes."

"Forgive me for not understanding, but why couldn't you just ask me that over the phone?"

"Because being my personal security guard involves a lot more than just protecting me from harm. It often involves committing crimes I tell you to commit."

Ray's eyebrows pressed together. "Like what kind of crimes?"

"Like murder for instance, or sometimes not something that drastic, like delivering a warning to someone."

Ray's mouth hung open as he considered what he was being asked to do. "Wasn't Garrett your personal security guard?"

"Yes, but he's dead now."

"How do you know that? I haven't seen anything in the news."

"Come on, Ray. You're not an idiot. I was forced to kill him. He's buried where nobody will find him."

Ray's face registered the sudden panic of a man figuring out his worst fears for why they were in the middle of nowhere were true. Now, he looked out the windshield and the passenger side window as if trapped. Looking back at Paulson, he said, "Why me?"

"Why not you? You have a juvenile record, so I know you're at least morally capable of committing a crime."

"Murder?"

"Yes, I know that's extreme, but it's a necessity, and one you will be paid handsomely for."

"How much?"

"This position comes with a raise of thirty grand a year on top of what you already make."

"Thirty grand a year for a hit man?"

"Well, thirty grand a year, plus you and your family get to stay alive."

"My family?"

"Yes. If you say no to my offer, I will have to kill you right here and leave your body to be found by some passing motorist, though that could take a while. This isn't a well-traveled road. I mean, look around."

"But why would you kill my family?"

"I'll only do that if you double-cross me after accepting the position, or if you refuse to do what I tell you to do once you accept the offer."

"And if I say no, you kill me?"

"You'll be dead within sixty seconds of saying it," Paulson said, opening the center console of the car, withdrawing a .38 caliber pistol, and clicking the safety off. "Or you can say yes, start making almost three-thousand more a month, and get to have supper with your family this evening instead of making them suffer through wondering where you are and the pain of finding out." He smiled at Ray. "Seems like a simple choice to me."

"Basically, you'll own me."

Paulson shrugged. "I guess that's true, but it's like growing old. It sucks, but it beats the alternative."

Tears spilled over Ray's eyelids as he stared out of the windshield at nothing. Paulson could see he was lost in thought, as if he had a choice in the matter.

"You chose me because I have a juvenile record?"

"Well, there were other factors. Your wife and three kids were the biggest ones. You see, I need the insurance that comes with owning their lives, too."

"Did you have to threaten Garrett's life to get him to take this job?"

"Of course."

"And his family's?"

"Hey, if it works, why change the hiring process?"

"You're a horrible man, Mr. Paulson."

"I came to terms with that when I was a teenager," Paulson said. "Now, do I kill you, or do you start making a lot more money and protect your family while you're at it?"

"What keeps me from packing up my family and disappearing?"

"The fact that you know I would find you eventually and the deaths would be slow and painful. Furthermore, you know that I'd make you watch me kill your family before killing you."

"Then I don't really have a choice at all, do I?"

"That's sort of the point, Ray."

"What would prevent me from killing you?"

"If I die, Circe would come for you, and she wouldn't be as nice as I am."

"Circe? You mean the French lady who owns Circe Enterprises?"

"Yes."

"She's part of this?"

"Ray, she's worse than me, and that's saying something."

Paulson watched Ray swallow hard, his Adam's apple bobbing. "Okay. I'll take the job."

27

While Paulson was going through files to find his next personal security guard, Pantera drove away from Gene's and stopped around the next corner. After making a brief call, Pantera waited several minutes until he was sure his request had been handled before heading back to the station. Once there, he started a new search warrant for all of Gene's electronic communications and to allow a search of his home. After an hour, he was finished. He called Harry to fill him in.

"Hey, we might be getting closer to at least getting a handle on this," he said.

"Yeah? What was in the envelope?"

"Don't know yet. He said he'd burned it, but I could see from his expression that would be the last thing he'd do."

"You think he might actually burn it while you're gone?"

"I don't think so, but I can't be sure. Depends on whether there's something in it that incriminates Gene in some way.

"What if he hides it?"

"I figured he'll definitely do that. If he burns it, there's not much we can do about it, but I called Stovall and had him come watch the place to see if Gene goes anywhere. He'll tail him if he does."

"Good thinking."

"Well, Gariepy wouldn't approve you for comp time, so I had no choice."

"You have the warrant?"

"Not signed yet, but I've included a request for

electronic information, both from his cell and his computer, as well as requesting a wiretap in the warrant. We should even be able to follow him through his phone's GPS if we want."

"That's a lot. You think you can get the warrant signed?"

"Yeah, I do. I'm saying that he has crucial evidence in a double homicide that could even incriminate him. Judge Lazlow will sign it. I'm stopping by to see him on my way to The Watering Hole."

"When will we serve it?"

"First thing tomorrow. The famous Childers no overtime rule."

"We could have someone else serve it."

"Gene will have removed it by now anyway, I'm sure. Taken it somewhere for safe keeping in all likelihood."

"Then you don't think we'll find anything at his place?"

"I didn't say that. With Stovall following him, we'll know where to look if he moves it. We'll just need another search warrant before going there."

"You don't think Gene will notice the tail?"

"Nah, Stovall's good at that."

"I hope you're right. See you at The Watering Hole."

"Yeah, see you there," Pantera said and disconnected.

He called Lisa. When she answered, he said, "Are you on your way to town?"

"I will be, but I have a few things to do first before I can come over. You might want to have dinner without me. Maybe you can invite Nancy and the girls over until I get there."

"Actually, I'm headed to The Watering Hole and hoped you could meet me there."

"I would, but I really have to do this first. I'm still in D.C. I should be at your place by nine."

"Okay. Maybe Nance can come join me. I'd like to find out how the house search is going." He didn't try to hide his disappointment.

"Sorry, Harry. We each have our work responsibilities."

"Oh, I understand. But that doesn't stop me from being disappointed."

"Invite Nancy over. She's still staying at the Days Inn?"

"Yeah. I'll see you this evening, Lisa."

"Okay. Keep a bottle of wine handy."

"I will." He disconnected just as he was pulling into the driveway of Judge Edgar Lazlow's home. He hated to stop at a judge's house to get a warrant signed, but he needed to act on this first thing in the morning. He had played down the urgency with Harry and considered serving the warrant that evening—the Hell with Childers—but he knew that Gene would have moved the envelope and its contents out of the house by now anyway. Still, there was no telling what they might find in a search, and they could hold that over Gene's head until he surrendered the letter.

Lazlow was happy to sign the warrant after Pantera explained its urgency and the likelihood that Gene was somehow involved in a crime or at least had knowledge of one.

Leaving the judge's expensive home, Pantera called Nancy.

"Hey, Tony," she said when she answered.

"What are you doing tonight?"

There was a pause on the other end, and Pantera wondered if she might have a date.

"Just going to curl up with a book."

"Sounds like a boring evening."

"It's a good book."

"Maybe so, but I was wondering if you wanted to join me for dinner later, maybe even join me at The Watering Hole first for a drink, then dinner. Not a late one, though. Lisa's coming over around nine."

"What about the girls?"

"They'll be happy with a pizza. When Lisa arrives, they usually retire to their rooms to give us some time alone."

"Okay. I can be at The Watering Hole in a half hour."

"See you then. Harry will be there, too."

"Okay. It'll be good to see him."

After the call, he drove to The Watering Hole and parked. Walking inside, he found the owner, Dean, behind the bar and Pete, Dean's brother-in-law and resident barfly, in his usual seat. It was still early enough that no other customers were there, but Pantera knew that wouldn't last. Dean's bar was one of those local bars with a strong base of regular customers.

"Hey, you old bastard! What's cookin'?" Pantera called upon entering.

"My nuts on summer days," Dean answered, his usual response to the question.

"Pete!" Pantera said. "Been sober lately?"

"Why would I want to do that?" Pete laughed and held out his hand to shake Pantera's.

Pantera had wondered for months after becoming a regular customer how Pete could sit in the bar all day and not become drunk until he watched long enough to learn that Pete would nurse one beer for hours. The only drink he downed quickly was the glass of ice water that sat on a coaster next to his beer.

This was where Pete could be found whenever the place was open. He was retired and financially comfortable and spent his days with the brother of his wife, who had died from breast cancer ten years ago. By the time Dean closed up, Pete might have consumed four beers. Pete may be a barfly, but he wasn't a drunk.

"The usual?" Dean asked.

"Sounds good to me."

At that moment, Harry entered the bar and the usual greetings were repeated. They bought their drinks and went to a booth.

"Nancy will be joining us. I hope you don't mind."

"Why would I mind? She's a lot better looking than you."

"Careful. You're a married man."

"Hey, I'm married, but I'm not blind. Besides, you should see how Ashley drools over some of the actors on TV."

"Glad that doesn't bother you."

"As long as my wife sleeps in our bed and nobody else's, it's not a problem. It's natural to look. It's like appreciating a beautiful work of art. Beauty is what it is. Guys who get jealous about that have something wrong with their thinking."

"Generally, guys who get jealous about that have self-esteem issues and are frequently projecting."

At that moment Nancy walked in and sat beside Pantera. The usual greetings with Dean and Pete were not exchanged. Pantera smiled at the image of Nancy calling Dean "you old bastard." Nancy would use such words when alone with people she knew well, but never in a public setting.

"Hello, Harry," she said.

"Hi, Nancy. Found a house yet?"

She smiled. "As a matter of fact, I have."

Pantera arched his eyebrows. "You have?"

"Yes," she said, smiling. "That's one reason I was going to just relax with a book tonight. House hunting causes a lot of tension to build up."

"Where's the house?"

"First, what are the girls doing? Are you going to make sure they have dinner?"

"Of course. They're probably at my place. They spent the day with friends, as usual. I plan to let them order a pizza. I'll pick it up on the way home."

"Okay."

"So, are you going to tell me where your new house is, or not?"

She smiled at him. "I decided to go ahead and buy the place near your house. The one I looked at first."

"You'll be living just down the street?" Pantera wasn't sure how he felt about that. He knew he'd been relieved when she said she wasn't sure she wanted to live that close to him.

"Yep. I put in an offer today. My realtor thinks they'll accept it. The house has been on the market for three months, a long time in the Richmond area."

"Well, that's nice. The girls will be living a five-minute walk from my place."

"You don't look happy," Nancy said. "In fact, you look disappointed."

"Why would I be disappointed?"

She frowned at him. "I don't know, but you do."

"Just this case we're working on right now has me chasing my tail." It wasn't a lie, but it also wasn't the reason for his disappointment.

"Oh?"

"Yeah. Basically, it's a triple homicide, though one of them may have nothing to do with the other two."

"Any suspects?" Nancy asked.

"For the two that were killed together, yeah, but no proof. At least not yet. So far we have nothing on the other one. She was a prostitute found in an empty lot. We have some semen from vaginal swabs, but getting DNA results can take months."

"The lab has the swabs?"

"Yeah, we use a lab in Fairfax. They'll get to it when they get to it."

"Can't you request a rush job?"

"Yeah, along with a hundred other cops. It's not like a blood sugar test. A good lab tech can only do a few per day because of the process involved."

"What if this is a serial killer? He could kill more girls while you're waiting for results."

"Even when we get the results, we have to match them to someone. If that person's DNA is in the system somewhere, it won't take that long, but if it isn't, it could be years. Gotta have a suspect and a sample of his DNA first," Harry said.

"The wheels of justice move slower than a snail's pace," Pantera said. "We work with what we have."

"I hope the guy's DNA is in the system," Nancy said.

"So do we," Harry said.

They talked over their drinks for the next half hour. After Harry left, Pantera called his house to speak to the girls about a pizza. When Beth answered, he said, "You two up for a pizza tonight?"

"Sure!"

"You're not going to ask your sister?"

"Are you kidding, Dad? She's always up for pizza."

"Pizza?!" he heard Andrea say in the background.

"Yeah," Beth said to her. Then she was back on the phone. "We're both up for it."

"Okay, call Dominos and place the order. I'll pick it up on the way home."

He disconnected the call and drove to Dominos. Nancy drove to his house to see the girls.

28

After the pizza, Nancy drove back to her hotel. Lisa arrived soon after Nancy left, and they were sharing a drink when Pantera received a call from Detective Stovall. He was in the middle of a conversation with Lisa but cut it off with, "I have to take this."

"Hey, Stovall. Whatcha got?"

"After meeting you around the corner from the subject's house and you left, I waited perhaps two minutes, keeping my eye on the house. The subject came out with a manila envelope and drove past me. He did not notice me that I could tell. I followed him until he pulled into a driveway about ten minutes from his home. He went inside with the envelope and stayed for about seven minutes. At that point, the subject returned to his car without the envelope and drove straight home."

Pantera smiled. "Excellent work. What's the address of the house where he left the envelope?"

Stovall provided the address. "Is this about the double homicide out at that fancy house?"

"Yep."

"Glad I could help, Tony. Catch you later."

After disconnecting, Pantera returned to the living room and Lisa.

"Good news?" she asked.

"Great is more like it."

"What happened?"

"I went to a home to see about getting an envelope with information in it that likely had something to do with a double homicide we're investigating. The guy with the envelope told me he'd burnt it, but I could tell he was lying. I got the feeling my arrival was the worst thing to happen to him today. I couldn't get a black and white to watch the house because it would stop the guy with the envelope from trying to hide it, so I had Detective Matt Stovall come watch the house to see if the guy left to leave the envelope with someone else. He knew we were coming back at some point with a search warrant. Sure enough, just a couple of minutes after Stovall arrived, the guy leaves his house with the envelope, drives to another house nearby, goes inside with the envelope, and comes back out a few minutes later without it. He thinks he's pulled a fast one, but he's been caught red-handed."

"So, case solved?"

"I don't know about that, but we'll know a lot more once we see what's in that envelope."

"Well, then. Are you up to some relaxation exercises?" Lisa asked with a smirk.

"Absolutely," Pantera answered, standing and extending his hand to help her up. He kissed her and they went to the bedroom.

The next morning, Lisa had to leave early to get back to Washington. The girls were still asleep when Pantera left the house. He knew they would probably wake up around nine or ten. They had the sleeping habits of most teens.

Pantera waited around the corner from Gene's house until Harry arrived. Just as Harry pulled up behind Pantera, two patrol cars stopped in front of the house, and the detectives joined them.

As Gene came outside to meet them, Pantera said, "I told you we'd get a warrant." He pulled the document from his pocket and handed it to Gene. Pantera couldn't help noticing the man's smug look.

Gene looked over the warrant and said,

"Electronics? What does that mean? You didn't mention electronics yesterday."

"That's your cell phone and any computers you have inside the house. I guess I forgot to mention those," Pantera answered.

Two hours later, they had seized his cell phone and computers—a laptop and a desktop. They found nothing else worth confiscating. Just as they were leaving, Stovall arrived. He held out another search warrant.

"What's that?" Gene asked.

Pantera looked at the warrant in his hand. "It looks like a search warrant."

"But you just searched my house. Why would you need a second warrant?"

Pantera couldn't help himself. "Well, I don't know. Let's see what it says." He pretended to read the warrant and said, "Oh, this is for the house you went to yesterday after I left. Seems you were carrying a manila envelope when you went inside but you didn't have it when you came back out."

"You had me followed?"

"You must have a very low opinion of my intelligence, Gene. I thought better of you than that."

Gene gave a growl of anger and frustration.

"You want to go with us to retrieve it? Maybe you could relieve the home's occupant of having to clean up after us by getting what we're looking for instead of having us go through his home room by room, drawer by drawer, and closet by closet? Save everyone the time and trouble."

Gene's cheeks puffed as he blew air through his pursed lips.

"Fine. Let's go. I'll get it for you. But why do you need my computers and phone?"

"Just to make sure there's nothing else you're hiding from us regarding this investigation," Harry said.

"Want to ride with me or Pantera? He drives like a maniac."

"You," Gene said and followed Harry to his car.

Fifteen minutes later, they were all standing in the bedroom of Gene's cousin, Andre. Gene had phoned Andre and asked him to meet them at his house, but Andre couldn't get away from work. He told Gene where to find a key and where to find the envelope once he was inside.

Gene lifted the mattress and reached under it. Pulling the envelope from its hiding place, he handed it to Pantera.

"Now, that wasn't so difficult, was it?"

"Actually, it was harder than you think."

Pantera turned to Harry. "Video me," he said.

Harry pulled out his phone and opened the camera app. "Okay," he said once the camera was working.

Pantera opened the sealed envelope and took out the previously opened envelope from Buddy Garrett containing the papers. As Harry captured what he was doing, Pantera read the document aloud. When he had finished, Pantera looked up at Harry and placed the papers and both envelopes in an evidence bag and sealed it. Harry stopped the video app and put his phone away.

Pantera again looked at Harry and could see the same disappointment in Buddy Garrett that he was feeling. On the one hand, Garrett was being threatened, but on the other hand, he could have come to the police and set up a sting instead of doing what he'd done.

"Tell us about the envelope," Pantera said to Gene.

"What do you want to know?"

"Everything. How you came to have it. When you opened it. Who else knows about it. Everything."

Gene said, "I need to sit down." They followed him into the kitchen, where they sat at the cheap, Formica-topped dining table.

"Buddy gave that to me over a year ago. He told me not to open it unless something happened to him."

"What did you take that to mean?"

"That he had died."

Harry said, "We saw the text from Ericka where she told you that disappearing was something happening to him. Is that when you opened it?"

"Yeah. Buddy had been real explicit about not opening it until I was sure something had happened to him. He told me he knew he could trust me to do that."

"Why not his ex?"

"I asked the same thing. He said she'd open it. He called her 'a regular Pandora' and she'd have it opened five minutes after he left it. He said he knew I wouldn't do that."

"You two were pretty tight?"

"Not so much, really, but he knew I could be trusted because I once told him about something that happened when I was a teenager and he was impressed that I had kept my word about something."

"What?"

"It doesn't have anything to do with this. It was just something where I kept my word even when it would have helped me to say something."

"Okay," Pantera said. "Go on."

"Anyway, I swore to him I wouldn't open it unless something happened to him. After I opened it, I started worrying that maybe he was just taking some time away from everything. That he'd show up and wonder why I opened it. Still worried about that, in fact. More than I was before because now you guys have it, and he'll be arrested and tried for murder and a lot of other crimes."

"You don't have to worry about that," Pantera said. "We found his body yesterday."

Gene looked weary. "He's dead?"

"Yep. Murdered."

Gene sighed and said, "That's what happens if you get owned by the wrong person, I guess." He looked at Pantera. "Did Paulson do it?"

"We think so, but we don't have much in the way of proof, just circumstantial stuff, but it's pretty damning."

"Can you convict him on what you have?"

"We might be able to now, but it's not anything close to open-and-shut. Do you think Paulson knows about this letter?"

Gene hesitated a moment before answering. "I doubt it."

Pantera said, "If he finds out you have it, watch your back. If he did kill Garrett, he won't hesitate to come for you."

"When was the last time you heard from Ericka?" Harry asked.

"When she texted about how disappearing was something happening to Buddy."

"Do you think she'd talk to us if you asked her to?"

"I don't know. I haven't been able to get her to answer her phone or text me back. I texted her I'd opened the envelope and what was in it. No response."

Pantera glanced at Harry, and his look of concern matched how he felt about that answer.

"Detective Overmeyer will give you a ride home," Pantera said. Looking at Harry, he said, "I'll meet you at the office."

"Sure thing," Harry said, and they left, Gene locking the deadbolt behind them and returning the key to its hiding place.

Gene climbed into Harry's car, and Pantera motioned for Harry to come close.

"Ask him to try calling Ericka again. If she answers, talk to her."

"Got it," Harry said, getting into his car and driving away.

LIKE AN UNTIMELY FROST

29

When Harry arrived at the station, he found Pantera at his desk, sipping a cup of fresh coffee from the breakroom down the hall. Pantera pointed at a steaming cup on Harry's desk to show he'd made one for him, too. The evidence bag with the envelope and its contents sat on Pantera's desk, and Pantera stared at it as if it were a jigsaw puzzle he had no idea how to put together.

"Any luck with Gene's call to Ericka?"

Harry said, "No. It went to voice mail. I could hear it. It's odd that she isn't answering his texts or calls. Do you think something happened to her?"

"No telling. I can see her not answering our calls since either the number is showing up as Richmond PD, or it's a number she doesn't recognize, so she doesn't answer. But she knows Gene and knows when he's calling. I hope she's just ignoring him."

"She was a hooker. Wouldn't she be used to answering calls from unrecognized numbers?" Harry asked.

"But Gene says she's out of that business now. That would be added incentive to ignore those calls. Why spend time explaining a hundred times that you're no longer in that line of business?"

"Good point."

"And she'd recognize an 804 area code as Richmond. Roanoke's a 540. A Richmond call would equal a former Richmond customer to her."

"Still, it's weird she doesn't answer Gene's calls."

"Maybe one of us should take a trip to Roanoke," Pantera said.

"Flip you for it," Harry said.

Taking out a quarter, Pantera said, "Heads or tails?"

"Tails. If I win, you go, right?"

"Yep." Pantera tossed the coin up and caught it, slapping it on the back of his hand and lifting his hand. Tails.

"Have fun on that drive," Harry said.

"I hope Childers doesn't mind springing for the trip."

"Maybe you can use the lieutenant's car."

Pantera laughed. "Yeah, or maybe he'll buy me a brand new Lexus to take."

"That's what? About a three-hour drive?"

"About that. At least it's a scenic one."

"Guess we ought to go talk to Gariepy."

"Yeah. Let's do it," Pantera said.

A minute later, they were sitting in Lieutenant Dan Gariepy's office.

"Roanoke?" Gariepy said. "What's in Roanoke?"

"A person we absolutely must talk to."

"Ever heard of a phone?"

"She's not answering it."

"Can't we get Roanoke PD to go talk to her? Get her to phone you?"

"They can't force someone to make a phone call, Lieutenant. We've been trying to get in touch with her for a couple of days now. She's either ignoring our calls—as well as calls and texts from someone she considers a good friend—or something has happened to her."

Gariepy sighed. "Call the Roanoke PD and see if they have any info on her. If there's nothing, you can go. Will you be back in time to take that comp time?"

"Forget about the time, Lieutenant. Consider it a gift from me to you," Pantera said, and they left the office.

A call to the Roanoke Police Department only served to take time. They had no idea who she was, and there had been no accidents or other mishaps involving her to their knowledge.

Pantera signed out a vehicle and left for Roanoke, figuring he'd be back to Richmond by seven that night. He knew asking for overtime would be a waste of breath.

He called Nancy and asked if she could get the girls for dinner. Two straight nights of pizza wasn't a good plan.

"Sure. Where are you going to be?"

"Roanoke."

"Why there?"

"Because that's where the case is taking me."

There was silence on the other end, and Nancy finally said, "Okay."

"What is it?" Pantera asked. He could tell something was bothering her.

"Nothing really. I just felt you were getting more— well—accessible, but you're still married to your job."

"Nance, I gotta do what I gotta do. I have no choices here." He didn't mention that Harry could have gone instead, but she did.

"Harry could have gone, couldn't he?"

"Nancy, what is this? We're divorced, you know. You have no say in my life anymore."

"But your daughters still need their father."

"And they have me. I'm not some deadbeat dad. I have made time to be with them, and they know that. They also understand there are times I have to do my job and that it can sometimes interfere with other plans. They're not little kids anymore. They get the concept of job responsibility."

"I know that, Tony!"

"Can I ask you a question?"

"What?"

"Does this involve any ideas of getting back together?"

"Who said I wanted to get back together?"

"Your daughter."

"Beth?"

"No, Andrea, but Beth agreed with her."

For a moment, Pantera listened to the silence on the other end of the call. Then, she spoke up.

"I can't say that hasn't crossed my mind. I've always loved you. I just couldn't take not knowing if you would come home alive or not."

"I still have that same dangerous job, Nancy. I've always loved you, too, but we're a bad match."

"I'm sorry. You're right. I just—"

"What?"

"I just get lonely, that's all. Waking up in a half-empty bed is—half a life."

"I know. It was lonely for me for a long time until I met Lisa."

"Are the two of you serious?"

"You sound like Andrea and Beth. We're serious enough, I guess. We don't have any plans in the works, but they could happen one day. Who knows? Life's a crap shoot in the best of times. I just do my best to take it one day at a time."

"You always were a sucker for clichés."

"They're clichés because they fit the situation."

"Tony?"

"Yeah?"

"I love you."

"Yeah. I know. I love you, too."

"Be careful out there, okay?"

"I'll do my best. That's worked for nearly twenty years. Maybe it will keep working until I can retire."

"Are you still considering going into business for

yourself someday? Become a private investigator?"

"Yeah, but I'm not ready for that yet. Figured I would retire first and take that up. That way I'd have my pension to pay the bills and could make some extra on the side."

"Tony, you have your trust fund. You got that when you turned twenty-five."

"Yeah, I know, but I don't touch that money."

"Why not?"

"I'd rather leave it to the girls."

"How much is it worth, now? Fifteen million? Twenty?"

"You know too much about me."

"I was married to you for fifteen years. Of course I do. So, how much is it worth now?"

"Honestly, I have no idea."

"Tony, retire early. Take some time to be with your family."

"Nance, you're not a member of my family anymore."

"I could be if you weren't a cop anymore and I could count on you coming home every day."

"We're talking in circles here. You know I don't want to leave the force, and you know why."

"Tony, being on the force won't bring your parents back. The men who killed them are rotting in prison, largely because of you. You did your good deed for your parents. Let it go."

Pantera felt his anger beginning to rise and knew he needed to end the call before he said something he would regret.

"Look, this isn't getting anyone anywhere. I'm gonna hang up now. We can deal with this later, but I have a job to do."

She was silent for a moment, then said, "Okay. Have fun in Roanoke. It's a beautiful place."

"It is, but I won't be enjoying the scenery. I'll be back sometime this evening, probably get home by eight or nine."

"Will you call me when you're back home?"

"Sure."

"Bye, Tony. Talk to you then."

"Bye."

As he drove, he tried to forget the conversation, but it wouldn't go away. It was like something he'd eaten that wasn't agreeing with his stomach, but he couldn't do anything to alleviate the discomfort.

By the time he arrived in Roanoke, he had managed to put the conversation in a compartment in his mind to be brought out later.

As he'd told Nancy, he had a job to do.

30

They had been supplied with the cell phone billing address for Natalie Oliver, who had called herself Ericka while in Richmond. Using that information, Pantera used his GPS to find the home. When he arrived, he found a small vinyl-sided home nestled among pine trees. Pantera judged the home's size at no more than a thousand square feet, an inexpensive rental property.

Climbing out of the car, he walked up the dirt pathway that led to the front door of the house. Stepping past the old Ford Taurus parked in front of his car, he placed his hand on the hood, feeling the heat from the engine. Someone had recently driven it, and that person would be here.

Before he arrived at the door, a young woman opened the door and stepped out, pointing a rifle at him.

"Stop there," she said more calmly than Pantera would have expected. "What are you doing here?"

Pantera raised his hands and stood still, doing his best to look nonthreatening. "I'm looking for Ericka Oliver. Are you Ericka?" Pantera noticed the slight furrowing of her brow when he mentioned the name.

"Never mind who I am. Who are you?"

"My name is Tony Pantera. I'm a detective in Richmond. I've come to talk to Ericka. Or should I say, Natalie? She isn't in any trouble. Or again, should I say you aren't in any trouble?"

The girl squinted at him, obviously making up her mind as to whether or not to talk to him.

"I've driven all the way here from Richmond. It's that important."

"You got a badge?"

Pantera reached for his back pocket.

"Careful." She adjusted her grip on the rifle.

Pantera slowly withdrew his badge and held it up for her to see.

"Put it on the ground and step back."

He did so, and she stepped forward, keeping the rifle aimed at him as she stooped to pick up the badge. Glancing back and forth from the badge to Pantera, she seemed satisfied that he was telling the truth.

"Why do you want to talk to me?"

"I think you already know. Your friend Miranda was murdered a few days ago, and we're trying to find out who killed her. We don't suspect you. We just need some information about Circe Enterprises and your job there."

"I ain't talking about that."

"Look. I couldn't care less what your job was unless it was as an assassin, which I doubt seriously. We know that Miranda was working as a hooker of some sort, but we don't know if she worked on her own or had a pimp. If you could help us with that, it might go a long way toward solving her murder."

"What if what I did at Circe was illegal?"

"Like hooking?"

"Let's just say that would be a good example, though I'm admitting to nothing."

"I'm not with vice. I'm with major crimes, which includes things like murder and armed robbery. As long as that wasn't the kind of things you did for Circe, and again, I doubt very much that you did, I really don't care. To be honest, we are fairly certain that you were a prostitute in Richmond, though we have no actual proof of that."

"What makes you think that?"

Pantera shrugged. "Call it a hunch."

"What? Are you saying I look like a whore?"

"No. Listen, Ericka, I—"

"I don't go by Ericka anymore."

"See? That's one reason we think you were hooking. Using a different name. Even Gene Crawford calls you Ericka, meaning he didn't know your real name. And from what we can tell, the two of you are fairly good friends."

Pantera watched as she stood there, still thinking whether to do anything beyond telling him to get in his car and drive back to Richmond, with a "sorry for the wasted trip."

He continued while she was still listening to him. "In any case, I'm certainly not going to harm you, so you think you could lower the rifle? I know the safety's on, but your finger is on it, and I'm afraid you might accidentally move it and fire. My daughters especially wouldn't like that, and I wouldn't be too thrilled either."

She took a deep breath and let it out slowly, lowering the weapon. "What do you want to know? I reserve the right not to answer any question I don't want to."

"Okay, but it's been a long drive. Do you think we could go inside? Maybe get some cold water or something?"

She jerked her head toward the front door and he entered it with her following.

The house was small, but Pantera could see she had done what she could to make it homey and comfortable, despite the worn furniture. Several vases of fresh flowers sat on various tables in the front room. When they entered the small kitchen, he saw a plaque on the wall announcing, "This is my kitchen. Don't like the fare? Go elsewhere." A gray tabby cat lazed on the floor under the small dining table, and he rose and left the room as if insulted that the company was not to his liking.

They sat in chairs facing each other after she brought out two bottles of water from the refrigerator.

"So, what's your first question."

"What was your job at Circe? Again, I am not here to arrest you. I'm here to find out what I can about the case."

"Do you think someone at Circe killed Miranda?"

"We're not sure. We're just checking what leads we have. So, what did you do there?"

"Have you met Paulson?"

"Yes."

"Well, he's the pimp. He has what he calls his 'stable of girls' that he rents to high-paying clients, or sometimes, it's a perk for some of the big shots who do business with them on a regular basis. Like this one guy would always have me and Miranda together. I think you get the drift."

"So Paulson pays you on the company's books?"

"It wasn't strictly like that. We were paid as 'consultants.' That way, what we were doing wasn't listed on the company's books, just our income."

"How do you know that?"

"Because I asked him one time. I was like, 'how do you get away with paying us to be high-priced call girls?' and he said, 'because I list you as consultants on the payroll.' I actually thought it was kind of clever. We got half of the money the men paid—those who did pay—as a sort of monthly bonus. That was paid in cash. The payroll part was to keep us employed at Circe, if you can call what we did being employed. It was mostly just so we would do what he asked."

"Other than you and Miranda, who else was working as 'consultants?'"

"I really don't know. It's not as if we had staff meetings. There were other girls, but I only saw them once in a while. I never knew anything other than the first name they used. I only knew Miranda because we became friends outside of work."

"So you were basically paid employees whose only job was to sleep with clients?"

"Yeah. We had to sign some papers saying we couldn't do that kind of work anywhere else. Paulson said it was to avoid spreading diseases. We were checked for STD's every month. One girl was fired when she came up positive. She said it must have been her boyfriend who gave her the clap, but me and Miranda didn't believe her." Ericka paused for a moment. "Come to think of it, another girl got all scared because she said she couldn't find the girl that got fired. She was scared something had happened to her. You know, something bad."

Pantera jotted this down, wondering if there might be another one of Paulson's girls lying dead somewhere.

"Do you think Paulson could do that? Maybe kill that girl?" Pantera asked.

"I don't really know. He's not a nice person, though. I can tell you that."

"What makes you say that?" Pantera asked. He didn't believe she was wrong but wanted her take on it.

"He'd have these orgies with the girls. It was either come to it or get fired. The money was really good, and the working conditions were better than standing on street corners hustling johns. That's where Miranda and I met was one of those orgies of his."

"Where did he have these orgies?"

"Mostly at his house, but one time he had one in his office in the middle of the day. It was weird. He and his executive assistant took turns with several of us girls."

"What was the assistant's name?" Pantera asked, thinking he knew who it was.

"I don't know her first name, but her last name is Davidson. I remember because she had one of those desk plates with 'Ms. Davidson' on it. She was at the desk in the outer office when we came in, and after we were all involved with Paulson, she invited herself to the party."

"Okay," Pantera said, noting that.

"Oh, wait. I remember now. He called her Doreen. So it's Doreen Davidson, I guess."

"Was anyone else there?"

"No. Just Paulson and Doreen and four of us girls including me and Miranda."

"Okay, how is it you know Gene Crawford?"

"How do you know I know him?"

"He admitted as much," Pantera said, not yet wanting her to know they had subpoenaed her phone records.

"How did he say we met each other?"

"He didn't. Were you two lovers?"

Casting her eyes down for a second, she hesitated long enough to tell Pantera the answer was yes despite her answer. "No."

"Then how did you meet?"

"He was a security guard for Circe. Miranda introduced us when we arrived for that private office party. He was working the desk at the main entrance."

"Wait. So he and Miranda knew each other?" This was news to him. Gene had suggested they barely knew each other when they showed him her picture.

"Yeah. They dated."

Pantera nodded, thinking he couldn't wait to share this bombshell with Harry—and talk to Gene. "How do you know that?"

"Look, I'd rather not get into all that."

"Your friend Miranda was murdered. Anything you can tell me about the people she knew or had contact with helps. If nothing else, it helps eliminate some of them."

"Or point the finger at them."

"It's a simple question, Ms. Oliver. How did you know they dated? I can't see how answering that will hurt anyone."

"Okay. We did a threesome once. She set it up to surprise him."

"How does that equal 'they dated'?"

She huffed her breath, obviously unhappy about telling him about this. "Because we talked about it after when he wasn't around. He was kind of jealous of me. Said we spent more time making each other happy than making him happy. Sorry, but when your job is to let just any man have sex with you, you tend to get sexual enjoyment elsewhere. At least, that's how it is with me."

"Do you have anything to corroborate that they dated or knew each other?"

"Why don't people believe me?" She stood abruptly and left the room for a moment, returning with her phone. Opening her photo app, she showed him a picture. It was of Gene and Miranda at a bar, laughing at something.

"Could you email me this picture?"

"Sure. What's the address?"

He gave it to her, and moments later the picture arrived in his inbox.

Moving on, he asked, "Who do you think killed Miranda?"

"Isn't it obvious? She must have pissed Paulson off and he killed her. Or had her killed."

Pantera reached in his pocket and pulled out the sheaf of papers with her cell phone records and texts. He held them up for her to see what it was. "These are your phone records. That's how we found where you live."

"I was wondering how you found me," she said, staring at the papers and reaching for a cigarette. "Pardon me. This whole thing has me in knots." She lit the cigarette with trembling fingers and blew the smoke in his direction. She held out the pack. "Want one?"

"No, thanks. I quit."

She flicked the ash and said, "Sorry. I guess the smoke bothers you now, huh?"

"Not that much," he said. It was a lie, but he didn't want her knowing it was an irritation. He wondered if she had lit up to see if it would bother him enough to make him wrap this up sooner. When she stubbed it out after two puffs, he decided he was right. "These records include your texts, which is how we found out about the envelope."

She froze while stubbing the cigarette out. "You know about that?"

"Yes."

"What was in it?"

"Sorry. Can't say."

"Does it implicate Paulson?"

"Again, I can't say."

"Wow, you're not much for sharing, are you?"

"You're not much for it either."

"Does Gene know?"

"Yes."

She stood and began pacing. "Does Paulson know he has it?"

"I don't think so. And it's 'had.' We have it now. Why do you ask?"

"Because if it's something incriminating, which Gene and I both thought it might be, Paulson would kill him."

"Ericka?"

"My real name is Natalie. Call me that, please. Ericka was my 'work' name."

"Sorry." He took a swallow of water. "Natalie. Are you sure you weren't Gene's girlfriend and you introduced her to Gene?"

"What makes you say that?"

"Just a hunch."

"Well, your hunch is wrong this time." She plopped back in the chair. "Listen, are we about through here? I have a shift to work."

"Where?"

"Trixie's Café. It's a little diner in Roanoke."

"Yes, we're about done. Are you leasing this house?"

"Yes. Is that a crime?" When he ignored the sarcasm, she continued. "I'd appreciate it if you didn't let anyone in Richmond know I'm here. I'm doing my best to get away from there."

"You trust Gene not to tell anyone?"

"He didn't tell you, did he? If he didn't tell you, he won't tell Paulson or anyone who knows him."

"Are you afraid of Paulson?"

She sat back. "Damn straight. He's dangerous."

"You don't have to worry about me saying anything to anyone other than my partner, who already knows where to find you." Pantera took out his card and gave it to Natalie. "If you decide you want to talk more about this, call me. And if you change your number or leave town, we'll come looking for you. So, don't do that, okay?"

She looked at the card as he stood. "I have no intention of leaving, but I gotta tell you, if Paulson or someone he sent shows up, they won't live long enough to get through the door." She looked in his eyes. "I want you to know that so if something does happen, you can say I feared for my life and killed whoever it was in self-defense."

He put away the phone records and said, "I'll at least tell the Roanoke PD that much if something happens." As he stepped out the door, he added, "And if you get a call from the number on my card, answer it, please. Don't make me drive all the way here again."

She actually smiled at that. "Maybe I'll answer."

After he left her home, he drove back to Richmond, thinking about what he'd learned before calling Harry with the details to catch him up.

Once Pantera had left, Natalie locked her door and sat at the table, thinking about the conversation. There were things she hadn't told him. For one, she didn't think Paulson had killed Miranda, but she would never tell the cops that, though she had shared her thoughts with friends at work. Her relationship with the cops wasn't good—never had been—and she always felt it best to keep her mouth shut around them about what she thought. Besides, they would never come to talk to her co-workers since they believed they would know absolutely zero about Miranda's death. She had to talk to someone about it, though. It gnawed at her, and talking always helped with that kind of thing.

She lit another cigarette and stripped down for a shower. She felt dirty after talking to the cop. She prayed she would never hear from him again.

31

When he was away from Roanoke and on his way back to Richmond, Pantera phoned Harry through the vehicle's CarPlay to catch him up on what he'd learned from Natalie Oliver.

When he'd told him about what she had called "Paulson's stable of girls," Harry said, "Wow. So he was pimping and paying the girls out of company payroll?"

"According to Natalie Oliver, he was. It's only her word about that, though I don't doubt that he was doing those things."

"Holy shit!" Harry said.

"That wasn't all I learned."

"Oh? What else?"

Pantera told him about the relationship between Miranda and Gene.

"Really?" Harry said. "But he said he barely knew her. Why would he say that?"

"Good question. Suppose we visit him and ask. He must be hiding something."

"First thing tomorrow. If he's not home, we can go by Ledbetter Place. Did she tell you anything else?"

"She mentioned that she and Miranda had a threesome with Gene, and he was jealous of the attention they paid each other."

"So he's the jealous type?"

"I guess. But I'm still wondering why he said he barely knew her. He must be stupid or something, thinking we wouldn't find out."

"Maybe that's why he didn't tell us where we could find Ericka," Harry said.

"Maybe."

"Do you think he had something to do with her death?"

"Everyone's a suspect until they aren't. We could talk the entire drive back to Richmond with the questions as to why he didn't admit he knew her—dated her even—if Natalie is to be believed."

"So she was evasive?"

"Let's just say she was less than cooperative. When I first saw her, she had a rifle pointed at me." Pantera went on to describe the encounter.

"She sounds scared."

"She's scared out of her mind. She doesn't admit she is, but she nearly begged me not to tell anyone where she was. Anyway, when I asked if she and Gene were lovers, she said they weren't, but I got the impression she was being evasive at best and outright lying at worst. Listen, I need to hang up and concentrate on these mountain roads."

"Sure thing. I'll see you tomorrow."

"Yeah. See you then," Pantera said and clicked off.

When he arrived home, Nancy and the girls were waiting for him.

When the girls had gone to their rooms, Nancy said, "I'm sorry about what I said on the phone. I don't want to create more stress in your life."

"It's okay. You were being honest," he said, sitting beside her on the sofa.

"I made dinner and kept a plate warm for you."

"Thanks. You didn't need to do that. You could have taken them out for something."

"It was my pleasure. Besides, what would you eat after your drive? A baloney sandwich?"

'Hey, on good bread, they're not that bad."

She gave him a sad smile. "I'll go now. Was your trip to Roanoke worth it?"

"Very much."

She leaned forward and gave him a peck on the cheek before standing to leave. "Take care of yourself."

"I will."

On the drive to the hotel, Nancy thought about how dangerous her feelings for her ex-husband were becoming. When she'd given him the small peck before leaving, she could feel herself wanting to turn that kiss into more—much more. She knew most of her emotions about Tony were a result of recently losing her second husband, who was killed by a madman Tony had been pursuing. She was lonely and needed some human contact beyond conversation. Tony was convenient. Or at least, she hoped that was all it was. Yes, if he had turned the small goodbye kiss into more, she would have gladly stayed the night, but he had Lisa now. She would have to deal with having nobody in the intimate portion of her life now.

She loved Tony—always would—but he was right. Their life together was over. She had ended it, and for good reason. She had realized she needed to divorce him when she was getting almost no sleep from worrying about his safety and whether or not he would be coming home the next day.

Then again, if he would leave the force and go into private practice or some other job, she would be back with him in a second if he asked.

Her mother had warned her about marrying a policeman. She had foreseen how Nancy would end up feeling, telling her she was an emotional child and had become an emotional adult, and with her emotions came worry. "You were always a worrier," her mother had said.

Yes, she was. She could admit that to herself. Still, even when she had been married to Phil, she could feel her heartbeat pick up a bit when Tony came around. She could recall the elation when he had first asked her out in college. After that first date, she had told her roommate that she would one day have his children. She had fallen quickly and totally in love with him.

Although she had divorced him, the worry had not stopped. True, she didn't lose sleep over it the way she had before, but the worry was still there. She was fully aware that if something happened to Tony, she would be devastated. Their daughters would be, too.

For the first time since the days after burying Phil, she cried herself to sleep that night.

The next morning Pantera arrived at work to find Harry had beaten him there. Pantera could see how anxious Harry was to get out to question Gene about his denials about knowing Miranda.

Pantera phoned Gene and asked if he was working today.

"Yeah, headed there right now. Why? What's up?"

"We just need to talk to you."

"Is it about the envelope?"

"Yes and no. We'll be there in about a half hour."

When they arrived at Ledbetter Place, Gene was at the guardhouse. "So what is it?" Gene asked when they pulled up.

"Let me park first. This could end up taking a while."

Pantera noticed the worry cross Gene's face.

When he had parked in a space just past the guardhouse, he and Harry stepped over to Gene.

"So what do you guys need to know?"

"I went to talk to Ericka yesterday," Pantera began.

More fear flashed through Gene's eyes. "And?"

"She said you and Miranda dated."

"What?"

Harry said, "Yep. Funny thing is you said you

barely knew her when we showed you her picture, and now it turns out you knew her intimately."

"I never dated Miranda!"

Pantera said, "I guess if I were in your situation, I would say that, too. She even told me that the three of you had a little fun together. A threesome."

"I—what?!"

"Come on, Gene. Why did you lie to us?"

"I didn't."

Pantera took out his phone and opened the email Natalie had sent him. Holding the phone out, he showed Gene the picture of him and Miranda. Gene's face fell.

"So, you want to tell us the truth now?"

"Okay, I did know her."

"Why wouldn't you say that before?"

"Because she had just been murdered, and I didn't want to become a suspect."

"Ahh," Pantera said, "so you wanted to wait so you could board the express train to suspect instead?"

"I didn't kill her."

"Well, Harry," Pantera said. "Glad that's cleared up. A guy who's told us several lies just said he didn't kill Miranda. I guess he's off the list of suspects now."

"Well, here's something to consider," Gene said. "I dated Ericka, not Miranda. Why would she say I dated Miranda?"

"You dated Ericka?" Harry asked.

"Yeah. For about three months. She's the one who arranged the threesome with Miranda. Said we'd all have a load of fun, but mostly it was the two of them who had fun."

"Is there anyone who can corroborate that story?"

"That the three of us had sex?"

"No, that you were dating Ericka and not Miranda."

He shrugged. "Why would that matter anyway?"

Pantera said, "You said yourself, and I quote, 'why

would she say I dated Miranda?' Honestly, if she was lying, I'd like to know why myself."

"Buddy knew, but he's dead. And of course, Miranda knew."

"Can't ask them."

He thought for a moment. "Wait! Andre! My cousin who was holding the envelope for me. He knew. We went out with him and his girlfriend once."

"Where can we find Andre right now?"

"He's probably at work."

"And where would that be?"

"Henrico Hardware."

Pantera looked at Harry. "You mind staying here to make sure Gene doesn't use the phone while I go pick up some nails I've been needing to get?"

"No problem."

When he arrived at Henrico Hardware, he found Andre behind the counter, checking out a customer.

"Hey, Andre. My name is Detective Tony Pantera. We're investigating the murder of—"

"I know who you are," Andre said. "Gene told me about you when he left the envelope."

"Okay. I just have one question. Gene dated a young woman who worked at Circe for a few months. He says that you and your girlfriend joined them on a sort of outing once—nothing illegal that I know of, so I'm not trying to bust anyone—but I need to know the girl's name."

"How recent?"

"Not sure, but not long ago."

"The man dates a lot of women. Most of them get a clue about how jealous he is and split."

Pantera nodded, reminded how easily Gene had talked to them the first time they'd met. He'd not meant to tell them anything important but had. Perhaps this tendency ran in the family. "You remember her name?"

"Yeah. It was Ericka, with a 'ck.' I remember because she introduced herself like that. You know, 'I'm Ericka with a ck.' That kind of thing. I remember wonderin' if she thought I might write her name down sometime and she wanted to be sure I spelled it right. Is that who you mean?"

"Yeah. So, did he date anyone named Miranda?"

"You mean that was killed?"

"Yeah."

"Naw, man, but he knew her." Andre grinned and winked. "Told me about some fun he had with her and Ericka."

"Did you know that Ericka was a hooker?"

"Yeah. So? Lots of girls make their livin' that way."

"But you mentioned Gene was jealous. An odd thing for him to date a hooker, isn't it?"

"Well, that was business. Gene gets jealous if the girl actually likes someone else. Fuckin' is just fuckin'. It ain't like she's actually enjoyin' it. To Ericka, the guys she was hookin' up with were just that. Guys. Sometimes girls, according to Gene. He was jealous of Ericka's relationship with that girl Miranda, but the people she got paid to do somethin' with didn't matter to Gene."

"He was jealous of Miranda?"

"Yeah. He didn't like that chick at all."

"You mean more than just jealousy?"

"Not sure. One time he pointed her out to me and said, 'right there is a class A bitch.' I asked him why he thought that, but he wouldn't tell me anything. Just said he'd rather not talk about it. I mean, he wouldn't kill her because he didn't like her or anything. Hell, if he did that, he'd kill half the women in Richmond."

"You're sure he didn't date her at one time?"

"Her? Naw, man. It wasn't like she broke his heart

or anything. He just didn't like her for some reason. I guess it was because she and Ericka would hook up sometimes."

"Okay, thanks," Pantera said.

After he arrived back at Ledbetter Place, he told Gene they would be in touch and that his cousin had verified his claim that he'd dated Ericka.

Pantera turned back to Gene as they were leaving and said, "By the way, do you know Ericka's real first name?"

Gene looked confused. "Ericka. Or maybe that's her middle name and she uses that because she prefers it."

"Okay," Pantera said, climbing into the car. "Don't leave town, Gene. We'll find you."

"I don't plan on it," Gene said.

As the detectives drove off, Gene wondered about the conversation and considered what he would say to Ericka when he talked to her again.

32

As they drove, Pantera filled Harry in on what he'd learned from Andre.

"So he hated Miranda?" Harry asked.

"Yeah, but Andre doesn't think he'd kill her. I also think it's odd that Gene dated a girl and didn't know her real first name," Pantera said as he drove away from Ledbetter Place. "Why would she keep that from him?"

"Maybe that's her real name, and she's lying to you."

"I doubt that. The date on the phone number goes back to high school, and the records show her name as Natalie. She must have switched the account into her name after she turned eighteen."

"How old is she now?"

"Twenty-three."

"Maybe she changed it when she turned eighteen."

"Naw. Too complicated. Rule number one of detective work: if the standard explanation fits, go with it until you have proof that it's different. She used Ericka for her life as a hooker. That is much more likely."

"Maybe," Harry said. "Still, it bothers me."

"Same here, but I'm not going to lose sleep over it."

"I guess."

"There is something that is bothering me more, though."

"What?"

"Why did she tell me Gene was dating Miranda and not her?"

"Yeah, that is odd. It's not like we would care one way or the other."

Pantera pulled over into a Lowe's Hardware parking lot. "We have to look at it from the viewpoint of motive. Why do people lie?"

"To cover something up."

"Bingo. Then what was she covering up when she lied about dating Gene?"

"No telling, but I'll bet that's something we should find out," Harry said.

"Agreed," Pantera said and pulled out his phone.

"Whatcha doing?"

"Calling her to ask that very question."

He dialed her number and waited while the call was put through. When it was, it went straight to voicemail. He checked his watch. It was after ten.

"Her phone must be off," he said. "She knows she needs to answer a call from me."

"Or she's on another call."

They looked at each other, smiled, and said simultaneously, "Gene."

Once Pantera had driven away, Gene took out his cell phone. As he opened to his contacts, a car pulled in and the driver said she was there to see a resident. Gene checked the log of expected visitors the residents would phone in but didn't see the name of the woman, so he called the resident, who told him the woman was expected and she'd forgotten to call that in.

Gene let the woman through the gate and returned to his phone. Pressing the button to call Ericka, he waited until she answered on the fifth ring just as he thought his call would go to voicemail.

"Yeah, Gene? What is it?" she said in greeting.

"I hear you had a visitor."

"Oh?"

"Yeah, Detective Pantera from Richmond PD?"

"Oh, yeah. He was here yesterday."

"It would have been nice if you'd told me. They came to see me this morning."

"They?"

"Yeah, Pantera and his partner, Detective Overmeyer."

"Why would they come see you? They said they had the envelope."

"Yeah, about that. I left a message for you to call me, but you didn't. I needed to talk about that with you."

"I got busy."

"They suspect me of killing Miranda!"

"Don't shout at me, Gene! I told you about that."

Gene took a breath and watched another car approach the gate. He needed to go but wanted Ericka's reassurance that she would answer if he called her back later. "Listen, I have to go for now, but I'm gonna call you when I get home this afternoon. It's very important that you answer, okay?"

"Okay, I get off work at five today. I promise I'll answer."

"You better," he said. "I'll call at 5:30."

When Gene arrived home, he waited until 5:30 and called Ericka. This time it rang only twice before being answered.

Instead of "hello," she answered with, "I'm sorry, Gene. I had no idea they would suspect you."

Gene decided to start out easygoing. "I understand. How's Roanoke? You still at that diner?"

"Trixie's?"

"Yeah, Trixie's," he said, jotting down the name.

"It's okay. Beats hooking for a living."

He ignored her response since he'd been angry she had left that position. It had made a lot of money, and he'd made plans based on her income, but of course, they all fell through.

CHARLES TABB

"I need to know something," he said. "Why would you tell them I was dating Miranda and not you?"

"I don't know. I just didn't want to be a part of all this shit. I figured if they knew we dated, they would have more questions for me. I figured they already suspected you of something since you had the envelope and didn't say anything about it. I just wanted to be left alone. Moving to Richmond was the worst decision of my life, and I just want to get away from everything about that place."

"You made good money when you were here."

"Yeah, and you got your fun for free."

"I don't recall you complaining."

"Sorry. I'm on edge." She changed the subject. "What happened with the envelope?"

He didn't want to admit Pantera had it, so he said, "I hoped it would be my own ticket out of here."

"How?"

"I'd rather not say."

"Come on, Gene. We've come this far. Tell me. Did you ask Paulson to pay you for it?"

He paused, then sighed.

"Oh, my God! That's it, isn't it? You were blackmailing Paulson!"

"Yeah. I just hope I don't end up like Buddy."

"What about Buddy?"

"Pantera didn't tell you?"

"No, what about him?"

"He was murdered. They found his body. Shot in the back of the head."

"Holy shit! What about the envelope? What was in it?"

"Buddy had a long letter in it explaining that he'd been forced to do Paulson's bidding, which included murder."

"He said that?"

224

"Yeah. He even described in detail a killing of a guy up in Pennsylvania."

"Then give it to the cops, Gene! With the letter, they'll have proof that Paulson, at least, was involved in the murder, and that would mean he probably murdered Buddy and Widner, too."

Gene let out a breath. "It's not that simple. I could write a letter detailing how Paulson forced me to kill someone. If I'd done the killing, that would really only prove that I did it. Saying someone else made me do it wouldn't mean shit."

"Oh, God. You're right."

"Yeah, but mostly I'm worried about them saying I killed Miranda."

"They don't know that. They can't prove it, anyway."

"Why would I kill her?" There was silence on the line. "Ericka?"

"I'm here."

"I asked you, why would I kill Miranda? You gonna answer?"

"Come on, Gene. We both know how jealous you were of her relationship with me, which is really weird since you knew I was banging men and women for Paulson."

"Yeah, but there wasn't anything emotional in that. That was just your job—and a lucrative one at that."

"You're pissed that I left, aren't you?"

"It was good money, Ericka! We could have moved into Ledbetter Place together, and I wouldn't have to be cow-towing to the rich folks at the gate like some freed slave or something! Besides, I might have been jealous, but not enough to fucking kill her!"

"Okay, I'm going now. I told you not to yell at me."

"Fine! Who needs you, anyway?" He yelled and clicked off before tossing the phone on the sofa table.

As he sat back, he thought about what to do next. He might go strangle Ericka. She deserved as much. He thought about doing that for nearly an hour, planning how he could get away with it. Yes, he would kill Ericka for leaving him, something that bothered him more than anyone other than him knew.

It would be as simple as killing Miranda had been, though the reasons for doing that were better than jealous rage. Yes, he'd been jealous of Ericka's relationship with Miranda, but his reasons for killing her had been about survival, not rage.

Now that he knew where Ericka worked in Roanoke. He figured it wouldn't be hard to find her.

An hour later and seven miles away, a man sat at a computer, listening to the recording of Gene's conversation with Ericka Oliver. That afternoon, they had begun using an easily obtained spyware to tap into his calls, which were automatically recorded and shared to his computer's hard drive. When he finished listening to the recording, he called his boss, Leland Braxton.

"Mr. Braxton? Davis here. We have a call from Gene Crawford to Ericka Oliver. Apparently, she used to work for Circe."

"Forward me the audio file," Braxton said.

Hanging up, Braxton felt his adrenaline kick into high gear. If this were something important, he would let Paulson know. It was Paulson, after all, who had ordered the wiretap on Gene Crawford's cell.

After listening to the recording, he phoned Paulson, who was thrilled with what they had learned.

33

Three days later, Ray Foster sat in his car watching the door to Trixie's Diner in Roanoke. Paulson had called him into his office that afternoon and told him what he would have to do. His plea not to be forced to follow the instructions was met with a glare and a reminder that he could choose to either carry out the plan or watch his family being murdered. That was what his life had come down to—do the bidding of a man the devil himself would admire or watch his wife and children being slaughtered like cattle. Of course, he would also be killed after being forced to watch the carnage.

Now, he watched for the doomed young woman to come out of the diner to drive home to her death.

Ray was a big man, six-four and 240 pounds with only seven percent body fat, the result of working out in a gym every day between work and going home to his family. He'd had a difficult childhood, leading to various run-ins with the law, but he'd turned from that path once he'd met Shannon, his wife. She was probably the only reason he wasn't in prison today. He could never let her be harmed in any way, so he'd made the only choice he could.

When the door opened and the girl he knew as Ericka stepped out, he watched as she climbed into her car. Starting his own, he followed her at a distance until she pulled into an unpaved driveway. As he drove past, she climbed out of the car and started towards her door.

Ray had seen a small convenience store that was closed for the night about a quarter mile from Ericka's house. Ray returned to it and drove around the back to park the car out of sight. He walked the short distance back to Ericka's house, a razor-sharp hunting knife strapped to his thigh. Two cars passed him as he walked, but he kept his head down and continued walking.

Natalie had undressed for a shower when a sudden crash came from her front room. Panic gripped her for a moment before she ran towards the closet to retrieve her rifle. When she opened it, she realized her mistake. She had left it in the kitchen, and whoever had just crashed his way into her house was between it and her.

Slamming her bedroom door closed and locking it, she went to the window and struggled to open it, fighting against the paint or rust that had long ago sealed it shut.

She heard the bedroom door being smashed open, and a large, powerfully built man she vaguely recognized stumbled through with the force of his body slamming into the hollow door.

Grabbing her around her neck from behind with a choke hold, he forced her onto the bed and lay atop her, his weight pinning her petite frame down.

She tried to scream, but the force of his arm around her throat prevented her from doing more than squawk, the sound a dim plea for help that wouldn't come.

Just as her vision began to melt into blackness, she felt the blade begin to slice into her neck.

Ray stood over the body of the young woman he'd just killed. All he could think about during the assault was that it was either her or him and his family.

Ignoring the tears running down his cheeks, he walked back to his car, climbed in, and drove back to Richmond, ignoring the blood that now covered him.

He had one more stop to make before going home.

A few hours later, he was standing at Gene

Crawford's front door. His shoulder ached from the previous job, so he looked around and saw a fist-sized rock near the door beneath the shrubbery, intending to smash the window open. As he lifted the rock, it was instantly obvious that this was not an ordinary rock. It weighed far less, for one thing, and did not have the feel of a rock. Turning the rock in his hand, he saw in the light from the porch that this was a fake rock that had a compartment for storing a key. Considering the rock's location, this one had to hold a key to the front door.

Removing the key, he opened the door. He knew an alarm might sound, but he doubted it would happen. What could someone like Gene Crawford, whose house wasn't much bigger than Ericka's, have that would warrant a costly alarm system?

He returned the key to its hiding place. Taking out his flashlight once the door was closed, he found the hallway leading to the bedrooms. One room's door was open, and he peered into it first, but it held only a mostly bare desk and a small desk chair. Wires that looked as though they had once been connected to a computer snaked behind the desk. Several boxes were piled nearby.

Carefully opening the door across from that one, Ray found his target asleep, snoring lightly. His face was half buried by a pillow, so even if he opened his eyes, he wouldn't see Ray approaching.

Ray had known Gene, though he would not consider him a friend, just a former co-worker. Still, killing him would be difficult. Once again, he thought of his wife and children and entered the dim room, lit only by the moonlight coming through the window.

When he'd been a teenager, he had broken into a few homes, burglarizing them for small items and an occasional snack or even a beer. Now, he had come to take a life, not a beer or some trinket or pocket cash he

229

thought was worth the effort of committing what he'd considered a minor crime as a teen. And it really had been minor. In the three burglaries, he'd probably taken a grand total of less than $100 worth of stuff.

Now, he would take the most valuable thing there.

Switching off the flashlight, he approached the bed and the sleeping man, using the light of the full moon that streamed through the window to see. He took in a deep breath, held it, and let it out slowly without a sound. The floor beneath him in one spot creaked as his weight forced the boards beneath to depress slightly. He froze and moved his foot forward a few inches before stepping down completely. He began to breathe again as the floor remained silent. He inched toward the bed and the sleeping body.

Raising the knife above his head, he thrust it into the chest of the man he'd been forced to kill, feeling the blade slice into the dying body with a clarity that was frightening.

The body heaved, and Ray pulled the knife from the deep wound, hearing the sucking sound as it was withdrawn, and plunged it a second time into his chest. The man lay back, dead or nearly so, his heart pumping the blood through the open wound that had severed his aorta.

As Ray watched him die, it occurred to him that if this kept up, he would kill himself. He wouldn't be able to live with himself. Looking now at the knife, he considered plunging it into his neck, severing arteries and bleeding out in minutes.

He raised the blade, intending to make a quick exit from this life, when an idea struck him.

Looking at the dying man, he removed his left glove, reached down with his bare hand, touched the pooling blood, and pressed his fingers into the headboard, leaving clear prints.

Perhaps they would listen to his story and give him leniency. That he was willing to go to jail rather than continue with this job made him wonder why he didn't make that decision earlier, saving the lives of the two people he had killed in Paulson's name. He had no answer to that question. All he knew now was that if he went down, he would take Paulson with him. Maybe they could be in the same prison. If that ever happened, he wouldn't kill Paulson, not at first anyway. He would torture him for years first. Ray was much bigger and would be able to do whatever he wanted to the man.

That was the only happy thought he'd had all night.

34

Pantera was driving to work when his cell rang. When he saw the 540 area code, he thought it might be Natalie Oliver. She was the only person in Roanoke that he knew who might call him on his cell.

"This is Pantera," he said as he pressed the button on CarPlay to answer.

"Detective Pantera? This is Detective Sergeant Miles Hoffer with the Roanoke PD."

Pantera felt an internal alarm go off. "Yes?"

"Do you know a Natalie Oliver from here?"

"We've met. I was at her home a few days ago asking about a situation here in Richmond."

"Detective, I'm afraid Ms. Oliver is dead. She was murdered sometime last night. When she didn't show up for her shift and wouldn't answer her phone, her employer called, requesting a wellness check."

Pantera took in a deep breath and slowly exhaled. Paulson. "Dear God," Pantera said. "And you found my card," he said, figuring out how Hoffer found him.

"Yes. The killer must have been a large man. The front door and bedroom door were smashed in. Neither were that sturdy, but it still would have taken a large man to bust them down."

Pantera pictured Paulson, who was slender. He would not have been the person who committed the murder unless he had someone bigger with him. If he did it, he must have sent someone to do the job, meaning he had a new "right-hand man" to replace Buddy.

"Can you tell me the reason you were interrogating Ms. Oliver?" Sergeant Hoffer asked.

"It wasn't an interrogation exactly. She just had some information about a case we're working on, three murders."

"Is it a serial killer situation?"

"No. She knew one of the victims."

"Was she any help?"

"Yes, but not to the extent that we had enough proof to arrest anyone."

"This murder was very violent, a lot of blood. Seems the killer used a large knife, which does not appear to be here. The victim's knife block in the kitchen was full, and luminol shows no traces of blood on them, so we think the killer brought the weapon with him."

"She owned a Remington pump action 30-30. Was it there?"

"We found it in the kitchen. Hadn't been fired."

They talked a moment longer before they clicked off, and Pantera drove the rest of the way to work thinking about Natalie and her promise to shoot anyone who tried to get into her house. She must have been in her bedroom when the killer busted the front door down. He imagined her locking the door to her bedroom before discovering her weapon was in the kitchen.

Arriving at his desk, he sat and stared across at Harry.

"What is it?" Harry asked.

"Natalie Oliver was murdered last night. Some hulk broke down her front door and used a knife to kill her."

"Oh, my God."

"Did we get her killed by my going there?" Pantera mused. "Did someone, probably Paulson, get spooked and decide to end whatever threat she might pose?"

"I doubt it, Tony. If she was a threat to him, he would have her eliminated whether we talked to her or not. We can't go beating ourselves up if a witness is killed. The killer is responsible, not us."

"Yeah, I know that, but if the killer is responsible, why do I wonder if we led him to her?"

"If we were the ones who led him there, he had the means to find her himself without our help. Let it go, Tony."

At that moment, Lieutenant Gariepy stepped out of his office and called to them. "Guys, you want to step in here a moment?"

"Now what?" Pantera said.

"I guess we'll know in a minute," Harry said.

Closing his door, Gariepy said, "We have another murder that relates to your case on Widner, Garrett, and the girl."

"Miranda Buckhorn," Pantera said. "She deserves to have her name spoken, not just 'the girl,' okay?"

"Fine. Widner, Garrett, and Miranda Buckhorn. There's been another murder that involves that case, or at least it seems to."

"Roanoke called you?" Pantera asked, wondering why they felt the need to do that.

"Roanoke? What are you talking about?"

"The friend of Miranda Buckhorn's that I went there to talk to about the case was murdered last night."

"Holy shit," Gariepy said. "No, this is local. A body was found at Gene Crawford's home. Murdered as he slept, apparently."

"Gene?" Pantera felt a knot growing larger in his stomach.

"I guess. You two need to hightail it over there. An officer has the crime scene secured. They're waiting on you. The M.E. was contacted and he's sending Aimee Wells to handle it."

"Son of a bitch," Pantera said, moving to the door.

"We're on it, Lieutenant," Harry said and followed Pantera to the elevator.

When they arrived at Gene's they found a young

officer outside the residence, sitting on the front steps.

"What do you have?" Pantera asked as he approached.

He shook his head as if trying to clear the memory of what he'd seen and said, "A neighbor noticed the door standing open for over an hour this morning and called it in. When I arrived, I entered the house and looked around. Nothing is disturbed, and I touched nothing, of course. Found a body in the back bedroom on the right down the hall. Looks like he was stabbed with a large knife while asleep."

Pantera looked at Harry, who said, "A knife. Same way Natalie was killed."

Steeling themselves for what they would find, Pantera and Harry entered the home and stepped down the hallway to the bedroom. Entering, they were greeted by the grisly scene. Blood covered the sheets where the body lay.

As they stepped over to view the corpse that held their full attention, they heard the officer arguing with someone. Just as Pantera looked down at the face, he realized who was now making a commotion at the front door.

The dead man was Andre, Gene's cousin. Gene was announcing loudly to the officer that he lived there and needed to find out why the officer was standing guard.

They left the bedroom and strode to the front of the house, where Gene looked ready to punch the officer to get into the house.

"Gene," Pantera said.

When Gene saw Pantera, he tried to push past the officer again but was held back.

"Calm down, Gene. We need to talk," Pantera said as he and Harry stepped outside.

"What the hell's going on?" Gene demanded. Why are you two in my house? Do you have another search warrant? Where's Andre? He stayed here last night."

"Why didn't he stay at his house?"

"His girlfriend kicked him out. That's her house. He needed a place to stay, so I made arrangements to stay at a girlfriend's. Where is he?"

"Who was the girlfriend you stayed with last night?" Harry asked.

"Her name's Sheila. Sheila Canfield, if it's any of your business."

"Where can we get in touch with Sheila?" Pantera asked.

"What?! What's going on, man?"

"Gene, it's in your best interest to give us her number right now so we can verify what you say."

"Where the fuck is Andre?" Gene asked. "Is he here?"

"Yes, he's here," Pantera said, "but he's dead."

Shock crossed Gene's features as he was struck silent, his mouth agape as he was about to say more when confronted with his cousin's death.

"Wha—" He swallowed hard. "What happened?" Pantera watched as tears filled Gene's eyes.

"Somebody stabbed him. He's in your bed. Apparently, he was asleep when he was attacked."

Harry stepped to the front door, examining the door's edges and jamb. Stooping to inspect the lock, he looked at Pantera and Gene. "The door doesn't look jimmied. Neither does the lock, though it will take a bit more to verify that. Looks like whoever it was had a key." He cast an accusing glance at Gene.

"Wait. You think I killed him?" Gene asked.

"Right now, we don't know what to think," Pantera said. "Now, what's Sheila's number?"

Gene took out his phone and scrolled through his contacts, tapping Sheila's name to call her before handing the cell to Harry, who stepped away.

"Shit!" Gene said. He looked at Pantera. "They meant to kill me."

"Sort of looks that way," Pantera said. "Anything you want to tell me?"

Gene sat down on the steps as if his legs could no longer hold him. He sobbed for several minutes, saying nothing but Andre's name and a series of apologies.

Harry returned to stand beside Pantera. "She confirmed it. He was with her from around 6:30 last night until about a half hour ago."

"He could have snuck out in the middle of the night."

"I asked her if he could have done that. She says she's a very light sleeper, and besides, her dog would have barked up a storm if he came out into the main part of the house in the night. The dog apparently doesn't like Gene very much, so Gene avoids him."

"Call her back. Ask if he could have crawled out a window in the bedroom."

Harry tapped the recall button on Gene's phone.

"Hi, Ms. Canfield. It's Detective Overmeyer again. Tell me, is it possible that Gene snuck out of a window?" He listened a moment. "Okay, thank you. You've been a great help."

Clicking off, he turned to Pantera. "She says the window creaks like crazy and the dog would have barked. Then she reminded me how she's a very light sleeper. She ended by telling me she would have known if Gene even got up to pee."

"Okay," Pantera said. "I seriously doubt he did this anyway, but we have to check."

35

When the crime scene techs arrived ten minutes later, they took control of the scene while Pantera and Harry gave the door and the jamb a more thorough inspection. Harry had checked the windows, and they were all locked from inside. The backdoor was also locked from inside with a chain in addition to the deadbolt.

They could find no evidence that force had been used to enter the house by the front door either. They did not even find the tiniest scratch to indicate the lock had been picked.

"What are you doing?" Gene asked from where he sat in a lawn chair nearby when he had composed himself.

"Trying to find evidence the lock was picked."

"Why?"

"Because, if it were picked, it would help us not suspect you."

"Man, I told you! I had nothing to do with this! I would never hurt Andre!"

"Mostly, we believe you, Gene, but it would just help if we could figure out how the guy who killed Andre got in. None of the windows are broken, and they're locked from the inside, as is the backdoor, so he had to use this one. It's not like he could beam himself inside.

"I leave a key outside," Gene said, pointing to a rock on the ground. "That's one of those fake rocks."

Using his handkerchief, Harry picked up the rock and found the small, latched doorway on the bottom.

Opening it, he found a key to the front door.

"Bingo," Harry said. "That rock surface is too rough to get a print from, but the bottom is smooth. Maybe we can lift one from there. He had to open the latch, right?"

"He probably wore gloves, but we'll check," Pantera said.

At that moment, one of the crime scene techs, stuck her head out the door. "Detectives? You'll want to see this."

They followed her into the bedroom, where she stepped over to the bed and pointed at the headboard. What they saw made both of them smile.

Four distinct and bloody finger prints, as well as a thumb print, were clearly visible. The prints were obviously from the killer's left hand. It would have been impossible for Andre to leave these prints because the person who left them had to be standing over the body.

As they stared at the prints, Harry said, "It almost looks like he purposely left these. No smudges, not even a partial of any of the fingertips. It's almost like he was being printed and someone held his fingers there."

"Yeah, like he wanted us to find it."

"What kind of person leaves prints like that?"

"That's a good question. Maybe when we pick him up, he'll tell us."

They left the room, allowing the techs to continue their work.

As they went outside, Harry said, "You think we'll find a match in the records somewhere?"

"Let's hope so. Then again, maybe he knows his prints aren't on record and he's toying with us."

"Maybe. I've never seen anything like it, though."

Pantera went to Gene. "Let me see your hands."

Gene squinted up at Pantera and held his hands out. Pantera took his left hand and looked closely at the fingerprints.

Harry knew what he was doing and asked, "Is it possible they're his?"

"Not a chance. Gene's prints are loops. The ones in there are arches," Pantera said, referring to fingerprint categories.

"Gene," Harry said, "unless you were using an accomplice, which I doubt, you're in the clear."

"I told you I'd never kill Andre. We were tight."

"Who knew about the rock?" Pantera asked.

"Andre."

"Nobody else?"

"No."

Harry looked at the houses surrounding Gene's. "What about neighbors? Couldn't they have seen you getting the key?"

"It's only there if I lock myself out. I haven't used it since I put it in there."

"Who would want to kill you?" Pantera asked.

"Nobody."

"Then who knew Andre would be here last night?"

"Besides me? His old lady."

"Is this 'old lady' his wife or girlfriend?" Harry asked, his distaste for the term evident.

"His girlfriend."

"Then call her that."

"I would if she deserved it."

Pantera said, "Are you sure nobody else knew he was here?"

"Not completely sure. It's not like he called me and said he'd told someone else he was at my place."

"Do you know of anyone else he might tell?" Harry asked.

"No."

"Do you know if Andre is a light sleeper?"

"Naw, man, he slept like the dead," Gene said,

240

unaware of the connection to reality.

"The killer might have mistaken Andre for you. Probably did. I'll ask again, who do you know who might want to kill you?" Pantera asked.

"Nobody!"

"Think, Gene. Someone came in here last night and thought he'd brutally murdered you. That wasn't on a whim."

"I know Ericka was pissed at me, but not enough to kill me."

Pantera and Harry exchanged glances.

Pantera said, "I have more bad news, Gene. Ericka's dead. She was murdered last night, too."

"No she wasn't! You're lying! Trying to get me to tell you something!"

"I'm afraid not. Her body was found this morning. I got a call from Roanoke PD driving to work. She was stabbed with a large knife. Same as Andre."

Harry said, "You think he killed her and then came here to kill Gene?"

"Gene, it's urgent you tell the truth. Did you talk to Ericka lately?"

"What?"

"We can find out by this afternoon, but you'd save us a lot of time if you would just tell us. Did you speak to her on the phone recently?"

"Are you gonna ask me what it was about?" Gene said, and Pantera had his answer.

"Gene, are you aware of how easy it is to listen in on a cell phone conversation?"

"No. You mean it's easy to do?"

"Like child's play."

"You mean someone's been listening in on my calls?"

"I don't know, but if you've discussed anything that may have gotten Ericka and possibly you killed, it seems possible, yes," Harry said.

Pantera looked at Gene. "It was Paulson, wasn't it? Did you tell him about the contents of the envelope? Maybe try to squeeze a little cash out of him? That's why you didn't give it up when we asked about it, isn't it? You saw it as money in the bank."

"That's attempted blackmail," Harry said. "Still, I doubt Paulson will press charges. He doesn't want what was in there to come out, so instead he just eliminates you and, because you told her, Ericka."

"Come on, Gene," Pantera said. "If the victim denies the attempt at blackmail, it never happened, so tell us. That's what happened, isn't it?"

Gene hung his head. "Yeah." He looked at Pantera. "But if you arrest me for it, I'll swear you made it up."

"Did he pay you anything?"

"No."

"And he doesn't know we know about it," Pantera said. "Or does he?"

"I didn't mention it to Ericka, no. I didn't tell her you had it."

"And Tony?" Harry said.

"Yeah?"

"If he's the one who set this up, he doesn't know Gene's alive. He'll think he's dead."

"Have you used your phone today?"

"I didn't. You guys did, though."

"If he's the one listening in, he'll know Gene's alive," Pantera said. "If he has someone else monitoring calls, he might not."

"Or if it's not Paulson in the first place," Harry said.

"That's possible, but I'd lay heavy odds it was Paulson. He's the only person I can name who would have reason to kill both Ericka and Gene."

"What are you guys thinking?" Gene asked.

Harry looked around. "I don't see the press here."

Pantera said, "He'd be at work now, and even if he knows, seeing Gene could trigger a rage or at least make him nervous."

Harry looked at Gene. "Gene? Let's pay Mr. Claude Paulson a visit."

"Why?" Gene asked.

"To get his reaction at seeing you alive."

Three hours later, Davis listened to the recording of a Detective Overmeyer on Gene's phone and mostly ignored the content of the call. Whether or not Gene was a light sleeper meant nothing. He wondered why Gene's phone was being used by a cop asking about that, but didn't think it was important enough to notify Braxton. He could imagine Braxton's reaction, which would basically concern the incompetence of calling about something that stupid.

36

Gene looked more like a person who has been told he must have a tooth pulled without anesthesia. "I'd rather not go see Paulson. Letting him know I'm alive might make him want to finish the job. He'll just send whatever goon he has in Buddy's old job to kill me tonight."

Pantera said, "We can put you in protective custody, and besides, if he did do this, he'll know within two seconds why we brought you. He'll know if something does happen to you, he'll be the first person we suspect."

"Protective custody? Where?"

Harry said, "You'd be put up in a hotel somewhere, maybe even outside of Richmond."

"A hotel?"

"Yes."

"Four star?"

"More like two," Pantera said, "unless you're willing to foot the bill."

"Will a cop be staying there, too?"

"Of course. Not very protective if you're alone," Harry said.

"Can it be a lady cop?" Gene asked.

"Not on your life," Pantera said. "Now, get in the car."

They drove to Circe Enterprises and entered the main lobby. When they did, the guard behind the desk smiled at Gene. "Gene! How you been?" His name tag read "Garwood."

"I'm hanging in there, Jon," Gene said. "These are

two detectives who need to see Paulson about something. It's okay if you tell them they're here, but don't mention my name. I want to surprise Paulson."

"Sure thing," Garwood said. "Where you working now?"

"Ledbetter Place. I'm at the gate there."

"Cushy job!" Garwood said, picking up the phone.

"Remember," Gene said, "not a word about me."

Garwood gave Gene a "thumbs up" and dialed the extension. After a moment, he said, "Ms. Davidson, there are two detectives here to speak to Mr. Paulson. It's rather urgent." Garwood winked at Gene as if he were helping with a monumental joke.

Garwood listened for a moment and said, "Oh? It's kind of important, they say." He frowned at Gene, who pointed to himself and shook his head.

"Okay," Garwood said and hung up, looking at Pantera and Harry. "She says he's busy today and can't talk to you. Maybe you can come back tomorrow."

Pantera said, "Call back and tell them we have a warrant." They didn't have one, but that wouldn't matter. They weren't planning to conduct a search.

Garwood frowned at this news. "Can I see it?"

"I'll only show it to Paulson," Pantera answered. "It lists some sensitive details that Paulson would not want anyone else to see."

Garwood frowned again as he picked up the phone and dialed the same extension. "Ms. Davidson? They have a warrant and insist on seeing Mr. Paulson immediately." He waited a moment before saying, "Okay."

Turning to the three men, he said, "Someone will be down in a moment to escort you up."

They moved to the familiar chairs and waited, figuring it would be a while before anyone came. However, just two minutes later, Braxton showed up.

"What can I do for you guys?" He didn't flinch upon seeing Gene, so they knew he had no idea he was supposed to be dead.

"Nothing," Pantera said. "We're here to see Paulson. I take it Ms. Davidson called you to play defense."

"You need to leave now, or show me the warrant."

"If I show you the warrant, Paulson will likely fire you by the end of the day."

"I'm chief of security here. I know about anything you might have on that warrant."

"Not this, you don't. I can guarantee that. If you do, we need to arrest you right now."

Braxton considered this and asked, "Are you serious?"

"Very."

After a brief pause, he lifted the receiver and dialed the extension to Doreen Davidson. "Doreen? Braxton. I suggest you let me bring them up." He listened a moment and said, "Okay. Be there in a few."

"Follow me," he said, hanging up and starting for the elevators without looking back.

Two minutes later, they were entering Ms. Davidson's office. Braxton led the way, followed by Pantera and Harry. Gene brought up the rear, trying to stay mostly out of sight.

"Thank you, Leland," Ms. Davidson said, dismissing him. She frowned at Pantera and Harry. When she saw Gene, her brow dipped but not in shock at seeing him alive. It was more questioning, as if she wondered what he had to do with any of this.

The door to Paulson's office opened, and Paulson stood there. When he saw Gene, he froze, but only for a second. He was obviously shocked to see him, and it wasn't in the same way that Doreen Davidson had reacted.

While it strongly suggested Paulson was guilty of setting up the murder, it wasn't proof. It was more like a strong nail in the coffin that would hold Paulson's freedom.

"Uh—" he stammered before regaining his control. "What is this about, Detective?"

Pantera had to hand it to him. He was quick to recover from the shock. Now he was angry, and Pantera wondered if he thought he'd been lied to by the person he'd sent to kill Gene.

"You remember Gene Crawford, don't you, Paulson?" Pantera said.

He nodded. "Yeah. How's it going, Crawford?"

"You son of a bitch!" Gene said and lunged toward Paulson, who stepped back and slammed the door to his office.

Harry grabbed Gene and a struggle ensued. When he gained control of Gene, Harry quickly escorted him from the room while Gene shouted curses and threats. Once they were in the hallway and the door to Ms. Davidson's office shut, Harry pushed him along the hallway. When they arrived at the elevator, Ms. Davidson came out of her office.

"You're not allowed to go anywhere in the building unescorted!" she said.

As the doors to the elevators opened and they stepped on, Harry said, "So call a cop." He watched a frozen Doreen Davidson disappear as the doors slid closed.

Turning to Gene, Harry hissed, "We warned you, Gene! You're going to blow the whole thing. His reaction to seeing you was what we expected, but he's no idiot. He quickly figured out that we had set him up and he recovered. The only good thing is you didn't mention the killing."

"I couldn't help it. When I saw his expression, I

knew he'd definitely been the one to send someone to kill me, but he killed Andre by mistake. I don't take that shit lying down!"

"You'll take this without doing anything. Let us do our jobs, Gene. We'll nab him and he'll spend the rest of his life in prison. Just knock it off!"

Gene leaned against the wall of the elevator as it descended. When they reached the lobby, he burst through the opening doors and made a beeline to the front entrance. When they were outside, Harry managed to grab Gene's arm and make him slow down. A bench sat at a bus stop nearby, and he escorted Gene to it.

"I know you're pissed, Gene. I would be, too. But that's not how we're handling it.

Gene took a deep breath, let it out, and said, "Okay. Now, what?"

"We wait for Pantera to come down and keep himself from punching you."

Doreen Davidson strode back into her office, obviously shaken. "I need to get in to talk with Mr. Paulson," Pantera said.

Regaining her composure, she said, "Okay." She dialed three numbers on the phone and said, "Detective Pantera is out here. The others are gone." She listened a moment and hung up. "You can go in," she said and rose from her chair, leaving without another word.

Once inside Paulson's office, Pantera told Paulson to have a seat, which given the man's shaky knees, he did without protest.

"When you saw Gene, you looked like you'd seen a ghost. Why was that?"

"Just serve your search warrant and do what you have to do."

"I was just wondering why you reacted like that when you saw Gene."

"I was wondering what he was doing here."

"I see," Pantera said. "Who was it you had visit Gene last night?"

"I don't know what you're talking about."

"Sure you do. Big fellow. Carries a knife."

"Where's the warrant?" he said.

"To be honest, I don't have one. I just needed to get in to see you and see your reaction at seeing Gene."

Paulson stared at Pantera a moment and said, "Get out of my office! If you show up here again, I'll file a complaint with the chief. He's a friend of mine, you know. So is Chief of Detectives Childers."

Pantera stood and walked to the door. Before leaving, he said, "We're going to be arresting you in the next day or two, whether you have friends in police administration or not. Count on it."

"That's it! You're harassing me. I'm calling both the chief and Childers. You won't have a job come sundown!"

"Whatever you say," Pantera said and stepped into Doreen Davidson's office, closing the door behind him.

Doreen was back at her desk. Looking at her, he said, "You might want to find other employment. Paulson and the girls you enjoy will be history very soon."

Her look of shock and the blush in her cheeks were all he needed to know that Natalie Oliver had been telling the truth.

37

Paulson was nearly in a rage. What was Crawford doing alive? Had Foster lied? Had he even killed Ericka Oliver? He'd said he did. What was he thinking if he lied? That Paulson wouldn't figure it out?

After a few minutes of stewing and wondering what he would do about this, he stuck his head through his door and shouted at Doreen. "Get Foster in here! Now!"

"Yes, sir." She picked up the walkie-talkie and clicked it. "Ray?"

Seconds later, he answered. "Yes?"

"Mr. Paulson wants to see you immediately."

"I'm in the can."

"Well zip up and get in here. He's not happy."

A minute later, Ray Foster walked through the door. "What happened?"

"Those detectives were here, Pantera and Overmeyer. I don't know what they said, but Paulson is plenty pissed off."

"Were the detectives looking for me?" Ray asked.

"No. Why would they be looking for you?"

"Nothing. Why is Paulson so pissed?"

"I don't know, but it may have had something to do with the security guard who was fired. Crawford? Mr. Crawford stormed out of here—well, he was actually escorted out by one of the detectives. He was yelling at Mr. Paulson about getting him back. I don't know what it's about, but Mr. Paulson wants to see you."

Ray wanted to run. Gene was alive? How could that be? At least he understood why Paulson was so upset. He'd told Paulson that morning that he'd done the job.

Had he gone to the wrong house? Had he killed some innocent person who had nothing to do with any of this? He wasn't sure he could live with himself if he had. Killing Ericka Oliver and the thought of killing Gene were bad enough.

Stepping to Claude Paulson's door, he knocked lightly and opened it while wishing he had chosen run away with his family instead.

"Get in here," Paulson said, his voice low but angry. "And close the door."

Ray did as instructed and stood there. "What is it?" he asked, preferring not to let Paulson know he already knew Gene Crawford was alive.

"Did you kill Ericka Oliver last night?"

"Yes."

"Are you sure? I mean, are you fucking positive?"

"Yes. I recognized her."

"Well, I hope you managed to get at least one thing right, because Gene Crawford just left my office a few minutes ago. He was threatening me, telling me he would get me."

"I—uh," Ray stammered, not sure what to say.

"You, uh, what?"

"I went to his house last night and stabbed him. Or at least I thought it was him. It was dark in the room, and he was asleep. It must have been someone else sleeping in his bed. Or maybe—"

"Maybe what?"

"Maybe I went to the wrong house, but I don't think so. I double checked the address because I didn't want to go into the wrong house and kill the wrong person. Unless you gave me the wrong address."

"Of course I didn't, you moron. Now the son-of-a-bitch is planning to get revenge. I don't know who you killed, but it must have been a friend of his or something."

Ray swallowed. "I'm sorry."

"Sorry doesn't cut it. I have to think about what to do. It's obvious the detectives think I sent someone to kill Gene."

"Well, you did."

"I know that! Shut the fuck up while I think!"

He sat at his desk, thinking of various solutions, none of them feasible. He couldn't kill the detectives, though he'd wanted to for a while now. A moron could figure out he'd done it, and he'd be in worse hot water than he was already.

Ray stood just inside the door, waiting to be dismissed. It occurred to him that Paulson might ask him to kill the detectives or threaten their families. He would kill Paulson before doing that. He knew he would be going to prison for killing whoever it was he'd killed last night. What was one more person? At least Paulson wasn't anyone who would ever do anything worthwhile for the world. Killing Paulson would be doing the world a favor.

But he knew he couldn't do anything until after he was arrested. He hoped to be able to turn state's evidence to get a lighter sentence and would offer to wear a wire and talk to Paulson. It was amazing how much clearer his thoughts were now that he had made his decision to turn state's evidence.

Finally, Paulson said, "What time is it in France?"

Ray shrugged. How would he know that?

"Never mind. Get out. I'll let you know what's in the works. I have to loop Circe in on this. I hope she doesn't fire me—or worse—for your fuck-up."

Ray left the office, and as the door closed, Paulson called out, "Don't go far. Be within a minute of my office!"

When Paulson's call to Circe was connected, she answered with, "What now?"

"I'm sorry to bother you, my lady, but my new bodyguard has fucked up royally, and I need some advice. I felt you would be the best person to advise me on how to handle this."

"*Merde*," she said. "Tell me what happened."

After an explanation, she said, "Why were you having them killed?"

"Because they had information that was going to be used to blackmail the two of us," Paulson said, including her even if the information they had did not exactly endanger her freedom.

"What kind of information?"

"About some of the less than legal things that were being done," he said vaguely.

"Can you have your bodyguard take the fall?"

Paulson considered this. "Maybe. I know I can have him take the fall for last night's murders."

"Then your problem is solved. Try thinking on your own without bothering me next time. *Au revoir*." The line went dead.

He hung up and sat there, planning how he would pin this whole mess on Ray Foster.

Ray didn't follow Paulson's instructions for once. Instead, he left the building and drove to the police station, figuring he would arrive not long after the detectives did.

When he stepped inside the entrance, he went to the woman at the reception desk.

"How can I help you?" she said.

"I'm here to talk to Detective Pantera."

"What's it about?"

"I killed a man last night, and I know it's his case."

The woman eyed him, not sure whether to believe him. "What man?"

Ray gave her the address where the killing had taken place. He finished by saying, "He'll have my prints from the headboard, I'm sure."

She picked up the phone and pressed some numbers. Moments later, she said, "Detective Pantera? There's a security guard to see you. Says he killed a man last night. He sounds legit."

Minutes later, Ray was seated in the detectives' squad room beside Pantera's desk.

38

Harry had taken Gene to a hotel in the nearby town of Midlothian, taking an officer with him to guard him until being relieved by another officer at 11 PM. They would arrange for five officers to stay with Gene over the next few days, alternating shifts. Pantera had phoned Lieutenant Gariepy on the ride from Circe Enterprises to receive authorization to spend the money on the hotel.

As Pantera sat with the security guard named Ray Foster, he tried to figure out if this was some kind of setup. The man had come in minutes after Pantera had arrived at his desk after turning the car over to Harry to take Gene to the hotel.

"So you're telling me that you killed a man you believed was Gene Crawford last night?"

"Yes."

"Your name is Ray Foster?" Pantera said, taking out a form for when someone was confessing to a crime. He wrote nothing yet.

"Yes, sir."

"What can you tell me about the crime scene?"

"It was bloody."

"Good guess. Anything else?"

"I purposely left my bloody fingerprints on the headboard."

Pantera could actually feel his body react to this. "Why would you do that?"

"Because I can't go on with this anymore. He's threatening my family."

"Who is?" Pantera asked, anticipating the answer he

expected.

"Paulson. He told me if I didn't do exactly what he told me to, no matter how bad it was, he'd make me watch while my wife and children were tortured to death. Then he'd kill me."

"And you believed he would do this?"

"Yes. He said he had already killed Widner and Buddy Garrett. He said Buddy was my 'predecessor,' and I could die too. He said Buddy died for much less."

"Did he say why Buddy died?"

"No. He just said he didn't want to kill him but had to, that he's sort of in the same situation that I'm in now. He had to do it or die himself."

"When did he tell you this?"

"Several times, really. He'd remind me my life was hanging in the balance every day just about."

"So you decided to get caught?"

"Yes."

Pantera believed him. It was basically what the information in the envelope claimed. However, with the envelope, they didn't have the person there to corroborate what was said. Now, they did. Still, he wondered about several things, the fingerprints chief among them.

"I have to tell you, this sounds ridiculous. You're going to prison, you know. We can match those fingerprints to you. Why would you do that? Why not run?"

"Because he'd find me eventually. Circe Enterprises is a worldwide corporation. He could offer a million dollars to anyone who found me and my family if we ran."

"What about WITSEC?" Pantera asked, referring to witness protection.

"Detective, he'd have every employee in Circe and anyone they knew looking for me. I'd be found in a year or two, maybe less."

"You don't think he can get you killed in prison?"

"Maybe, but I figure he'd be in prison himself. I doubt anyone else in Circe even knows what I do now. They wouldn't care. The only ones who might care are the families of my victims."

"Victims? As in more than one?" Pantera asked.

"Yeah. I killed a young woman last night as well. It tore me up all the way back to Richmond. She didn't deserve that."

Pantera could feel the hair on the back of his neck come to attention. "Who was she?"

"Her name was Ericka something. She lives in Roanoke." He took a deep breath and stared at his shoes. "Or she did."

Pantera leaned back in his chair. Part of him wanted to smash his chair over Foster's head, but Foster wouldn't have done what he had if Paulson hadn't told him to. At least, that's how it was if Foster was telling the truth, which Pantera believed he was. What reason did Foster have to kill anyone?

"So you left the fingerprints to end your being forced to kill people?"

"Well, that, but mostly to protect my family. If I was out of the picture, he would have no reason to harm them. They don't know anything about this."

"How can Paulson be sure of that?"

"He threatened worse if I told them. He said he knew a man who—" Foster paused and swallowed what must have been a sizable lump in his throat. "A man who liked little kids. He said if I told anyone, he'd call that guy first."

"Are you certain he knows someone like that? It's not a thing people talk about if that's their interest."

"I don't know, but I didn't want to find out either. I mean, would you?"

Pantera had to admit the threat was enough.

Foster added, "Wouldn't you go to prison to save your wife and kids?"

That was another thing Pantera had to agree with. He felt bad for the man. Yes, he'd made the totally wrong choice, but once he had, he was stuck. He imagined Garrett had felt much the same way.

"Why did you accept his offer in the first place?"

"Because he would have killed me on the spot if I didn't and left me on the side of the road."

This made Pantera think of Miranda. Had Paulson killed her or had her killed? Had she been a similar victim but refused to do what Paulson demanded?

"Forgive me for not understanding. You just said you were willing to sacrifice yourself for your family."

"I wasn't thinking like that at the time. It was all sudden. He took me out to this secluded spot and told me what I had to do if I wanted to stay alive. I just accepted. I didn't see a choice at the time."

Pantera considered his next move. "Does Paulson know you're here?"

"No, but I was thinking I could record him."

"I'd have to let you go, and I can't do that."

"Detective, I came in here by choice because if I waited for you to match my prints, you would probably think I was making this all up. I purposely left those prints, which should be kind of obvious considering how clearly I pressed my bloody fingers on the headboard. I'm not running. If I do that, I'm unlikely to get any sympathy from a judge or jury. You can let me go. I'll record Paulson and come back with the recording. If I don't go back to work, there's no way he'll talk to me about this."

"You think he'll talk about it?"

"I'm certain he will."

Pantera sat back, considering the offer. If he ran,

which Pantera thought unlikely, Gariepy would have a cow, and Childers would have him on traffic detail at best and suspended at worst. It was risky, but he didn't believe it was a bad idea.

After a moment, Foster sat forward and looked Pantera in the eye. "I want this son-of-a-bitch as much as you do. A lot more, probably."

Pantera glanced at Gariepy's door, wondering if he should get permission before throwing his career in the toilet, but he knew he'd get an answer he didn't want to hear. This was his decision, and his alone. He didn't even want to involve Harry because if it went south, he didn't want Harry in Childers's crosshairs.

"If you run, I'll hunt you down, and it won't go well for you. My career is on the line here."

"I won't run."

"We're lucky Virginia is a single-party state."

"What's that mean?"

"It means that only one party has to give permission to be recorded, so it will be legal to admit as evidence, even without a warrant."

Foster gave a weak smile.

Pantera opened a drawer and took out a recorder that would fit easily into a pocket. He sometimes used it on a case. He removed the batteries and pulled a couple of fresh ones from another drawer, inserting them. The device could be set to voice-activated or continuous record. Setting it to continuous, he handed it to Foster.

"Put this in your pocket and stand up."

Pantera stood about three feet away from him and said, "Testing 1-2-3. Test." He held out his hand. "I need to check the quality."

Foster pulled it out of his pocket, handing it to Pantera, who pressed a series of buttons and listened. His words were slightly muffled but clear enough for a jury.

He instructed Foster on its use and told him to make sure it was ready before being in the room with Paulson. "You'll know it's working by the blinking red light when it's on voice-activated or a solid red light if on continuous record. Keep it on continuous to avoid creating gaps, which could become a problem for the jury. The light will stop showing after ten seconds so there's no chance he sees a light and knows he's being recorded."

"Does this record on tape or a chip?"

"A chip, but still, don't use voice-activated. We want the jury to hear all of the sounds on the recording once it's played for them."

Foster placed the recorder in his pocket.

Pantera said, "I don't have to tell you what will happen if he discovers you're recording him. It's okay to sound worried in the conversation. Frightened, even. In fact, if you're too calm, it could alarm him."

"Don't worry. I won't have to pretend to be scared."

"And not returning is not an option."

"I know. Thank you, Detective."

As Foster turned to leave, Pantera said, "You're really okay with going to prison over this?"

"I killed those people. Don't I deserve it?" Foster left the room without looking back or saying another word.

39

While returning to Circe Enterprises, Ray checked to see if Paulson had texted or called him. He hadn't. Ray figured Paulson might not want to see him, which helped make sure Paulson didn't try to find him. He needed to record the conversation today. If he didn't, Pantera could get suspicious and haul him in.

He had left the building through the loading dock area to avoid anyone knowing he had left work in case someone asked Garwood about it. He'd thought about telling Garwood not to say anything, but felt sneaking away was a better option.

When he arrived at Circe, he entered the building through the loading dock for that reason and took the stairs to the third floor before using the elevator to take him to the executive suite of offices. He didn't worry about the cameras monitoring his movements in the building. If anyone ever did have reason to look at them before they were erased, he would already have the evidence he sought.

As he stepped into the corridor that led to Paulson's office, he pulled out the recorder and switched it on. Because he was shaking, it took three tries to flick the small switch. Checking that the solid red light was on and watching it until it went out ten seconds later, he pocketed it and stepped into Ms. Davidson's office.

Looking up as he came in, Doreen said, "I'm not sure you want to be here right now. He's very angry, and apparently it has something to do with you."

"How do you know it has to do with me?"

"He said he didn't want to see you again today."

"Really?"

"Yes. He said if you showed up to tell you to go home and wait for further instructions."

Ray felt as though the walls were closing in and suffocating him.

"I really need to see him."

"I can't let you in there."

Ray glanced around for a second before coming up with an idea.

"Don't you need to go to the bathroom?"

"What are you going to do?"

"Just go in and talk to him. See if I can get him to calm down."

She considered his suggestion. She could claim to have been in the bathroom when Ray came in, and they hadn't seen each other. Paulson was in a horrible mood, and ordinarily she wouldn't do this for fear of his anger. But if Ray Foster meant to calm the waters a bit, perhaps it would make this horrible day get a bit better. She enjoyed the perks that working for Paulson garnered, especially being able to join in on the fun with the girls that practically nobody else in the firm knew about. But days like today made her think of putting out her resumé. Perhaps she could suggest another office orgy to see if that would help change Paulson's mood once Ray was finished calming him down. It might be just what Paulson needed. She could sure use the stress reliever of having sex with Paulson and a few of the girls. A fun party was always a great mood-changer, provided Paulson's mood could be changed enough to consider it. She hoped Ray could do that.

"If he asks, I wasn't here when you came in," she said. She didn't worry that Paulson might hear their conversation in her office. His office was soundproofed.

She grabbed her purse and exited the room, walking down the hall to the ladies' room.

Ray stepped over to Paulson's door, took a deep breath, and walked in.

When Paulson saw him, he pointed a finger at him and said, "I don't want to see you!" Standing, he shouted, "Doreen!"

"She isn't in her office. She must be in the bathroom," Ray said, surprised at how calm he sounded.

"Then get the Hell out! I'm trying to figure out how to fix the mess you created!"

"You're the one who sent me to kill them, so it's partly your fault, too."

"I'm not the one who fucked up and killed the wrong man!" Realizing the door was still open, he said, "Shut the door!"

Ray closed the door. He was in, and he might already have enough to convict Paulson of more or less hiring him to kill.

Sitting across from Paulson, he said, "The girl, Ericka, came off without a hitch. I stabbed her in the chest. It was still early enough that she was up. If I had the right house, then whoever was in Gene Crawford's bed was asleep. I didn't want to wake him. Gene may not be a big man like me, but he would be harder to control physically than a small girl like Ericka. How did I know Gene wouldn't be there? It's either that, or I fucked up and went to the wrong house."

"Gene Crawford has something that could land me in a lot of trouble, if not prison. That has to be dealt with."

"Maybe I could make it look like an accident," Ray said.

"After what happened? The police know Gene was the target." Paulson paused. "That must mean it was Gene's house but someone else in his bed."

"It was dark, Mr. Paulson. It could have happened if you were the one who went there to kill him just as easy.

I wouldn't have been there if you weren't threatening my wife and kids if I didn't do whatever you tell me to do."

Paulson glared at Ray. "I'll be honest. When your fuckup came to light, I considered taking one of your kids out as a lesson to you not to fuck up again. You remember my friend, right?"

Ray had to restrain himself from leaping over the desk and pummeling Paulson to death. There was no gun aimed at him now, and he was going to go to prison for the murders of the woman in Roanoke and whoever was in Gene Crawford's bed last night anyway. The only reason he didn't was he wanted Paulson to suffer every day of his miserable life in prison. Paulson wasn't a muscular man, and he might end up being passed around once he was where he belonged.

"How do you know a guy likes molesting kids?"

"He's my uncle. It doesn't take a genius to figure out how I know."

Ray thought how he could kill two birds with one stone—or one recording. "What's your uncle's name?"

"You think I'm going to tell you and let you hold his freedom over his head?" He looked at the door. "Get out. I'll consider your offer to make Crawford's death look like an accident. I guess if you make it good enough, they can suspect all they want. Without proof, they have nothing."

Ray stood to leave, praying that the recording would be good enough to get Paulson convicted. Maybe it wouldn't take much to figure out the identity of the uncle as well.

Ray opened the door and turned back to Paulson. "In either case, I'll eventually see you in Hell, Paulson."

Paulson said nothing until Ray was beyond the closed door. "We're already there, Ray. You haven't figured that out yet?" he said to the empty room.

Ray switched off the recorder once he was in the

elevator and left the building through the front entrance, stopping to speak to Garwood as he left. Garwood was a nice enough guy, and he had something to say to him.

"See you around," Ray said, knowing it was a lie.

"Sure, man! You headed home early? What? You sick or something?"

Ray nodded. "Or something. But don't worry. It's not contagious."

"Hope you feel better," Garwood said.

"Maybe I will," Ray said. "We'll have to see. And Jon?"

"Yeah?" Garwood said.

"You might want to find somewhere else to work. This isn't a great place."

Jon Garwood's expression of bewilderment would have been humorous not that long ago. Now, however, nothing seemed funny anymore.

Ray called his wife and told her to leave work early and meet him at home, telling her he was headed there himself and wanted to cuddle—their term for making love. He would enjoy what little freedom he had left before taking the recording to Pantera. He knew he had several more hours available to him. She protested that they could just do it that night, but he insisted, telling her to fake illness.

He made love to his wife for what he knew would be the last time unless the prison allowed conjugal visits. She could sense something was wrong, but he wouldn't tell her what, only professing his love for her, telling her how meeting her was the best thing to ever happen to him and marrying her was the best decision he had ever made. He didn't bother mentioning the worst one.

When they were finished and lay together holding each other and engaging in the pillow talk he knew he would miss more than the sex, she said, "We need to get up. Kids will be home from school in about a half hour."

They dressed and waited for their children to walk through the door. He pulled them both onto his lap and talked with them about their day, cherishing each word, each second. He somehow managed not to burst into tears until he was on his way to meet with Pantera. He knew his wife's sister would be able to bring her to retrieve the car once the reality of his life came to light.

He hated not telling her what was going on, but he wanted her to enjoy her day until he called her from jail. He knew her life would never be the same either and hoped she didn't come to hate him, choosing instead to see he did what he did because of his love for her and the children.

Instead of telling her why he had to leave, he told her he had some work to do and would let her know more later.

Walking into the squad room where Pantera waited, Ray could see the detective breathe a sigh of relief.

When Ray sat down, Pantera introduced him to the other detective, Harry Overmeyer.

"Did you get it?" Pantera asked.

"Yes. I hope it came out clear enough."

"Then you haven't checked it?"

"No. I was afraid I'd mess up and delete it instead."

"What's this about?" Harry asked.

"Sorry, Harry, but I had to keep you out of the loop on this one for your own protection. If Ray here hadn't returned, I'd have been forced to retire, probably." He went on to explain what he'd learned from Ray Foster earlier that day.

Ray pulled the recorder out of his pocket and handed it to Pantera, who clicked it to play the most recent recording.

They listened to the conversation with Doreen Davidson and heard Ray walk into Paulson's office. As with the test recording, the voices were slightly muffled but clear enough for the words to be understood, especially when Paulson was doing them the favor of shouting.

Pantera and Harry smiled at each other.

"We got him," Harry said.

Pantera said, "Caught like a lion in a cage."

Pantera turned to Ray and said, "You did good. I'll testify in court about your turning yourself in and taking steps to make sure the person who forced you to do this was caught. You won't be exonerated, but it should help."

"Thanks, Detective."

"Any idea who his uncle is?" Harry asked.

40

After finishing with Ray Foster, Pantera had an officer take Foster for processing before taking him to a holding cell. They allowed Foster to call his wife and fill her in on the details. Harry and Pantera left him alone during this conversation, which lasted nearly an hour. Based on the look on Foster's face when the call ended, things had not gone well.

As Foster was taken away for processing, Pantera asked, "Do you have Paulson's home address? He's likely left work for the day."

Foster provided it and said, "If he's not there, he could still be in his office. He often works late, sometimes until midnight or later. There's a security guard at the desk 24/7, though."

"I'll handle that. We're there to arrest Paulson, so refusing to let us see him won't wash. And if I still can't get in to see him, we'll monitor both exits and get him when he comes out."

When Foster was taken away, Harry said, "So, are you ready to arrest Paulson?"

Pantera smiled. "I've been ready for a week. Let's go."

Taking a uniformed policeman with them, they left.

Arriving at Paulson's house, they rang the doorbell at the magnificent residence located in one of the city's nicest areas. A middle-aged woman answered the door.

"May I help you?" she said.

Pantera said, "We're here to see Claude Paulson."

"He's not here."

"May I ask who you are?"

"I'm his cook and housekeeper."

"Do you know where we can find him?" Harry asked.

"I imagine at his office. He doesn't keep me informed of his comings and goings."

"Thank you," Pantera said. "Sorry to bother you."

"No bother at all," she said, closing the door as they walked away.

"You think we should have suggested she start looking for another job?" Harry said.

"She'll figure that out soon enough."

Arriving at Circe Enterprises, they went to the main entrance and found the doors locked. A security guard they'd not met was at the desk.

Pantera knocked loudly on the heavy glass door, holding up his badge. The guard rose slowly and sauntered to the door, peering at the badge as if he couldn't figure out what it was.

"We're Richmond PD. Could you let us in?"

"What's your business?" the guard asked.

Pantera looked at the guard's name and said, "We're here to arrest someone, but we can always add another for obstruction—Mr. Hodges."

The guard shrugged as if he didn't care and unlocked the doors, allowing them inside.

They immediately started for the elevators that would take them to the executive suite.

"Hey, you can't go anywhere until I get you an escort!" the guard shouted after them.

Pantera pointed at the uniformed cop. "He's our escort." He glared at the guard again. "Or do you really want us to take you in for obstruction? We'd rather not have the subject of the arrest be informed we're coming to get him. Sort of ruins the surprise."

"I could lose my job!"

"Get arrested for obstruction, and you'll lose it, too.

Your choice." He left, not waiting for an answer.

As they entered Doreen Davidson's office, they were greeted by a clean, empty desk. Stepping to the door to Paulson's office, Pantera tried the knob. It was locked.

Lifting the phone's receiver on Ms. Davidson's desk, he dialed the three numbers to Paulson's office having memorized them when she'd called Paulson earlier that day.

"Who is this?" Paulson said when he answered, obviously upset and surprised by the call.

"I need to talk to you, Paulson."

"Again, who is this?" Paulson asked.

"Detective Pantera."

"I don't have time for you right now."

"I'm afraid you'll have to make the time."

"Since when do you tell me what to do, especially in my office?"

"Since now. Open up, or we bust down the door."

"You're not alone?"

"No. I have my partner, Detective Overmeyer, with me." He didn't mention the uniformed officer.

"Hello, Paulson!" Harry called out, as if they were old friends.

"Unlock the door, Paulson," Pantera said.

He heard a click and turned the knob.

As they entered, Paulson was backing away from the door, a Smith and Wesson .38 in his hand. It was aimed at them.

The uniformed officer immediately pulled his weapon and aimed it at Paulson. "Drop it!" he shouted.

Paulson's momentary indecision allowed both Harry and Pantera time to step away from each other, making it more difficult for Paulson to shoot all three of them. Each pulled their own weapons, aiming them.

"Do what he said," Pantera said. "You might get

one shot off, but not three. You'll be down before you can squeeze the trigger for a second one.

Paulson was sweating, the perspiration running down his cheeks. "You're here to arrest me!"

"All we said was we wanted to talk. You're the one who pulled a gun."

Harry said, "Give it up, Paulson. Nothing good can come from anything if you shoot. The way your hands are trembling, you'd likely miss anyway, and you'd be down before you know it."

"Are you here to arrest me?"

Pantera felt it was time for a lie in an effort to calm Paulson down. "We just want to talk."

"If I put the gun down, what are you going to do?"

"First, we'll take the gun to make sure you don't pull it again," Pantera said. "Then we'll have a seat and talk about what we came to talk about."

Paulson slowly lowered the weapon. Both Pantera and Harry rushed him, Harry grabbing him and Pantera taking the gun. The officer stepped forward, handcuffing Paulson.

"What are the cuffs for?!"

Harry said, "For the protection of everyone here."

Pantera smiled and said, "Claude Paulson, you're under arrest for arranging the murders of Natalie Oliver and Andre Crawford, as well as the attempted murder of Eugene Crawford."

"What? You said you weren't here to arrest me!"

"So, I lied to get you to calm down. You have the right to remain silent. If you give up that right, whatever you say can and will be taken down and used against you in a court of law. You have the right to have an attorney present before any questioning. If you wish for an attorney but cannot afford one, one will be appointed before any questioning. Do you understand these rights?"

"Yes. I need to call my lawyer."

"Fine. We won't ask any questions until he arrives. You will be taken to the city jail and processed. In the morning, we can get your attorney and ask questions."

"Let's go, Paulson," Harry said, and they led him to the elevator.

When they stepped off the elevator, Hodges was once again seated at the entrance desk. His look of shock was nearly comical as they walked by. He had obviously not expected them to have Paulson in tow.

"See you around, Hodges," Pantera said as they left the building. Harry sat beside Paulson in the back and Pantera drove the four of them back to the station to have Paulson processed and placed in a holding cell until morning.

41

Paulson refused to talk until his lawyer arrived, which was no surprise to Pantera or Harry. The uniformed officer processed Paulson, taking him for his mug shot, fingerprinting, and the other activities necessary when a person was booked into the jail.

When he made his phone call, Paulson called the criminal attorney Riley Newsome, a well-known criminal attorney and the most expensive one in the city. Newsome specialized in white collar crime, not murder, but Paulson must have offered enough money to get him to come to the police station after his usual working hours.

When Newsome showed up, he was wearing a suit that would have cost Pantera a month's pay if he bought it at a consignment store. The lawyer and the detectives were familiar with each other from their encounters in court. Neither Pantera nor Harry liked Newsome, and the feelings were mutual. Pantera had once called him the equivalent of a criminal defense ambulance chaser who only chased ambulances that came to the richer neighborhoods of the Richmond area. Newsome had just smiled while preening his full, white, handlebar mustache and said, "I don't chase the ambulances, Pantera. The ambulances come to me."

When he entered any room, it became a stage for Newsome, a room to command. He was 6' 4" and weighed over 300 pounds, much of it around his waist, and he used his bulk to harvest the attention of everyone in the room. His voice did not seem to understand the concept of quiet.

After informing them, as well as anyone else within earshot, that he had been hired to represent Claude Paulson, he sat down in a chair barely large enough to hold him and in his booming Southern drawl said, "So, what trumped-up crime are you saying my client allegedly committed?" He said this as if Paulson had not told him the charges. It was all part of Newsome's theatrics.

"He threatened one of his employees to get him to murder two people," Pantera said.

Newsome laughed as if this was the funniest thing he'd heard all day. "Seriously, Pantera, what's the story on my client?"

"That is the story, Riley. He forced one of his security guards to murder two people by threatening the security guard's life as well as the life of his wife and two young children." Pantera called Newsome by his first name because he knew it irritated the man.

"I suppose you think you have proof."

"Yep. Solid."

"Yes, well, the cops thought they had solid proof against O. J., but it turned out they didn't."

"First, we're not arresting O. J., and second, the legal system learned a lot from the mistakes made in that case. Believe me, we have him dead-to-rights. The evidence is so strong you might end up suggesting he confess."

Newsome laughed again. "Confess," he said to himself as if repeating the punch line of a good joke. "I've never told a client to confess in my life, and I'm not about to begin now."

Pantera smiled back at Newsome. "I was indeed joking there, Riley. Confessing doesn't earn you much money, does it?"

"That's beside the point. It's the principal of the thing. I never admit defeat, Pantera. You know that."

"Okay, then maybe take a plea bargain."

"I only do that late in the game, and then only when it's absolutely necessary."

"Of course," Pantera said. "After all, you have to pay for your next suit."

"You're just jealous, Pantera."

"You might not believe it, Riley, but I could afford suits like the one you're wearing. I just prefer not to spend my money on things like that."

"Where in the world would you get money like that, Pantera? Are you on the take?"

"Inheritance."

"Ahh, I see." Newsome looked around the squad room. "Yet you choose to do this for a living anyway."

Pantera shrugged. "I'd rather leave my money to my daughters than spend it on me."

"Good for you, Pantera. Me? I make the money, so I want to do the spending."

"Whatever makes you happy, Riley."

"So, what is the ironclad evidence you have against my client?"

"You'll get it in discovery, Riley."

"That's okay. I'll just ask my client."

"You do that," Pantera said.

"So, when do I get to speak to my client? I'm on the clock, and I doubt he'd be happy if I spent the entire time chatting with you fellas."

"I've not said a word," Harry said.

Newsome smiled. "You have now." He gripped the head of his expensive cane and said, "So, In which room will you be eavesdropping on my conversation with Mr. Paulson?"

"We don't do that," Pantera said. "Take interview room C. I'll have Paulson in there in a few minutes. You can have five minutes with him and we'll be in to ask questions ourselves with you present."

"You can ask all the questions you want. He won't be answering any, unless you want his recipe for chicken and dumplings or something."

Newsome knew the office layout well and rose, shuffling down a hallway to the small room and taking a seat. Paulson was ushered in a few minutes later.

After Newsome had spent five minutes talking to Paulson, Pantera tapped on the door and stepped in, Harry behind him.

"As I said, Pantera, he won't be talking."

"That's fine. He needs his beauty sleep, though."

"You need it more than he does," Newsome said.

"That might be the first thing you've said that makes sense. He'll be arraigned at ten tomorrow morning. See you in court."

The next morning, Pantera received a call from Miles Hoffer, the Roanoke detective. Pantera mentally kicked himself for not calling when they found out who had killed Natalie Oliver. With everything else going on, it had slipped his mind.

"Pantera," he said as he answered the call.

"Detective Pantera, this is Detective Hoffer in Roanoke. How are you?"

"Great. I think we may have something for you."

"Okay, but I have something for you first."

"Alright, you first."

"While investigating the murder of Ms. Oliver, we talked to two waitresses she worked with. They each told us independently that Natalie suspected someone of killing her friend in Richmond." Pantera heard some papers being shuffled. "Ah, here it is. Miranda Buckhorn. They each said Ms. Oliver felt strongly that another friend of theirs killed Ms. Buckhorn. A guy by the name of Gene Crawford. We'd like to come see Mr. Crawford and ask questions about Ms. Oliver's death, and I'm sure you have some questions as well."

Pantera blinked before replying, "That won't be necessary. I was about to call you. We have a solid case against the person who killed Ms. Oliver. It was a murder for hire situation. The killer confessed to the murder."

"Really? Is it solid?"

"Totally. We even have a recording of the man who arranged for Ms. Oliver's murder talking about it."

"Well, that's great news. Now I can work on the other five cases I have in front of me."

"Glad to help," Pantera said.

"Me too."

"Did the other women say anything about proof that Gene Crawford killed Miranda? Did they mention a possible motive?"

"No. They just said she was fairly certain he'd done it."

They disconnected, and Pantera sat in thought until Harry came back from getting his morning coffee.

Harry spoke first. "You're not going to believe this."

"Oh?"

"Yeah. They got a new coffee maker. A Kuerig, with a lot of great k-cup coffee, even vanilla bean."

"You know I don't care for flavored coffees."

"Well, I do," Harry said and sipped his brew as if it tasted like heaven.

"I think I can one-up you on that 'you're not going to believe this' comment."

"Okay, what is it?"

"Natalie Oliver apparently strongly suspected Gene Crawford of killing Miranda."

Harry froze, his coffee cup nearly to his lips. "You're shitting me."

"Nope."

"Why didn't she tell you?"

"I have no idea. Maybe she didn't say anything because she had no proof. Who knows? Can't ask her now, but the truth is she told at least two women she worked with that she strongly suspected Gene of the killing."

"You're right. I don't believe it."

"What do you say we go ask Gene a few tough questions?"

"As long as you drive," Harry answered and headed for the door.

Pantera stopped him. "Wait a second. I think we need to plan this and not rush into it. He's not going anywhere. He has no idea we suspect him, if only because someone he knew mentioned her suspicions to friends."

"Okay, what's the game plan?"

"Let me make a call."

Harry sat and enjoyed his coffee while Pantera dialed a number.

"Who you calling?"

"The lab. See if we can put a rush on the DNA results from Miranda's murder. I know they found semen in her vagina."

"But we don't have a sample of Gene's DNA to test it against."

"That can be arranged," Pantera said and held up a finger to indicate someone had answered.

"Molly? Detective Pantera here. How are you doing?"

"Swamped, what else? What case are you calling about?"

"You know me too well."

"I've been in charge of this lab for six years, Tony. I know a lot of people too well. Now, what's the case?"

"Miranda Buckhorn."

He heard her typing, and she said, "Not yet. I might have it for you next week, though."

"Listen, Molly, can you put a rush on it? We might actually have a suspect, and we need to either arrest him or rule him out so we can move on with the investigation."

He heard Molly sigh. "How fast are we talking?"

"Well, yesterday would have been ideal, but I'll settle for tomorrow."

He heard some more typing and waited.

"I can have it for you Friday, but that's the best I can do."

"You're an angel, Molly. Thanks."

"I'll expect a nice bottle of wine for Christmas for this, Tony. And I'm not talking about anything under fifty bucks."

"Hey, for you? A hundred will be the basement. Thanks, Molly. I owe you one."

"Yeah, one bottle of good wine. Later," she said and hung up.

"We can go see Gene on Friday," Pantera said.

"Hey, Tony," Harry said after a few minutes. "We ever get an analysis of the marks on Miranda's neck?"

"Yeah. It looks like the killer used a belt to strangle her."

"You think they can match the belt to the marks?"

"I would wager a lot that they can."

Harry smiled. "Be sure to include any and all belts on the search warrant for the DNA sample."

"I figured it was your turn to write up the warrant."

42

That Friday, the results arrived in a secure email. What was known was that the semen belonged to a black man who had been given a vasectomy since no sperm, alive or dead, was found in the swabs of Miranda's vagina. They had known there were no sperm already from preliminary reports, but they would need to find out if Gene had a vasectomy. Still, the DNA and belt pattern should be enough to prove that he was either guilty or innocent.

Harry had written the search warrant, seeking a DNA sample and all of the belts Gene owned. Pantera had even bought a cheap belt from Walmart to prevent any complaint that Gene's pants might fall down without one.

"We're getting slow," Harry said.

"What do you mean?"

"We should have at least looked at Gene's belts. You said yourself that everyone's a suspect until they're not."

"Where we're getting slow is that we never suspected Gene. Not enough to suggest we get a search warrant at least. 'He knew the victim' isn't enough for that, even when he misled us on how well he knew her. My question is, what was the motive? I know he suffered from extreme jealousy, but he didn't seem to mind that Ericka was a hooker."

"Didn't you say Andre said Gene was okay with that because of the money?"

"Yeah. But I still don't think he'd kill Miranda because she and Ericka were friends with benefits."

"You're probably right," Harry said.

"Who knows? Maybe we'll get his DNA and belts and end up back at square one."

"The case against him now is weak, Tony. All we have is the suspicions of his former girlfriend."

"Yeah, that sort of makes me pause, too. Why would she answer his calls and texts?"

"Maybe keep him from suspecting she thought he did it? Stop him from trying to kill her, too?"

"Maybe. I guess we'll see once we have the belts and DNA."

Pantera called Judge Lazlow's office and spoke to the judge before Lazlow entered his courtroom. He was told they could come by around noon and get the warrant signed.

They arrived at Judge Lazlow's chambers and the warrant was signed after a few questions, but the questions were mostly cursory ones.

As they left the courthouse, Pantera said, "We can serve our warrant after he gets home from work."

While Pantera drove, Harry called Gene. "Gene! What time do you get home today? We have some important stuff to discuss."

"What kind of stuff? I thought you had all you needed on Paulson."

"We do, but there are a few loose ends we need to tie up."

"It has to be today?"

"Yeah. Pantera and I are both off tomorrow, and Childers, our Chief of Detectives, won't allow even a single minute of overtime."

"Sounds like most every boss these days," Gene said. "Okay, I get off at three today. I can meet you there at 3:30. Will it take long?"

"I doubt it. Ten minutes. Fifteen tops."

"Okay. See you guys at 3:30."

At 3:25, Pantera and Harry arrived at Gene's house, parking at the curb. At 3:32, Gene pulled in. "So, what is it?" he asked as he approached them. Seeing that Pantera was carrying a shopping bag from Walmart, he said, "And what's that?"

"It's a little gift for you, but we need to go inside. Hot out here anyway," Pantera replied.

"A gift?"

"Yeah, I'll give it to you inside."

Gene led the way into the house. Once they were seated at the kitchen table, Harry pulled out the warrant.

"What's this?"

"It's a warrant. We need a cheek swab to obtain a sample of your DNA and all of the belts you own."

"What for?"

"An allegation has been made. Mostly, we think the evidence will exonerate you, so our Lieutenant will let us move on."

"What kind of allegation?"

"You've been accused of being Miranda's killer."

"What? Are you kidding me?"

Pantera had confronted hundreds of suspects in his time on the force and had a fairly good feel for when a suspect was nervous and the denials rang as false. Sometimes the feeling was minor. Other times, it was as if the subject was saying outright that yes, they were guilty but they are going to deny it anyway. Part of Pantera had hoped this was a wild goose chase. He liked Gene and didn't want to think he had killed Miranda, so when the alarms went off in his head that told him Gene was nervous that the evidence they sought would end up convicting him, he felt his stomach tie itself into knots.

"We're not kidding, Gene. We need a sample of your DNA and every belt you own. I have a new one for you to hold up your pants until they are returned to you." He held out the Walmart bag.

"Who's saying this shit?" Gene demanded.

Harry said, "Apparently, Natalie Oliver, though you knew her as Ericka, told some friends she worked with she was fairly certain you were the killer. Because we really don't have anything else to go on in the investigation, we had to at least look into it."

"Can I refuse?" Gene said.

"It's a valid warrant. It basically forces you to comply," Pantera said.

"Should I get a lawyer?"

"If you feel like you need one," Pantera said. "But he'd tell you that compliance with the search warrant was mandatory. You could fight it—pay a lawyer a few thousand dollars if you can get one on the cheap—but in the end, you'd still have to comply.

Harry pulled out a sealed package and removed a test tube from it. He broke the seal on the test tube's top and withdrew a cotton swab. "Open wide."

Gene inhaled deeply and let it out before opening his mouth. Harry swabbed thoroughly along each inner cheek. Replacing the swab in the test tube and sealing it shut, Harry opened another sealed package and removed another swab inside a test tube. He inserted this one and swabbed both inner cheeks again, sealing that tube once he had finished. Taking out a felt-tip marker, he wrote Gene's name, the date, and the time on the paper adhering to the outside of the wide test tubes. He signed below this information, and Pantera signed below Harry's signature.

Pantera removed the belt from the shopping bag, along with an evidence bag.

"The belts?" he said. "We'll need every one of them you own, starting with the one you're wearing."

Gene removed the belt and handed it to Pantera, who placed it in the evidence bag.

Pantera said, "Now, let's explore your bedroom, all

your closets, and your drawers."

They went into Gene's bedroom. "Here's where I keep my belts." He opened a drawer and pointed. He had four more belts. Pantera put them in the evidence bag.

Harry said, "We'll have to look around anyway."

Gene sat on the bed. "Have at it, but if you don't need to make a mess, I would appreciate it."

Forty minutes later, they had searched everywhere they thought a belt might be. They doubted they would find any others since Gene had obviously not expected to have a warrant served asking him to turn all of his belts over to them.

"Why do you need the belts anyway?"

"She was strangled using a belt," said Pantera.

"How would they know that?"

"Patterns left behind in the bruising," Harry said. "They'll compare those patterns to the patterns on your belts."

"There must be a thousand belts like mine," Gene said.

"It's a funny thing about belts," Pantera said. "As you wear them, they start developing small flaws that make them different from every other belt in the world. These are mostly invisible to the naked eye, but they'll show up under a microscope."

"And in bruising patterns left behind when someone is strangled with that belt."

Pantera could see that this discussion was making Gene extremely nervous. By the time they left Gene's house, he was convinced Gene had indeed killed Miranda. The big question now was why. Even with the DNA and the belt, the motive was missing, which could make conviction more difficult, though certainly not impossible. It was only that without motive, the jurors might wonder about the crime.

"Don't leave your house," Pantera said as they left.

"I didn't do anything, so of course, I won't."

As they drove back to the station, Harry said, "Yeah, I think our guy is guilty."

"I hate to say it, but I think you're right."

They dropped off the samples at the lab, speaking with Molly when they did.

"We need this ASAP," Pantera said. "We have a suspect who could run if we don't act fast enough."

"I can have the belt analysis for you fast, a preliminary one at least. I can be more specific by Monday. The DNA will take at least two days, probably three. I can give you an answer on that Monday, along with a more definitive analysis of the belt."

"Thanks," Pantera said.

Pantera pointed out the belt Gene had been wearing. "Look at that one first. Can we wait?"

"Sure. If it's not the belt, it won't take long at all, maybe five minutes. If it is, I can have at least a good idea in about twenty minutes. If I remember correctly, there was a significant flaw on the belt used.

About fifteen minutes later, Molly came out to where they were waiting.

"The first belt's a match. I'd say right now it's a 95% certainty it was used to kill Miranda Buckhorn."

"That high?"

"Yes. The belt used had a small notch on one edge, a blemish. Also, the hole used to latch the belt gets worn down, again in a unique pattern on every belt, though they are all very similar. That hole gets wider, and there can be small notching of the belt at the hole from the pressure exerted on the hole over time. The latching hole was against Miranda's neck, and the blemish on the hole matches the one on her neck. It takes a lot of pressure to strangle someone. Using his belt for the job was not a wise choice."

"Thanks, Molly, we owe you."

"Hey, you owe me from the last one. Now you owe me two bottles of wine, and I'm still not talking a twelve-dollar bottle."

"Fine. Harry can spring for one."

Pantera turned to Harry, who looked satisfied that they had solved the murder but not happy as to who the killer had turned out to be.

"Shall we go pick him up?" Pantera said.

"I guess so."

When they pulled up to Gene's house, he was carrying a box out to his car. When he saw them, he dropped the box and ran around to the back of the house. He obviously hadn't counted on the tests taking such a short time and had taken the time to pack before leaving.

"Go!" Pantera shouted, pointing to the right side of the house as he ran around the left side.

When they emerged behind the house, they saw Gene jumping the chain-link fence at the rear of the property and running between the two houses that backed onto his yard.

The detectives followed him, each hoisting themselves over the fence and running between the houses.

When they reached the street, they saw that Gene had disappeared. He was nowhere in sight, and he had not run across the street to the house on the other side. They had been close enough to see him if he had.

"Where is he?" Harry asked.

Pantera was catching his breath. "I don't know."

At that moment, they heard a scream of pain coming from behind the houses they had run between.

"He circled back around!" Harry said, and the two men ran back toward Gene's house.

Gene was attempting to pull his hand from where it had been impaled on the chain link that topped the fencing. The metal had been twisted into a point, and

Gene had apparently missed with his hand when rushing to hoist himself over the fence. His hand was bleeding, the metal points sticking up from the back of his hand. He grunted with the pain, his face a grimace.

Pantera arrived first, pulling Gene's good hand to the fence and handcuffing him to it. Then he grabbed the other wrist and said, "Hold still."

Lifting straight up, he managed to pull the hand from its trap, Gene howling as he did.

"Go get a small towel in the house," Pantera told Harry. "We'll wrap it and get him to the hospital."

Pantera told Gene his rights. Gene said nothing in reply.

Soon, they were at the emergency room of St. Mary's Hospital in Richmond. Gene, an obvious flight risk, was kept handcuffed to the bed while the doctors and nurses worked to clean and bandage the wound.

"Why did you do it?" Pantera asked.

"Do what?" Gene asked. "Run?"

"No, kill Miranda."

Gene was silent.

"We have ample proof it was you. I'm 100% certain when we get the DNA analysis, it will match yours."

"What kind of proof?"

"Your belt is a perfect match for the one used to strangle her."

Gene said nothing.

"When the DNA comes back, it'll be a slam-dunk. Your lawyer will be advising you to make a deal."

"I'll wait for the deal," Gene said and went silent.

Both Harry and Pantera looked at each other. It was all over but the legal end of the crimes. They probably wouldn't have to testify since both Paulson and Gene would likely take plea deals.

The next morning, the detectives arrived for work

and sat with their coffee before writing up the events from the previous day.

"What about Circe?" Harry asked. "Will she get away with it?"

"If Paulson will give her up, maybe we can get her extradited from France."

"And if he won't?"

"If that happens, I doubt we'll get her."

"What about our friend Reginald Hallwater?"

"Do you have any idea where he is?"

"No, but there are ways to find out."

"We can try," Pantera said, "but I doubt he'll testify against her. If we can find him, it's a cinch she can, WITSEC or no WITSEC."

"That's a shame."

"Yeah, but we have to go with what we can prove."

"But why would Paulson kill Widner if he wasn't more or less forced to by Circe? Killing Garrett can be explained as not needing him anymore and the threat that he would testify against him someday. But Widner?"

"Good question, but if he doesn't give her up, I'm sure he'll come up with something."

"Something plausible?" Harry asked.

Pantera shrugged. "Plausible enough, I guess."

"I guess it's like it always is. You win some, you lose some."

43

Weeks later, all three men—Paulson, Gene, and Foster—took deals, with Foster's sentence being the lightest since his crime had extenuating circumstances, which Paulson admitted. That was something Pantera had insisted be a part of Paulson's deal and allocution, and the DA agreed.

Paulson had refused to implicate the woman known as Circe, though Pantera was certain she had been a part of killing Widner and Garrett. There was circumstantial evidence to show it, but without Paulson's testimony, her conviction was far less than certain, and attempting to find Reginald Hallwater would be mostly a waste of time since he would very likely not testify, and even if he did, a good lawyer, which Pantera knew Circe could afford by the dozen, could raise a reasonable doubt about his testimony. Paulson was swearing he was the one and only killer of Widner. The fact he was able to corroborate the physical wounds inflicted during the torture without ever having seen a medical report on them spoke volumes about his involvement.

Arresting Circe would have to wait until she committed another crime in the U.S. Pantera knew Circe was the one pulling all the strings and would continue to do so, though he figured her Richmond office would be less involved in illegal activities for the next year or two. Still, Pantera would do his best to keep an eye on the company in case they slipped up. He also asked to be notified if Circe re-entered the U.S. He was uncertain how well that would work, given the ability of the very rich to escape notice when entering the country.

Paulson had received forty-five to life, but he would be eligible for parole in twenty-five years, so Paulson could be sixty-eight when he was freed. Pantera hadn't liked that aspect, but something had to be offered for Paulson to admit how he forced both Garrett and Foster to do his dirty work. Otherwise, he would have ended up serving life without the possibility of parole. The promise of breathing free air had an enormous appeal for those being sent away for a long time.

Gene was sentenced to eighteen to twenty years for killing Miranda Buckhorn. He claimed she was blackmailing him. He had been stealing from Circe Enterprises, and she had found out about it. He had paid her over $15,000 in the five months before killing her, money he'd made from selling what he had stolen. He also felt she was responsible for ending his relationship with Natalie, having urged Natalie to leave him even before she moved to Roanoke, citing his intense jealousy over their lesbian relationship.

Despite the brutality of the killings of Natalie Oliver and, by mistake, Andre Crawford, Ray Foster was sentenced to seven to ten years, The charges against Foster had been reduced to manslaughter with extenuating circumstances. This leniency was due to Paulson's confession that he had threatened Foster and his family with painful and humiliating murders, as well as how Foster had come forward before being caught to offer help in proving the charges against Paulson. Pantera had fought for the lighter sentence as well.

Paulson claimed he had no uncle and that his threats about Foster's children were just that—threats. A records search verified the lack of an uncle, and the district attorney let the matter drop. Pantera wondered if maybe the demon Paulson planned to send to molest Foster's children wasn't Paulson's uncle but someone else Paulson knew. Pantera hoped that wasn't the case.

Once the men were sentenced, Pantera took some time off to be with Lisa, who took a vacation herself. They flew to New Orleans and enjoyed the atmosphere and the cuisine that could not be replicated anywhere in the world, despite efforts to do so. Lisa claimed it was the atmosphere that made the difference. She was probably right.

Pantera noticed during the vacation that Lisa was sometimes distant, as if something was bothering her, or at the very least, something was occupying her thoughts. He would ask about it, but she would brush his concern off, claiming she was just tired and enjoying the ability to relax.

When the vacation was over and they were on the flight home, he noticed again that something seemed to be bothering her.

"Come on," he said. "It's obvious something is bothering you. Tell me what it is."

She sighed deeply. "It's my job."

"What about it?"

She took another deep breath and said, "They're transferring me."

"You mean a new job or a new place?"

"Both."

He suddenly understood the contemplations that seemed to plague her. "Where to?" he asked, knowing it wouldn't be close to Richmond.

"Seattle."

He was silent for a moment. The flight attendants were serving drinks from the pushcart they rolled down the aisle, and the serving cart had arrived at their seats.

"Would you like something to drink?" the young woman asked them, wearing a smile that seemed to mock his sudden misery.

Knowing they wouldn't have Writers Tears, he said, "Scotch on the rocks. A double."

Lisa said, "Do you have a chardonnay?"

"Yes, ma'am."

"I'll have a glass of that."

Pantera fished some cash from his wallet and paid for the drinks, and the flight attendant moved to the next set of seats. Pantera sipped his scotch, wanting to down it in one gulp but refraining. He didn't want to get drunk, just slightly numb.

He turned to Lisa. "I take it you're accepting the new job?"

"On the one hand, I don't want to. I'm going to miss you terribly. But turning it down would prevent me from ever moving up again, and I don't want to stagnate in this job forever."

"I'm rich. Just quit and move in with me."

"It's not that simple, Tony. I love you, but you're not my complete existence. This isn't the 1950s. My career means a lot to me. Just as yours means a lot to you."

He considered what she said. She was right. Her dedication to her work was part of what made her attractive to him.

"Would you drop your career to move to Seattle?" she asked.

"No."

"Why should it be different for me?"

"Can we try the long-distance relationship thing?" he asked, knowing her answer but wanting to at least suggest it if for no other reason than being able to say he tried.

"I'm not much for those, and I don't know how long a three-thousand mile relationship would last anyway. We'd likely only see each other twice a year, three times if we were lucky. That's no way to keep a romantic relationship alive."

"How long have you known?"

"I found out about a week before we left for New Orleans, but we were planning this trip, and I wanted us to have this last fling before I told you. If you hadn't brought it up, I was going to tell you on the flight to Richmond from Atlanta."

He started to take another sip from his scotch but stopped. Then he raised his plastic cup in her direction. She held up her cup of wine and he clicked his cup against hers.

He said, "Here's to one of the most wonderful ladies I've ever known. I'm sorry things didn't work out differently."

She smiled. "I love you, too, Tony."

They drank to each other and sat back to stew in their own private thoughts.

When they landed in Richmond after a smooth flight from Atlanta and retrieved their luggage, they caught the shuttle to their cars.

Putting their suitcases in their trunks, Pantera went to her. "Beth is going to be very upset."

"I know. I plan to keep in touch with her. With you, too, for that matter. I still consider you a cherished friend."

He smiled, but there was little joy in it. "I've played that part well before."

"I didn't want to hurt you, Tony."

"I know."

She flashed her own pained smile. "Or me either."

He held her for an eternity that lasted only ten seconds then kissed her softly.

"Goodbye, Tony. I do plan to keep in touch. If I change my number, I'll let you know."

"Bye, Lisa. Take care of yourself."

As she turned to climb into her car, he asked, "Did Harry know about this?"

"No. I told Ashley not to tell him. I didn't want this

coming from him second hand. Besides, it would have spoiled our fun in New Orleans."

"You told Ashley and she kept the secret?" She nodded. "Your sister should work for the CIA."

She smiled and climbed into her car. Starting it, she backed away from the curb and drove off. He watched her car turn at the end of the lane, wondering how long it would be before they saw each other again. He figured she would refrain from even calling for several months to allow the change to set in. He knew she was right to do that, despite knowing he would want to call her every day in the meantime.

Taking out his phone once he was seated behind the wheel, he called Harry.

"Hey," Harry said when he answered.

"You'll never guess what happened," Pantera said.

"Lisa got transferred to Seattle."

"When did you find out?"

"About an hour ago. Lisa apparently swore Ashley to absolute secrecy, saying she could tell me once you were on the plane coming home."

"Well, I found out more than an hour ago, so I guess I wasn't the last to know at least."

"What are you going to do?"

"What can I do? I'll keep waking up every day and doing the best I can."

"Sounds like a plan," Harry said.

"It's the only plan there ever was."

"Beth is going to be devastated."

"Yeah, that's what I told Lisa. Didn't change her mind, though. Anyway, Beth's tough. She'll get over it. Lisa says she plans to keep in touch with her, and at least that will make Beth happy. Or at least take out some of the sting."

"Where you headed?"

"Home. I'm tired. Funny how a vacation does that."

"Yeah. Will you be in tomorrow?"

"No, I arranged for another day when I put in for the time. A vacation from my vacation. Maybe we can meet up at The Watering Hole for a drink after you get off tomorrow. Enjoy Dean's and Pete's company. Have a few laughs."

"Sure thing. See you there around six."

"Okay. Later."

When Pantera arrived home, Nancy's car was in the driveway. He'd asked her to park at the curb so he wouldn't block her in when he got back. She had found an apartment to rent month-to-month to give her a place to live while the deal on the house closed, but the apartment was a tiny one-bedroom, not big enough for Nancy and the girls, so she had bunked at his place while he was in New Orleans. She was returning to her apartment tonight.

When he walked in, the girls greeted him as if they'd not seen him in months instead of just a week. Nancy beamed at him, knowing how much he basked in his daughters' love.

"I fixed you pot roast, potatoes, and fresh green beans for dinner," Nancy said. "You hungry?"

"Sure." He wasn't that hungry but didn't want to disappoint her.

He talked about New Orleans, and by the time he finished the meal, he had eaten more than he'd thought he would. Now, both girls wanted to go there when his next vacation with them came along. He was happy to tell them to start planning.

He mentioned nothing about Lisa to any of them, but when the girls went to bed, Nancy said, "I talked to Ashley Overmeyer today."

"Oh? What did she have to say?" he asked, knowing full well what she'd said.

"She told me that Lisa is moving to Seattle."

He could see a shade of hope in her eyes.

"Listen, Nance. It's way too early in this to make any kinds of plans. Let's just see where life takes us, okay?"

"That's all I can ask."

"Are you sure you still love me, and this isn't some kind of reaction to losing Phil?"

She stared into his eyes for a moment and said, "Tony, I loved you even when I was with Phil. I just couldn't live with the wondering. I told you that."

"Yeah, I know."

"I'll see you tomorrow evening, okay? You'll need me around to help give Beth the news her favorite adult woman in the world will be living three thousand miles away."

"You're her favorite adult woman in the world, Nancy."

"Parents don't count in that. She knows neither of us would ever move that far away."

"True. I'll be going to The Watering Hole to meet Harry at six. Can we tell her after I get home? That'll be around 7:30."

"Sure."

When Nancy was gone and he was finally lying in his own bed, he considered his life. Nancy was right about one thing. He could retire from the force. He had enough time in, and he had inherited an estate that was now worth around twenty million dollars. He just chose not to live as though he had. His work was important to him. It gave him a sense of worth.

But for the first time, he began to seriously contemplate going into private practice. He could certainly afford it, and maybe there were people out there needing his help before someone did something horrible to them. It was only after something bad was done that the police could do anything, really.

Perhaps being a private detective would put him exactly where he needed to be to help others, and maybe he could talk Harry into joining him.

For the first time, such a change seemed attractive, despite the big change that had just occurred in his life. He wasn't sure what he would do. For now, he was tired.

He would sleep on it.

If you enjoyed this book, please leave a review at Amazon and/or Goodreads. To find other books by Charles Tabb, visit charlestabb.com.

Charles Tabb is available for online and in-person presentations and discussions of his books, with online meetings being free-of-charge. In-person meetings are usually free as well. Contact him through his website, above.

As a retired teacher, he is always eager to talk to student groups about goal-setting and how to follow through on those goals.

Made in the USA
Middletown, DE
28 November 2024

65584672R00188